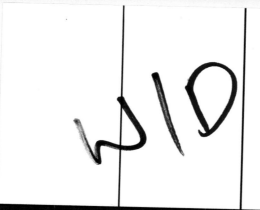

WID

D1337577

C016940842

RAMSEY CAMPBELL

THE WISE FRIEND

This is a **FLAME TREE PRESS** book

Text copyright © 2020 Ramsey Campbell

FLAME TREE PRESS
6 Melbray Mews, London, SW6 3NS, UK
flametreepress.com

Distribution and warehouse:
Marston Book Services Ltd
160 Eastern Avenue, Milton Park, Abingdon, Oxon, OX14 4SB
www.marston.co.uk

Publisher's Note: This is a work of fiction. Names, characters, places, and
incidents are a product of the author's imagination. Locales and public names
are sometimes used for atmospheric purposes. Any resemblance to actual
people, living or dead, or to businesses, companies, events, institutions, or
locales is completely coincidental.

Thanks to the Flame Tree Press team, including:
Taylor Bentley, Frances Bodiam, Federica Ciaravella, Don D'Auria,
Chris Herbert, Josie Karani, Molly Rosevear, Will Rough, Mike Spender,
Cat Taylor, Maria Tissot, Nick Wells, Gillian Whitaker.

The cover is created by Flame Tree Studio with
thanks to Nik Keevil and Shutterstock.com.
The font families used are Avenir and Bembo.

Flame Tree Press is an imprint of Flame Tree Publishing Ltd
flametreepublishing.com

A copy of the CIP data for this book is available from the British Library.

HB ISBN: 978-1-78758-404-4
PB ISBN: 978-1-78758-403-7
ebook ISBN: 978-1-78758-405-1
Also available in FLAME TREE AUDIO

Printed in the UK at Clays, Suffolk

RAMSEY CAMPBELL

THE WISE FRIEND

FLAME TREE PRESS
London & New York

For Don D'Auria –
champion of horror, champion editor

CHAPTER ONE

The Journal

I could never have believed I would wish my son loved books less, let alone dread the consequences. That August afternoon he'd been in my apartment less than half an hour before he ended up in the room with shelves on every wall. He was sprawled in a leather armchair several times his age, and leafing through an exhibition catalogue, when his phone gave its vintage ring. A glance at the screen let him say "It's mum."

"Shall I leave you to talk?"

Roy's features – the long sharp-nosed face and thin lips he'd inherited from me – twitched in a fleeting grimace. Just the deep brown eyes were his mother's, but their habitual preoccupation was all his. "You can hear," he said.

Just the same, I turned to the window. Double glazing fended off much of the noise from New Brighton Station down below, but I was being told a train was late. On the far side of the railway, beyond a cluster of chain restaurants at the bottom of the hill, the sea led to a crowd of windmills spinning like cogs of the sky. A microscopic oil rig and the distant filament of Blackpool Tower might have been components as well, helping maintain the pellucid blue. None of this distracted me from hearing Julia say "Are you at your father's now, Roy?"

"Have been for hours. Do you want to talk to him?"

"I will when I've spoken to you. Are you settling in all right?"

"Don't know what you mean."

I could tell this meant yes in a fifteen-year-old's parlance besides protesting at the question, but Julia persisted "Will you be comfortable there while I'm away?"

"Mum, dad can hear."

"Then I'm sure he understands."

"I'm good." As I hoped this wasn't dutifully aimed at me Roy added "I'm reading in his book room."

"No need to bring any of those home. That's what your tablet's for."

"The modern librarian," I murmured and felt sly at once.

"I didn't hear that," Julia said, which generally meant she had. "What's your reading, Roy?"

"A book of dad's aunt's paintings."

"Just don't let them tempt you to imitate her. You make sure he doesn't, Patrick."

"I haven't done paintings since I was little," Roy said.

"You know perfectly well what I mean," Julia retorted forcefully enough to be rebuking both of us. "All the things she was mixed up with obviously harmed her mind, or she wouldn't have done what she did to herself."

"It was never proved she meant to," I said.

"I'm not having this argument again," Julia said, a response familiar from the last years of our marriage. "Please keep an eye on what Roy reads and what he does while he's your responsibility. I'll be home once the conference is over."

As our son took refuge in the book, which didn't save his face from growing mottled with embarrassment, I said "I think we're both responsible for him."

Someone unfamiliar with Julia might have thought she'd grown briefly deaf, since she said only "Call me whenever you need to, Roy. And make sure you two don't get into any mischief."

"Yes, miss," I said but heard no sign that she'd taken it as a joke.

When a further silence made it plain that she'd gone, Roy slipped the phone into one of the several pockets of his elongated shorts. As he reopened the catalogue at Thelma's best-known painting – the red London bus perched on the highest Himalayan peak – he said "What was your aunt like?"

"She'd have encouraged you to look further than people ordinarily do. That's what she did to me when I used to stay with her, though I can't say my parents were altogether in favour."

"That's how all the books with her pictures on them used to make me feel. Have you still got them?"

"They're over in the corner where the sun can't get at them. All the books with anything to do with her are, just in case they fade."

Roy was making to replace the catalogue when he peered into the corner I'd devoted to my aunt. "What's back here?"

Reaching into the gap the catalogue had left, he coaxed out an item. He might have been extracting a slice of darkness, a concentrated essence of the shadows in the corner, but just the covers of the exercise book were black. I had no idea when I might have trapped it behind the other volumes, and it touched off memories I hadn't visited for years. "That was Thelma's," I said.

Roy perched on the edge of my desk while he leafed through the book. "What's it meant to be?"

"I was never really sure. Maybe they're notes for some of her work. I thought the names were places she based paintings on."

"It's more like a diary at the start, but it doesn't end up much of one."

As he passed me the journal it emitted a faint earthy smell, presumably of age. My aunt had made an entry on the inside of the front cover, which suggested she'd written it later than she'd begun the journal. *21st March, first year*, the elaborately cursive writing said. *Met A on walk.* I glanced at a few of the place names she'd annotated with obscure quotations – Monks Cross, Slatevale, Goodmanswood – and then let Roy have the journal, since it intrigued him. "Why did she give you her book?" he said.

"She didn't, but I think she'd have liked me to have it. She tried to inspire me whenever I stayed at her house. She thought her sister, that's my mother, didn't bring my mind out enough." With a twinge of guilt I said "Maybe I should have passed it on to her biographer."

"Do you think they'd have understood it?"

"If anybody could." As the railway station's voice turned female, warning listeners to be aware of suspicious items, I said "I was hoping it would help me understand what happened to my aunt, but that's one more thing I don't think we'll ever really know."

Roy blinked at the journal and laid it on my desk with a thump as muted as the voice below. "We could go and see some of these places," he said, and now I wish we'd never found the book.

CHAPTER TWO

Absences

"Mummy, what did grandma say about dad's auntie?"

"Roy, you've been really good all day." Julia's delicate but determined face barely hinted at a frown. "Don't spoil it now," she said. "You know you shouldn't interrupt while grown-ups are talking."

"But I only nearly heard what she said." His quirk of language earned him an indulgent smile from an art critic. "She said something was a pity," Roy insisted.

"She wasn't talking to little boys. Would you like to play in the back garden? Just don't go out of the gate."

"I don't like playing there by myself. Someone kept looking at me over the fence."

"Now, nobody could do that, could they?" My mother lowered her round face, which routinely resembled a badge of concern, towards him. "It's taller than you and your daddy put together," she said and told the rest of the family "Someone looking over it, that's the kind of thing my sister would have made up, and our parents would have encouraged her."

"No need to squash his imagination, Astrid." While my father's face looked weighted by generous jowls, his slowness denoted thought. "I expect they were up a tree, were they?" he told Roy, adding an unhurried smile. "That'll be what you saw, son."

"They were in a tree, but—"

"That's settled, then," Julia said. "If you don't want to play out, why don't you see if anybody wants a sandwich? You were so good taking them around before."

"You needn't send him away, Julia," my mother said. "He's not too young to know what I was saying, and the sooner the better.

Roy, sweetheart, don't you ever get up to the kind of thing my sister did."

"But mum and dad like me to paint."

"Not painting, lovely. Don't go in buildings nobody lives in, and never go up too high. We don't want you falling over, do we?"

"Didn't dad's auntie mean to fall?"

"I'm sure she didn't, son," my father said. "She just didn't take enough care."

"That's right, Jonathan," my mother retorted, though not as if it wholly was. "Cared too much about her art and not enough about how we'd feel for losing her."

"I shouldn't think that crossed her mind, dear."

"Too much didn't that should have." My mother appeared to recall Roy was listening. "Your family's the most important thing in your life," she told him. "Your mummy and daddy care for you and each other, and I know they always will."

"I know too," Roy said with a seriousness that seemed concentrated by his size and youth. "Dad's auntie's paintings are important, aren't they? Lots of people said they were in church."

"They're very important," Julia said, "to people who like them."

"Don't you, mummy?"

"I prefer art to be more like real life, I'm afraid."

Perhaps I shouldn't have felt provoked to respond. "As the lady from the Tate was saying, Roy, my aunt made people look again and further."

"I don't need to be told how to look," Julia said.

"Don't we all take things for granted sometimes?"

"Oh yes, Patrick," Julia said. "You've been known to do that."

"Now, children," my mother intervened. "Shall we just talk about Thelma? That's why we're here, after all."

Roy gazed around the room full of my aunt's friends and colleagues, more of whom were audible in the kitchen and the hall. Beside the redundant red-brick hearth, above which hung a Leonora Carrington print apparently depicting a witch and her familiar, Thelma's one-time husband Neville was arguing with an art critic. "Shall I tell everyone they have to talk about her?" Roy said.

"I'm sure they are already," my mother said, only to look as if she'd missed the chance to send him away on a mission. Neville had finished disagreeing and was making for us.

His wide not quite shaven face with its greying hair and equally shaggy eyebrows looked unkempt with suppressed grief. "I hope nobody thought the worse of me for not speaking at the funeral," he said. "I wouldn't have trusted myself."

"Neville," my mother said like her handclasp shaped into a word. "I'm certain everyone understood."

"And sorry if you thought I should have lined up with you outside the church."

Since my mother had relinquished my uncle's hand, my father dealt it a manly squeeze. "You could have if you'd liked, old chap."

"I didn't want to presume." Having hesitated while he glanced at Roy, Neville said "No, the truth is I didn't know if you'd have someone else with you."

"This little fellow's mother took him for a walk, but even if he'd been there—"

"Not your grandson. My replacement. Thelma's man."

"I don't see how you could have thought that," my mother objected. "We wouldn't have wanted him."

"We had quite a few words with her about him," my father said.

"Well, thank you," Neville said, though the reason for his gratitude wasn't clear. "Was he here today? You might know better than I would. I don't even recall what he looked like, not that I've any wish to."

"I don't myself too well," my father said. "Can you improve on us, Astrid?"

"I don't think I'd know him if he walked into the room, and I shouldn't think Patrick would either."

"I only saw him once like you," I said and immediately wondered if I was mistaken. As we'd entered the chapel I'd noticed someone among the trees on the far side of the graveyard. I couldn't tell whether it was a man or a woman, but I'd thought the loiterer was watching us. "And I heard him one night while I was staying here," I said. "I don't think I was meant to."

"He was good at skulking all right. Made for it, he was so thin." Neville stared around the room, presumably in search of him. "I kept hoping Thelma just wanted a break from me," he said. "I know I wasn't the easiest person to live with."

"None of us are," I said.

As Julia gave me a look more meaningful than I entirely welcomed, Neville finished surveying the room. "I've never seen the house so tidy," he admitted. "I know some of that was my fault."

"That was Astrid and me," my father said. "We cleared up for the wake."

"Did you throw much out?" Neville was anxious to learn.

"We've tried to keep everything that might mean anything to someone," my mother said. "Some things we don't think would. There's a kind of diary Thelma started, but it might as well be blank for all the sense it makes."

A memory prompted me to blurt "Where is it?"

"Where we found it. In her studio."

Neville was focusing on Roy as if he'd just noticed him. "You look like a grand chap," he said, delivering a large loose handshake. "My grandnephew, will you be?"

"He's our little helper, aren't you, Roy?" my mother said.

All this felt like my excuse to be elsewhere. "Back in a few minutes," I said and sidled through the crowd.

Outside the room a man appeared to be miming a bird, his arms held behind his back while he cocked his head at a framed painting. Three guests seated on consecutive stairs reminded me of plaster poultry mounted on a wall. In the bathroom a woman I didn't think I'd ever seen before was restoring her makeup in front of a mirror. The bedroom I used to stay in looked diminished, stripped of memories, awaiting some visitor other than me. My aunt's studio faced it across the landing. As I stepped into the large room scattered with paintings and the makings of them a woman said "Can I help?"

She might have been addressing a potential customer at her gallery, which had been the first to support my aunt's career. In the church she'd spoken at length about Thelma's achievement – how the intense lyricism of her early landscapes had grown hallucinatory before advancing into a highly personal form of surrealism, where enigmatic elements recalled the magical suggestions of Leonora Carrington, Thelma's favourite painter. Towards the end Thelma

Turnbill seemed to grow dissatisfied with her success, perhaps feeling too much of her fame depended on her early painting of a bus up Everest, used by London Transport for their *Taking You Everywhere* poster. In the pulpit Barbare had sounded close to proprietary, but I wasn't going to let her treat me like an intruder in the studio. "Just looking for an item," I said as firmly as I could.

Barbare thinned her eyes, lowering her multicoloured eyebrows. They and her cropped rainbow hair might have been designed to contrast with her severely funereal suit and polo-neck. "May I ask what?" she said.

I didn't answer until I located Thelma's attempt at a journal, lying on the sill of the broad high window that overlooked the woods behind the house. Leaves rusty with autumn massed into the distance, where their tints were diluted by mist. My son's complaint about a watcher made me peer into the forest, but I'd seen nothing except trees when Barbare said "Excuse me, could you leave that? It was Thelma's."

I picked up the book I'd laid my hand on. "I'm her nephew."

Barbare narrowed her eyes further before letting them relax. "I do know you. I haven't seen you for years, or much."

"Thank you for everything you said today. I'm sure everyone would want me to say so. I'll leave you to it, then."

I was giving her permission to explore the studio, but she said "I wish you wouldn't take that. Do remind me of your name."

"It's still Patrick."

"I should have remembered. One of the few men in her life."

Remembering the discussion downstairs made me ask "How well did you know the last one?"

"Her inspiration, you mean."

"That's what you think he was."

"That's what Thelma said he was, and her work did take a new direction."

"You sound as if you weren't so happy with it."

"It sold. It must have spoken to people, even if they weren't sure what they were being told." Barbare left her mouth ajar as a preamble to adding "It felt as if she'd started hiding details in her work she didn't want the rest of us to understand."

"And you're blaming her partner."

"If that's what he was. I don't know what else he could have been. She did say she wouldn't have visited quite a few of the places she painted without him."

"What did you make of him yourself?"

"Do you know, I thought of mentioning him in the church, but I couldn't find a single thing to say about him. I'm sure I met him several times and yet it feels as if I hardly did."

I had a disconcerting sense that the imprecision of her memory had infected mine, and I turned to my aunt's last canvas, a version of the woods beyond the window. Every season of the year was represented by foliage or its absence. Just one detail looked incomplete, a figure beneath a distant tree that was skeletal with winter despite bearing blossoms on some of its branches, not to mention leaves in every state a year would bring. The figure had been left without a face, and even its gender was unclear. "What do you think she was trying to do there?" I said.

"I'm afraid we'll never know, even if we think she finished it. I'm not sure she meant to fill in whoever's in the background."

The longer I gazed at the rudimentary shape among the trees, the more it suggested a bid to erase or at any rate lessen the power of a presence. I was making to leave it and the studio behind when Barbare said "Do you really need that book, Patrick? What does it mean to you?"

I was increasingly unsure but equally determined not to give it up. "It reminds me of staying here with her."

"I just think we should keep as much as possible together for posterity. Someone's already had her landscape specimens."

Now I realised there was no sign of the jars of earth my aunt had taken to keeping on the windowsill, apparently samples of settings she planned to paint, an eccentric species of reminder if not inspiration. A memory glimmered, but I suppressed it at once. "I'll keep this safe, I promise," I said, hugging the book so hard it exuded an earthy smell. "If you need it you'll know where it is."

I took the journal down to my car and locked it in the boot. I felt oddly surreptitious, as if someone was watching, but all the guests I could see were engaged in conversation. Julia and Neville were still talking about Roy, who looked impatient to contribute, and I took the opportunity to confront my parents. "Did you throw out those jars of earth Thelma kept in her studio?"

"We would have if they'd still been there," my mother said, a response that outraged me so much I failed to wonder who'd disposed of them or why they had.

CHAPTER THREE

Boys Together

"Down, boy. Lie down now, Basky, there's a good hound. You won't hurt Mr Holmes or the doctor, will you? You don't have to act the way you were brought up. You just guard Mr Holmes's rooms for him."

"Mrs Hudson, you're the hero of the day. She's more of a man than either of us, Watson."

"I'll let the world know when I tell this story, Holmes."

"You mustn't, Doctor Watson. Just say Mr Holmes solved another case, or it might harm his reputation."

I'd asked my students to analyse their choice of a classic from a feminist perspective, not retell the tale, but Veena's essay earned my approval. Too many of the others were less than grammatical, bereft of sentences and infected with nonsensical autocorrections, and quite a few read more like texts sent from a phone. At least some of the usage had improved during the year I'd taught this group of students, but my course was meant to deal with English literature, not the basics of the language. Reading the last essays of the summer term left me all the more grateful that Roy was so literate. I might have told him so, had he been home.

He should have been by now. I took my time over marking several essays, resisting an urge to underline every error, and as I turned an almost entirely unpunctuated page on its face I heard the last train from Liverpool arrive at the station. It was so close to soundless that it put me in mind of a teenager sneaking home late at night – more precisely, my son. Craning over my desk, I saw a few people leave the station and recognised none of them. As I took out my phone I told myself there was no need to panic.

Roy's phone rang long enough to make me hold my breath.

When he spoke at last, it wasn't what I hoped to hear. "It's Roy. Don't know who you are or what you want, so say. Your number would be good as well."

"It's me. It's your father. I take it you missed the train. Just let me know where I need to pick you up."

I was hoping he would interrupt my message, but his phone stayed mute. I rang off to await his call. Down in the station the windows of the darkened train resembled slabs of slate. I peered across the bay until I fancied I was making out the dormant windmills, which looked as if the night had clogged the works of the world. Everything felt silenced, not least Roy. How long ought I to wait before calling him again? I assumed he was in a tunnel or somewhere else that cut off his signal, though not on a train or indeed a bus, since those had stopped running as well. When I tired of waiting I set about hunting for him. He wasn't in the station; whoever was sitting in an unlit corner wasn't him. He wasn't in the nearest carriage of the train, though the solitary passenger was unidentifiable in the dark. There was one in every carriage I walked through, though surely not the same occupant every time. Now I was at the front of the train, where the seated figure resembled a propped-up section of a painting if not a sourceless shadow. Despite the absence of a driver, the train was crawling forwards. I swung around to shout Roy's name through the carriages, and a voice too soft for its gender to be plain spoke at my back. "He'll be with me."

This jerked me awake, or the muted thud of the front door did. Somebody was trying not to make much noise in entering the house. I heard a surreptitious creak of stairs and then a key searching for the lock. I was in my hall by the time Roy let himself in, edging the door open so gradually that I had time to check my watch. It was nearly two o'clock, and he blinked unfavourably at me as if I'd wakened him, except not quite. "How did you get home?" I said.

"Lift."

"From whom?"

Even more reluctantly he muttered "Friend."

Several of those had driven over from Manchester to spend whatever kind of evening they'd spent with him. "I hope the driver wasn't in your state," I said.

"Can I go to bed now?"

"I think you better had, and we'll talk in the morning."

I slept once he finished blundering about in the bathroom, an activity suggestive of wordless resentment. Now that I knew where he was I didn't dream. In the morning I was up well ahead of him. By the time I'd evaluated the last of the essays, he was still in bed. I took a fierce coffee to the spare room, where he peered blearily at me from his lair of a thin quilt, which concealed him up to his eyes on the converted sofa. "Will you be very much longer?" I said.

His voice was pretty well as indistinct as an announcement that came from the station. "Supposed to be the holidays."

"That's no reason to waste the day. Do you sleep this late at your mother's?"

His eyelids sagged shut, reaching for sleep or so he wouldn't have to look at me. "Thought you wouldn't care."

"If you mean I won't mind, I rather do. You mustn't think I'll let you get away with everything she doesn't like you doing. What will you have for breakfast?"

"Not much."

"You need to have something," I said as my mother would have. "I'll leave this here. I hope it wakes you up."

I planted the mug on the floor beside the sofa, where the aromatic steam made for his face. When an unenthusiastic hand strayed from beneath the quilt I went next door to the kitchen. As bacon sputtered in the pan I heard Roy stumble to the bathroom. I wondered if the smell had proved too cloying, but it appeared to have enticed him. I was setting out the rest of breakfast – rolls, mustard, orange juice – when Roy wandered into the kitchen, naked except for underpants patterned with miniature leaves. "Can I have some more coffee?" he said.

"Your medication is right here." I refilled his mug, which was lagged with an image of a book cover, Thelma's painting of a red phone box in a rainforest. Was a vague shape lurking upright in the box? Perhaps it was the shadow of a tree trunk. I watched Roy grimace as he took a gulp of coffee, after which he loaded a roll with bacon spread with mustard and gazed hard at the result. "How are you feeling?" I had to ask.

"Expect I'll feel better later."

"Just remember you did it to yourself. I'm sure I've felt like you do right now, but it wasn't at your age or even nearly."

"Shouldn't think you ever have."

"It's not a contest, Roy." His dully smug look prompted me to ask "Why wouldn't I?"

"It's too now."

"If we're talking about drugs, please stay away from them. You've no idea what the side effects may be." Since his silence admitted as much I said "What was it and where did you get it?"

"Didn't have a name." He bit into the roll, perhaps to delay answering. "It was just a pill," he said eventually. "We got it in a club."

"They oughtn't to have let you in. You must have been under age."

"They thought I wasn't."

"More like they didn't care." I'd felt proud that he looked older than his years, but not now. "Are you going to tell me the name of the club?"

"Doesn't matter. I won't go to any more if I get all this grief every time."

"I'm afraid I haven't finished yet. What did this substance of yours do for you?"

"Colours and patterns and shapes. Made me see them like I bet your aunt did."

"She was taking part in a controlled experiment run by a university, and she was twice your age. Your brain's still forming and you shouldn't interfere with the process."

"Nothing wrong with my brain."

"And we don't want there ever to be." Now I had to acknowledge "I'm not sure if the drug trial left my aunt with a problem."

"I wouldn't mind that kind of problem," Roy said and stared through the kitchen doorway. "Doesn't look like she had one to me."

He might have been invoking a presence, but he was gazing at some of her work. My aunt had sketched me every year I'd stayed with her, and now all the portraits hung in the hall. Behind two versions of my face a year apart I saw an impression of trees, which at that distance resembled part of a spider's web, and I was on the way to making out another detail when Roy's phone gave its nostalgic trill. "Mum," it announced as well.

"Just calling to say you won't be able to reach me while I'm in session today."

I suspected this was a way of checking up on him. Since he didn't answer, I did. "I'm sure there'll be no need."

"Isn't Roy there? Can't he speak for himself?"

Roy looked away from me before saying "Yes."

"Is that all?"

"What dad said."

"Sorry if I'm intruding. What are you up to today?"

As our son had no reply to this I felt I should explain "Some of us have only just got up."

"You roust your father out of bed, Roy. Make the most of your summer."

Had she really misunderstood my comment, or was she loath to hear anything against our son? He seemed to prefer to return to her question. "We were looking at his portraits his aunt made."

"The ones he didn't want to part with. Well, we don't need the money now." I knew better than to take this for absolution, having recalled how strident our disagreement had been. "It's a pity she didn't concentrate more on her family," Julia said.

"Maybe they should have concentrated more on her," I said.

"We won't argue," Julia said, which generally used to mean we would. "Must go, but you can always leave a message, Roy. Don't sit around reading, both of you. Get out and about and enjoy your day."

Once she'd gone Roy said "Thanks for not saying about last night."

"I didn't have the opportunity."

"You won't, though, will you? You don't want to bother her when she doesn't have to be."

"I'll refrain if you promise to do nothing of the kind again."

"All right."

"No, I want to hear you promise."

"All right," Roy said more reproachfully than I found appropriate, "promise."

"Don't sound so victimised. I'm only looking out for you. You've got a good brain, so take care of it. I'd have you as a student right now if I could."

"No chance of that. They wouldn't let me in."

"They're accepting people I'd say were less qualified than you. I'm sure you'll have your choice of university when the time comes."

"If I want one. I don't want to end up like you and mum."

I didn't know whether I felt more insulted or dismayed. "How have we let you down?"

"Not me, yourselves. You wish you were teaching better people and she hates books and wants to get away from them."

"I wouldn't say she hates them. She's a librarian, after all. She just has enough of them at work."

"She never liked us bringing books home. That's where studying got you both."

"She doesn't stop you reading, does she?" When his head admitted to a shake I said "I hope you'll never say any of that to her."

"I won't if you don't tell her about last night."

"You don't want to upset her when there's no need, do you?"

"You don't either."

I felt as if I'd strayed into a trap I'd set myself. "Then perhaps we'd better do as she suggested. What do you want to do today?"

"Don't know," he said as dully as only a teenager could, and then "Maybe I do."

"Anything at all." I didn't pause long before adding "Within reason."

"We were going to look at the places your aunt wrote in her book."

"We could, but not today. They're all some way off."

"The wood by her house isn't."

"I don't believe that's in the book."

"She painted it, didn't she? That's nearly the same." As if he'd exhausted his efforts, which in any case had proved pointless, Roy said "Don't if you don't want."

"I do. We'll go." Now that we'd fixed on an activity I was anxious not to let him lose enthusiasm. "I'd like to see what she saw in it," I said, and at once I began to remember.

CHAPTER FOUR

A Voice in the Trees

As I drove past the house that had been my aunt's the upstairs windows snatched at the afternoon sun. The light on the glass erased the room where I used to sleep, as though the anonymity of the suburb had spread into the house. My mother had expressed surprise not far short of a reprimand that Thelma and my uncle lived somewhere so lacking in character. My aunt had valued the northern light that the generous windows afforded her studio, but now I wondered how much the view had meant to her – the view of Third Mile Wood.

The suburb might have been designed to hold the forest back, in which case it was failing in its task. One roof sprouted a small shrub like a feather in a cap, however little of a token of achievement. Some of the fences behind the houses were scaly with ivy that had climbed out of the woods. In a drive a paving stone had tilted up, exposing a contorted knuckly root. A few cars were parked on an expanse of gravel by an entrance to the woods. Flyers for a local folk festival lay beneath the windscreen wipers, fluttering in time with restless foliage as Roy and I left the car. A board above the stout fence bore a map of the woods, so vandalised that the diagram of paths was indecipherable. It was just possible to discern four walks, often crossing one another: red, blue, yellow, green. "Let's go green," I said.

That path led directly behind my aunt's old home, where the shadows of the houses spread an unseasonable chill. The window that had belonged to her studio was full of leaves, a reflection of treetops. In my teens I'd thought this looked as if the woods were reaching for her. I was about to follow the path into the woods when a head reared up above the fence.

It belonged to a child on a swing in the back garden, but the sight reminded me of a remark Roy had made at Thelma's wake. I was making to ask him about it when the little girl sailed up again. Her pigtails were the last of her to vanish, and she left her voice behind. "You'll get lost in the puzzle," she said.

I wasn't sure I'd heard correctly. "Are you talking to us?"

Her voice reappeared before she did, pigtails flailing. "Get lost in the woods."

As I wondered if this was a clarification or a directive, another voice joined hers. "Are you talking to yourself again, Francie?"

"I don't ever, mummy. Now it's a man."

I heard footsteps tramping to the fence ahead of a plea: "Don't stop pushing me, mummy." A bolt clanked back, and the gate that used to let me into the woods swung inwards, revealing a large ruddy woman whose extravagantly herbaceous dress bared her muscular arms. "May I help you?" she rather less offered than said.

At the top of the sloping garden the little girl was trying to increase her arc. "Your daughter was saying we'd get lost," I said.

"You mustn't mind her. She worries for people, that's all."

"She needn't worry we'll be lost," I said for the child to hear as well. "I've stayed in your house."

"The gentleman means he came visiting, Francie." Considerably lower the woman said "We've had enough of her talking to people who aren't there. Who were you staying with?"

"My aunt. That was her studio." I indicated the window, and a woman looked out as if I'd summoned her. "Who's that up there?" I couldn't help blurting.

"My other mummy," Francie said with pride.

"It's our bedroom at the moment," the woman at the gate said. "We aren't sure about the view."

"Your little girl said it was a puzzle."

"You can still call her our daughter," the woman said with a look that searched for disagreement. "I don't know why she would tell you that."

"Because there are faces in the wood," the little girl called. "Really there's just one."

"You can see all sorts of things at her age if you go looking for them," the woman said. "Anyway, enjoy your walk. I'd better get back to my exercise."

She meant the swing. Its repeated squeak grew fainter as Roy and I made our way along the sporadically gravelled path. At least she'd given me an idea what he must have thought he'd seen during Thelma's wake. Of course children often saw faces in foliage. I seemed to recall doing so myself in Third Mile Wood, unless that had been a puzzle picture I'd pored over as a child.

Silence intermittently pierced by birdsong massed around the path as the green of the forest did: explosions of foliage, gatherings of moss and ivy on the tree trunks, elaborations of undergrowth. When I glanced back I couldn't see a single house, as if the woods were impatient to be themselves. "Why's it called Third Mile Wood?" Roy said.

"My aunt used to say it was because however far you thought you'd walked, there would still be a mile to go. Mind you, I don't know how much she used to make up."

"Like what?"

I felt oddly hesitant about remembering. "In the autumn the trees in here used to catch the wind, keep hold of it, I mean. You'd hear the leaves fluttering like bats in a cave. That's one thing she said."

"Why would she if it wasn't true?"

I was disconcerted by how eager to believe Roy appeared to be. "She may have thought it was. They'd given her the drug by then."

"Or maybe she wanted to lend you her imagination. What else did she tell you?"

"I remember once she said in the winter some of the leaves stayed on the trees when they ought to have fallen. Just their veins hanging in the air, she said. When the trees turned to skeletons their leaves would too. Maybe that was a picture she never got around to painting."

"Wish she had."

The path turned a bend, beyond which it curved in the opposite direction through the trees, quite like a mirror image. I'd assumed the woods might bring my memories alive, but now I had the odd notion that the process could be reversed. Had my aunt's fantasies affected me more than I'd realised? I felt as if something she'd shown me lay around the next bend. This was no reason to feel even slightly apprehensive, and I matched Roy's eager pace. As our stony footsteps seemed to hush the birds, I saw a long object lying beside the path. "I think I remember that," I said, only to feel absurd — it could hardly be the same log I'd seen decades earlier. I recalled thinking that one looked as if it was trying to hide in the grass, in which case it would have been thoroughly hidden by now. Just the same, it looked confusingly familiar — the four upheld stumps of branches situated regularly enough for legs, and the circular knots in the lopped end, suggestive of eyes blind with moss beneath a ragged smile in a flat inverted face. "She told me about something like that," I said.

"It's some wood." Rediscovering enthusiasm, Roy said "What did she say?"

"She said if you turned it over it would waken the wood."

"The wood," Roy said before gesturing around him, "or the wood?"

"Maybe it was supposed to be both. She said a friend told her."

"So did you turn it over?"

"You can see I didn't," I said and had to laugh at myself. "No, of course that's not the one. Whichever it was, I didn't touch it and she didn't either."

"Let's try it now, then."

I couldn't help holding my breath as Roy poked the toe of his trainer under the log and levered it out of the grass. It wobbled on two of its stumps and then came down on all of them. Either the impact stirred the grass around it or the departure of unseen insects did. When the activity subsided I couldn't quite see where it stopped, perhaps because I was distracted by the appearance of the log, crouching on all fours to thrust forward its round slab of a face. It might have been a carving of a guardian of the woods, blindly alert for intruders and poised to leap. "She should have put that in a picture," Roy said.

He was already striding onwards, and I made the effort to outdistance him, which gave me an excuse to glance back. Had the grinning log toppled over? At that distance I couldn't be sure, and the long grass didn't help, but I thought the stumps resembling a caterpillar's legs might be uppermost again, as though it had twisted onto its back to await the next visitor. While this was a notion my aunt might have had, I was happy to leave it behind.

Ahead the path split into a pair that appeared to be marked as green as the leaves that shaded them. I took the left-hand route, which was slightly more gravelled than its equally overgrown neighbour. My instincts suggested that it would eventually bring us back to the car park. It led through a tunnel of trees, beneath branches heavy with leaves. The foliage was so abundant that long before we reached the end I began to feel as though the laden boughs were about to nod towards us, lowering the leafy roof. The notion reminded me of a carnivorous plant, and I was glad to emerge into relatively unobstructed sunlight, even when I saw a pattern of stones beside the path. "What are you thinking now, dad?" Roy said.

The sight had made me falter. The four grey stones were bare except for a fur of lichen, which didn't lessen their resemblance to inverted hoofs. "My aunt showed me something like that in here," I admitted. "Someone's buried a horse upside down, she said."

"That's kind of what they look like," Roy said and scrutinised my face. "She said more stuff, right?"

"She told me there were places where the world could turn upside down or inside out. Supposedly her friend told her."

"Which friend?"

"I think it may have been the man she left my uncle for."

Roy's interest flagged or at any rate reverted to the sight beside the path. "Did she show you how turning things round worked?"

"There's her painting where all the trees you think are convex are concave, and all the spaces between them are inverted trees."

I assumed he was asking about Thelma's work, but I recalled how her suggestion had made me feel – as if I were on the wrong side of the globe, hanging by my feet towards the sky. She'd said that you didn't need to move the symbol, unlike the log – that just concentrating on it would be enough. Perhaps I turned away too fast, however ridiculously irrational my haste was. I almost lost my balance, and the world around me seemed to capsize, dangling the forest into space. I was about to grab Roy for support if not for some greater reassurance when I managed to regain my sense of how things ought to be. "Enough of that," I declared and waited barely long enough to make sure Roy came away as well.

The path was distinguishable only as a strip of paler grass, no longer emphasised by gravel. I felt as if the vegetation that had overwhelmed it was threatening my senses too. The sunlit greenery everywhere around us was so intensely present that I could smell and virtually taste it, leaving little room for thought. My aunt had never said how you would know if the world had been turned inside out, but the notion made the trees at the edge of my vision feel illusory, close to abandoning their substance to exhibit some kind of reversal, a hollowness eager to take on more life. Whenever I glanced aside I saw nothing my aunt would have imagined, which surely meant I needn't. A marker post next to the path heartened me, at least until we reached it. Was it painted green, or was that moss? When I looked back for reassurance that we hadn't wandered away from the official routes, I couldn't see the path. "Aren't we going further?" Roy said.

I should make the most of the time we had together. We had hours of daylight yet, and I said "Anywhere in particular?"

"Anywhere your aunt showed you stuff."

In that case we might as well find our way out, since nothing further came to mind — and then I recalled her saying the woods had a face. I'd never seen or grasped what she meant, but now I felt it could be anywhere around me. A sense that I might glimpse one, shaped by leaves or bark or the contortions of a fallen tree, distracted me from concentrating on the ill-defined path. Not seeing so much as the hint of a face only intensified the feeling that one was about to reveal itself, perhaps the first of many repetitions of a solitary face. Its imminence felt like an unseen shadow, and despite the sunshine that parched the track yellow I had to shrug off a shiver, as though we were walking through a marsh. At least a marker post ahead established that we were following an official path, except that as we came closer I saw it owed much of its greenness to moss. The post wasn't as regular as it had looked at a distance, and when I tried to strip away the moss, the stump disintegrated. It hadn't been painted at all. It might almost have been feigning artificiality, a trick played by the woods. "We need to find a path that's on the map," I said.

"I can't remember what that looked like." Less hopefully than as a challenge Roy said "Can you?"

While I had only a general impression, I thought the green path had circled left, eventually returning to the car park. The problem was that I had no idea how far back we'd strayed away from it or how we could find it again. Beyond the false marker there wasn't even a path. The nearest to a track that I could see led into the depths of the forest to our left, and I was about to propose heading for it when Roy said "What's that?"

I was more nervous than I'd realised. "What are you seeing?"

"Nothing." Before I could react he said "Listen."

At first I heard a vast protracted breath — a hot breeze passing through the woods. As the leaves very gradually regained stillness, I wondered when I'd last heard birdsong. Silence as oppressive as the unrelieved verdure settled around us, and I was about to ask Roy what he expected me to hear when I caught the sound. It was a voice, so distant that I had no idea of its gender. I thought it was singing a song, though I couldn't distinguish a word or even a melody. "Let's find her," Roy said.

"We don't know if that's the right way. It sounds like the folk festival."

"I think it's a radio at someone's house. Anyway, whoever's there can help us."

This surely was an option. I couldn't understand my hesitation, especially since the voice came from the direction I'd meant to follow through the trees. As we advanced into the forest I felt as if my mind could take in nothing except green. Even the tree trunks were fattened with green moss. I sensed growth progressing all around me, too measured to be visible, although suppose some aspect of it formed into a face? I did my best to focus on the route between the trees and the voice to which it seemed to promise it would lead. More of a tune was audible now, though it sounded as though the performer was searching for one. Every so often I caught a few words I took for a refrain: "Call me my name." This surely suggested a folk song, which might very well mean it was coming from the festival, but at least that would take us out of the woods. I had no idea how far we'd followed the nominal path when Roy said "Have we done the third mile yet?"

I wished he hadn't asked. "I hope we won't have to," I said.

The idea seemed to let the woods close in. When I looked back the far end of the path was indistinguishable from the trees. In the distance ahead it grew equally impossible to locate. The stillness all around us felt like the imminence of a transformation. We were crossing an elaborate mosaic of fallen leaves, who knew how many years of them, and I remembered my aunt saying there were places where leaves chased you even if there was no wind. Glancing back showed me nothing of the sort, but I could have fancied the path stirred underfoot, as if the leaves were restless. Perhaps I was treading on insects, not an appealing notion. I could have thought the sensation or its source had enlivened the woods, and here came the threat of faces in the trees again, a vision I wished my aunt had never lent me. I felt desperate to grasp the words of the distant song so as to rein in my consciousness, but could still hear only that same phrase: "Call me my name..." As I strove to bring the voice closer it seemed to lurch at me, only to fall silent. I was willing it or anyone to become audible when Roy said "Have we done it?"

I felt almost robbed of words, or nervous of understanding. "What?" I said like someone no more than Roy's age.

"Aren't we back? Isn't that a house?"

I peered where he was pointing. A mass of green beyond the furthest trees looked more solid than foliage, but remoteness could be lending that appearance to a bank of leaves or grass. Even when we halved the distance I was wary of embracing the illusion, and urged a voice to make itself heard. Instead I heard a door creak open, which could be the movement of a tree trunk, even if there was no wind. The sun glinted on a pool of water, though how could a pool be so high in the air? Perhaps it was on top of a ridge. Now I saw it was rectangular and upright, and felt as if the woods had lost their power to confuse my perceptions. The sight beyond the trees was indeed a house, painted an unhelpful green. My aunt's house stood to its left, and along the fence to the right was the car park.

I made for the entrance and didn't slow down until both of us were in the car park, from where I gave Third Mile Wood a last look. I saw trees absorbing the sunlight, and no trace of the fancies I appeared to have inherited from my aunt. "Well," I said, which felt almost like enough, "that was some kind of an adventure."

"Just the start, dad."

For once I might have preferred him to sound less enthusiastic. "I'd like to head home now."

"I didn't mean today." Having finished not much of a laugh, Roy said "Let's see more tomorrow. There's lots we could."

CHAPTER FIVE

On the Roof

On our return to Third Mile Wood Roy took the yellow path. At
first I managed to keep up with him, but soon I fell behind. I was
hindered by a sense that the forest was on the brink of turning into
a cartoon of itself. Already the trees looked flatter than they ought
to be, more like a painting that could render us just as motionless. If
they came to life I was afraid it might be a wrong kind. Perhaps they
would start to dance where they stood, unless they scurried on their
knuckly roots to clasp one another's branches before forming rings
everywhere around us in a ritual dance. The holes fallen branches
had left in the tree trunks looked about to gape if not to burst into
song, to surround me with the lyric I'd heard last time we were here.
Might my aunt have had visions like this during the psilocybin trial?
Could I have inherited the effects somehow? Constantly glancing
about for reassurance that the forest hadn't changed slowed me
down, and now Roy was out of sight. I was afraid I'd lost the path
until I saw a yellow marker post ahead. I was making for it when the
post turned green, as if moss had swarmed up from the undergrowth
to add the colour of the woods. Now I saw that the whole of the
forest – foliage, tree trunks, grass and other vegetation – was a single
shade of lurid green, the expression of a solitary underlying presence.
This frightened me more than I understood, and I tried to shout to
Roy, but I wasn't even sure what came out of my mouth. All the
same, it brought a response – a distant voice. "Call me," it said, and
I was reminded of yesterday's faraway song. Was there more to its
demand? "Call me, lad" or "Call me mad" or "Call me sad"? The
strain of trying to decipher it made my clenched jaws throb, and
belatedly grasping it jerked me awake. "Coffee, dad," Roy had said
at least once.

"Wealth, ankhs." Trying to take hold of my words while opening my eyes proved to be one task too many. "What tie miss it?" I mumbled.

"Getting on for eight."

Having managed to focus on my phone, I would have said it was closer to seven. "I'll leave it here, shall I?" Roy said.

He awaited a mumble before planting the mug on the bedside table. His question plainly contained the hope that I wouldn't linger in bed. "Have you been up long?" I felt prompted if not urged to ask.

"Maybe a couple of hours."

"I'm impressed. What did you find to do?"

"I've been reading about your aunt. I want to ask you about her."

This felt unnecessarily reminiscent of my dream about a vision she might have had. "Let me have a shower first," I said.

The shower was meant to help me wake up – surely not to put off the discussion. As the thin tilted storm drummed on my scalp, a kitchen aroma crept through the steam. I joined Roy to find he'd made a decent job of sausages, each of which poked out of the bivalve of a roll. While I was pleased he'd volunteered, I sensed he was anxious to get the task out of the way so that I wouldn't delay talking. "Tell me what you'd like to hear," I said.

"What really happened to your aunt?"

"I thought you'd have read that." This felt like an attempt to deny responsibility for his knowledge, and I said "Supposedly she felt she'd taken her vision as far as she could, and that's why she volunteered for the drugs trial. It turned out they gave her the highest dose of anyone, and she said she saw new meanings in the world."

"I read she felt her brain was opening up like a flower and her eyes were blossoming as well."

"Just remember it was a controlled experiment run by experts, and even that may have gone wrong for her."

Roy looked amused by my sally at an admonition. "Didn't you ever take anything, dad?"

"I may have smoked a bit of pot when I was at university." Although this minimised my experience, parenthood had lessened my liberalism. "That doesn't mean you should," I said, "and I hope you aren't and won't."

When Roy opened his mouth I thought I'd prompted a confession, especially since he didn't speak at once. "I wasn't asking about that part of her life," he said. "I meant the end."

"She died in a fall, Roy. She fell off a tower block."

"I know all that. How, though? Why?"

"Barbare, she's the owner of the gallery that first took Thelma on, she thought Thelma may have been looking for new ideas. She was seen elsewhere that day, so Barbare assumed she was scouting locations. She always took a sketch pad in her car, and it was there when they found her."

"Don't you think that's wrong? If she went up the high rise, why would she leave that in the car?"

"Maybe she'd have fetched it if she'd found anything worth sketching. Maybe she went up to look for places around the block."

"Do you think looking made her fall?"

"Nothing else that I can think of." Just in time I saw I'd almost missed the chance to say "Unless the drug did. Some people think they can fly."

"That was years after she took it, though."

"People can have flashbacks years later." It occurred to me that my panic yesterday in Third Mile Wood had felt not unlike a cannabis experience, and perhaps I'd just explained it to myself. "Maybe she had one on the roof," I said.

"How about the man she left your uncle for?"

"What are you saying?" I wasn't sure why this disconcerted me so much, unless I was troubled by Roy's way of thinking. "The drug couldn't have brought him," I said.

Roy laughed, but not much. "I'm saying where was he when she was on the roof."

"Presumably not with her, or someone would have said. We couldn't even track him down to get in touch after my aunt died. My parents thought he might have gone for good by then."

"Maybe she was screwed up because he left her."

"My mother thought that might have been part of it, but I don't think she ever really understood her sister."

"I'd like to. Did you ever go where she died?"

"It never occurred to me, and I have to say—"

"She says somewhere you never know what's anywhere till you go and look. It might help us understand her better. Don't you want to, dad?"

I'd begun to feel disloyal to my aunt's memory, and I didn't want to quash Roy's enthusiasm. "We can drive there if you like, but don't expect too much."

As my car unlocked itself on the drive hemmed in by rhododendron bushes, a thin insistent screech approached the station — the cry of brakes on the track. A concentrated sun appeared to have parched the sky, leaving it white as eggshell and even less substantial. In ten minutes we were travelling under the river, through the clinically pallid tunnel. On the far side the Liverpool streets had been robbed of all their shadows. Outside the city fewer buildings hid the flatness of the land. Extensive fields shone fiercely with the sun, and some looked drained of colour. Scattered spires marked the horizon, but when I turned off the motorway towards Stonefield there wasn't a church to be seen.

I was expecting less than I'd told Roy he should. The tower block where my aunt died had been derelict then, and I assumed it had been demolished since. Then the tops of several blocks rose ahead as if they were supporting the edge of the sky, and soon I saw they'd been renovated. The five of them dominated the overspill estate, which otherwise consisted of identical terraces of houses — ranks that resembled containers with windows — and ungenerous promenades of shops, quite a few of which were defunct or at any rate shuttered. An elongated concrete church with a perfunctory steeple lay low behind the first tower block, as though it had been flattened or designed to hide. It was no taller than its neighbours, a row of vintage cottages with thatched roofs and small gardens, the last remaining predecessors of the estate. For a moment they distracted me from realising "I don't know where it happened. It could be any of the blocks."

"Can't we ask?"

"I wouldn't know how. Let's walk around and see if anything suggests itself."

When Roy kept his seat I thought he was being adolescently stubborn until I saw him consult his phone. "There's a police station," he said, only for his eagerness to flag. "It's shut."

"Let's get a sense of the area, then. That's all we can do."

Roy confined his disagreement to a grimace as he left the car. I'd parked alongside the first cottage, where an old lady straightened up beyond the low hedge to fix us with a look. Her skin was on the way to growing as white as her hair. Green rubber gloves flapped around her elbows as she brandished a polystyrene carton she'd retrieved from a flowerbed. Once she decided that we weren't the culprits or potential malefactors she dropped the squeaky carton in a black bag and stooped with a disgusted grunt to collect more litter.

Characters like a giant child's stencilling identified the nearest tower block as **BLOCK FIVE**. Twenty storeys of communal balconies led up to the presumably flat roof, the kind from which my aunt had fallen, but I saw no way to establish whether this was the one. I was about to suggest moving on when Roy said "What do you think, dad?"

Before I could reply, someone else spoke. "Is he proposing to live there?"

I assumed the old lady meant Roy. "Not at his age."

"Not at any, I would hope." She was at the hedge, frowning to fend off a wince as she extracted an abandoned plastic wrapper from among the thorns. "You don't want him falling in with the wrong element," she said.

"I'm picky with my friends," Roy wanted her to know.

"You won't find many of the right kind here any more," the woman said, still to me. "Not since they built this soulless place around us."

"We aren't looking for accommodation," I assured her.

"Then may I ask what you are looking for?"

"Where my dad's aunt died. She fell off one of those," Roy said, jerking his head at the tower block. "Thelma Turnbill."

"He doesn't hold back, does he?" It was unclear whether the woman meant this as praise. "Were you even at school then?" she asked him.

"Nearly, and anyway it doesn't matter. My dad's her nephew."

"I'd gathered as much, thank you. I still don't understand why you're here."

"We're going where she did."

"I sincerely hope not," the woman said and turned on me. "What does the boy mean?"

"My aunt was an artist. We're researching her life." This felt like a bid to explain our behaviour to myself. "Visiting places she found significant," I said.

"Significant." After a pause that an examination of the word apparently required, the woman said "I suppose you could put it that way."

"He just did."

I was about to apologise for Roy when the woman said "You're where you want to be."

It could have been a question bereft of approval. Since her attention had settled on fragments of plastic she was tearing out of the hedge, I said "We won't distract you any further."

"I'm not distracted at all. I'm not entirely worn down yet," she said and glared at the tower block. "I'm advising you you're in the correct place. The lady fell from block five."

"Well, thank you." As she lowered her eyes to her thorny task I said "Roy, let's have a closer look."

We'd turned away by the time the woman said "Don't you care to hear anything further?"

Roy swung around at once. "Whatever you've got."

In case she found his eagerness impolite I said "Please, by all means."

"I saw your aunt make her way up the building. I only wish I'd realised something must be wrong and contacted the authorities in time."

Rather too much like my son I said "What are you saying was wrong?"

"I should tell you first of all the place was derelict. Some of us had been complaining for years to the council, but they simply allowed it to run down. It wasn't even made secure, and all the local louts were using it for mischief. Every window smashed, and fires on half the floors. I've no doubt there were drugs and rutting too. Why would anybody like your aunt seek out such a place?"

"Dad thinks she was after ideas."

"She would have had to be desperate. I fear she was."

With some care I said "Can you say why?"

"I can, yes." Having paused to make it plain she found my form of words uncouth, the woman said "Why else would she have struggled all that way up to the roof?"

"Isn't there a lift?" Roy said.

"All those had been vandalised." Almost entirely to me the woman said "I saw her go in by herself, but I heard her talking on the stairs."

"Maybe she was on her phone."

"She didn't have it with her, Roy, unless it was stolen afterwards. There's no evidence she made a call. Certainly nobody came forward."

The woman at the hedge cleared her throat, a sharp shrill sound. "I'm sorry if you think I should have."

Before I could respond more gently Roy demanded "Why didn't you?"

"Perhaps I was ashamed of failing to intervene." Just as defiantly the woman said "Or perhaps I didn't care to sully her reputation after I learned who she was."

"So who would she have been talking to?" I said.

"It must have been herself, I fear. I was surprised she could even find the breath when she had so much to carry."

I felt infected with surprise. "What was she carrying?"

"Two large bags full of jars of some kind."

"Have you any idea what she did with them?"

"I've every idea," the woman said and gave me time to imagine several. "As soon as she reached the roof she came to the edge and emptied the bags over. That's how I can tell you what was in them. And then she said something I couldn't hear, and the jars had hardly smashed when she threw herself after them." The woman held my gaze well after adding "I told you I could have harmed her reputation."

Rather than interpret this as a threat I said "I understand."

"Didn't you ever tell anyone?" Roy said.

"I phoned the services at once, of course." The woman was addressing me as though Roy hadn't spoken. "I told them I'd heard glass break," she said, "and I'd seen your aunt had fallen."

"I shouldn't think it would have helped if you'd said more."

I was trying to placate Roy – I didn't need anybody else's emotions troubling me while I came to terms with the information about my aunt – but he said "Did you see her face when she did it?"

"No, because she turned around at the last moment. She was looking back."

I had the awful thought that my aunt had changed her mind too late. "What at?" Roy said.

"Nothing I could see. I've said once that I'm certain she was by herself."

"Maybe she thought she'd heard someone and lost her balance."

"You may think that if you wish." To me the woman said "I tried to forget what I'd seen as soon as I was able. Till now I practically had."

"Thank you for doing what you could," I said and forestalled any comment Roy might have made. "Let's have that look."

As he followed me to the tower block the woman uttered another displeased grunt, which might have referred to us. Fragments of bottles glittered dully in the shadow of the block. They could hardly have belonged to the jars my aunt had thrown off the roof, but they reminded me that I had no idea why she'd behaved that way. I tilted my head back to stare up the tower, and saw a greyish object resting on the parapet. In a moment it toppled over the edge – no, took flight, revealing that it was a pigeon. No doubt a nearby movement meant another bird had hopped or flown out of sight on the roof. "Are we going up?" Roy said.

"What do you think that's likely to achieve?"

"We won't know till we see, will we? I'll go if you want to hang about down here."

The notion of leaving him alone on the roof made me feel I wasn't taking care of him. "We'll both go," I said at once.

The lobby was deserted. The whitish concrete walls were littered with graffiti, mostly names as large as the official letters outside but considerably untidier. A grubby plastic button occupied the gap between a pair of lifts. When Roy poked it the button flickered feebly as an ember. The right-hand lift staggered open, and as we stepped in I heard its neighbour gape. Once Roy thumbed the topmost of the buttons, most of the numbers on which were blurred if not erased by use, he wiped his hand on his shorts. "You need gloves like she had," he said.

He meant the owner of the cottage. I'd never seen my aunt wear gloves even when her hands had grown motley with paint. I felt oddly guilty for using the lift when she'd had to climb an entirely unreasonable number of stairs, even though the grey cage resembled a windowless cell. The metal walls were scraped and gouged, not to mention scrawled with extravagant spray-painted characters apparently unconcerned with forming words. Halfway up the shaft a smell of cannabis drifted into the lift, and Roy almost looked at me before glancing hastily aside, as if he wasn't sure he should own up to recognition. I wanted him to be more open with me, but the smell made me nervous that the lift might let in someone who wouldn't welcome our presence. It faltered more than once, emitting an ominous muffled twang, but stayed shut until we reached the top floor.

A concrete space distinguished from the entrance lobby by different graffiti led to a balcony lined with windows and front doors. A band was rehearsing in an apartment, with bass and percussion so fierce I thought I heard a window jangle. The stairs were on the far side of the lifts, where the last flight ascended to the roof. At the top a door on which the remnants of a sign spelled **KEE LOSE** had been wedged open. Beyond it the bleached sky looked unnaturally low. When I grabbed the handrail while avoiding beer cans on the steps it clattered in its crumbling sockets, and I let go for fear of alerting someone in the tower block. I pressed my hands against the cold rough walls instead as I clambered up to the roof. I felt nervous of encountering someone out there, but when my head cleared the doorsill I saw the roof was deserted.

Weeds sprouted from cracks in the concrete expanse, which was strewn with cans. The parapet was at least four feet high, and I couldn't imagine anybody falling over it by mistake. As I headed for the edge above the entrance to the tower block the band recommenced its performance, drums thudding harder than ever. I had the impression that the band was pounding a folk song so flat it was unrecognisable. I planted my hands on the parapet and leaned over, though not very far.

Little less than two hundred feet below, the microscopic occupier of a doll's house stooped minutely to a garden like a green inkpad. Except for a dwarf lorry tracing the horizon, I could see no other movement anywhere on the levelled landscape. As Roy joined me I straightened up, to be met by a surge of dizziness that made me grab the parapet. Despite my momentary panic, I found I was in no danger of toppling over the edge. Perhaps up to that moment I'd hoped the woman at the cottage had been wrong about my aunt. "I think we've seen all there is to see," I said.

"You saw that, dad."

This sounded like a question that wasn't quite sure of itself. When I looked where Roy was pointing, I saw an irregular line of greyish marks that led from the doorway, ending close to us. At first glance I could have taken them for footprints, which made no sense. There was just one set of marks, none returning to the stairs, and they were composed of lichen, however closely some of them resembled the prints of bare feet. It was even more ridiculous to fancy they'd been there since my aunt's fatal visit, and I could have done without the way they clung to the edge of my vision as I headed for the stairs. "Nothing to do with Thelma," I said, "and nothing to do with us."

CHAPTER SIX

Tales

"Another thing you can say the play's about, Patrick," my aunt said. "Trying to control magic."

"He's meant to be on holiday, Thelma. Give the poor fellow a chance."

"There's never harm in thinking, Neville. He'll have a head start on his class when they go back next term," my aunt said but appealed to me anyway. "You don't mind, do you?"

"I like talking to you about art and stuff."

"So Caliban's the product of a kind of magic but he's made into a slave, and Prospero binds Ariel when he sets him free of the curse."

"He lets him go at the end, though."

"What do you think would happen if you let your familiar loose? That's a spirit somebody's called up to help them."

"I knew that," I said with a hint of teenage pique. "Shakespeare doesn't say."

"There might be good reasons to limit its powers, do you think? Otherwise who knows how the world might end up."

"Sounds as if there's scope for somebody to write a sequel," my uncle said.

My aunt looked not just disappointed but frustrated, and I tried to help. "Maybe you could paint it."

I had a sense that she'd already finished talking about Shakespeare, but now she gave me the impression that I'd missed the point. So as not to leave my uncle out I told him "You could make a game of it."

"A tad too cerebral for my brand, old fellow. How are you finding the new one?"

"It's fun." In case this made it sound too easy I said "I'm not halfway yet."

"Take all the time you like and remember, never be afraid to tell me anything you don't think works."

For years now he'd let me preview his video games, and this was his latest creation – Scise Mice, a title he'd devised on learning Scouse Mouse was in use. Your comical cartoon rodent had to outwit cats and traps and seagulls on the way to collecting the Cheeses of Power and then finding the right labyrinthine route home from a honeycomb of mouseholes. Though I thought it was somewhat young for my age, I didn't want to hurt my uncle's feelings. Perhaps I was actually reacting against how hard some of the levels were, and so I said "Everything does."

"You're a pet to indulge our fancies, Patrick."

"I'm not." Unsure how much my aunt was joking, I thought it best to add a laugh, however awkward. "I like you asking what I think," I said. "Are there any more paintings to look at?"

"I've something in progress." As I opened my mouth my aunt said "Your uncle will tell you I never talk about those."

Her speed left me gaping like a fool, and my uncle said "You have sometimes."

"Not now, and I don't want it to be seen either. Patrick, would you mind not going in my studio unless I say."

"Don't feel singled out, old fellow. I'm barred too."

"I hope it'll be a good secret, anyway."

I thought my words had come out childish, but my uncle said "I think your aunt's keeping a few of those."

Though this sounded affectionate enough to me, my aunt retorted "What are you saying, Neville?"

"Some of your work has been making me feel I don't really know you at the moment. There are things in there I don't understand at all."

"Don't feel left out," my aunt said, and possibly in case I did "Now what shall we all do together? Who's for a walk?"

"So long as it isn't in the woods."

"Why, what's wrong with them?" I had to know.

"I just don't feel too welcome. I expect it's because Thelma's always looking for ideas in there and so she doesn't need me, but I feel as if I'm one too many somehow."

"I don't suppose anybody will object to a game of cards," my aunt said.

We took glasses and a jug of orange juice tinkling with ice cubes to the table under an umbrella at the far end of the back garden. As my aunt dealt hands of knockout whist, a dark shape leapt onto the umbrella, which quivered in the breeze that had brought the shadow of a tree over the fence. Whoever won each round chose trumps for the next one, where every player received one card less. When I selected diamonds, my uncle gave his cards a wry squint. "That's what I call a transformation."

I thought my aunt was about to speak, but she simply glanced towards the woods as if he'd reminded her of an idea. My uncle won the round and soon the game, and we played on. I'd liked whist ever since they'd taught me, but now I was distracted by a sense of being spied upon, which made the face cards I was holding look as though they were peering from behind one another. I kept having to glance at the trees beyond the fence, to see birds darting from branch to branch. They gave me the impression that a presence kept withdrawing into the foliage just as I looked up, and I was quite glad when dinnertime sent us into the house.

My uncle had made a chicken curry or at any rate a politely English approach to one, keeping its distance with the addition of carrots. Dinner was accompanied by a disc of Richard Strauss. "That's the sun coming up," my uncle told me. "He brings it up in *Also Sprach* as well. Now the climbers are shinning up the foothills. Now they've reached a meadow with cows in, hence the bells."

"It isn't just about climbing in the Alps," my aunt objected. "It's about going high so you can see further."

"That kind of high I don't mind. You could have told me when you were going up the mountain."

"I didn't know I'd need to go that far, Neville. I only knew when I was there."

"You're wondering what on earth all this can be about, aren't you, Patrick? Just your old uncle wishing he could join in like he used to."

"Neville, you still help me. You're in my work even if you can't see where."

I had a sense that he was unconvinced. Dinner finished as the sun sank back into the dark, in the symphony and more gradually outside the house. I helped my uncle wash up, a wordless process until he murmured "Forget that little disagreement, won't you? We didn't need to let you hear. Your aunt went looking for something to paint, that's all."

"I thought she just saw things that made her want to paint them."

"She goes looking now. That's the new Thelma. If it works for her, that's what matters."

Was he trying to persuade himself? He didn't speak again until we were in the front room, where he consulted the television listings. "Here's an old favourite we could watch," he said. "*I Married a Witch*."

"A bit twee for Patrick, I should think."

"See if you like it, Patrick. Your aunt's a fan."

"I used to like it," my aunt said. "I don't know how I'd feel about it now."

"One way to find out. You're always saying we should look again."

All this made me uncomfortable with the film, which in any case was too colourlessly vintage for my teenage taste. Since it was meant to be a comedy, I produced a dutiful laugh whenever my uncle's reaction suggested I should. My aunt didn't seem too taken with the prologue, where two witches – Jennifer and her father Daniel – were put to the stake, though they instantly returned as puffs of smoke. She seemed more engaged by Daniel's creation of a body for his daughter, which helped Jennifer plague the Wallaces, the family who'd caused their deaths. My aunt sat forward when Daniel took away his daughter's powers for falling in love with a modern Wallace. She sat back again once Jennifer regained her body, stolen by her father, and my aunt gave an odd laugh as Wallace trapped the magician's essence in a bottle, which sang the line "I'm going to leave you now" to end the film. "What did you think?" my uncle said at once.

"Long long ago, when people believed in witches..." My aunt was quoting the start of the film, not too favourably. "Well, it was meant to be funny," she said.

"I'm guessing it failed in that department."

"It was harmless." This sounded like a dismissal or at any rate an attempt at one. "What's your verdict, Patrick?" my aunt said.

"I liked her."

"Veronica Lake?" my uncle said. "I did at your age and a bit older too."

"I'm sure there were hordes like you." Having indulged us, my aunt said "But she was a body her father made. We never see what she actually looked like."

"I'll make do with how she did," my uncle said.

"You wouldn't give a witch a body," my aunt said with unexpected stubbornness. "They've mixed up their traditions in all sorts of ways."

"It's only a film, dear. Not even a serious one."

I saw my aunt suppress a response and then, I thought, another. Instead of speaking she retrieved a hefty almanac of British folk traditions from beside her chair. As she set about marking pages with a red pen, adding dots so delicate they were barely visible, she said "If you want to watch something else I'll be in the studio."

"Don't leave us," my uncle said. "We've got reading to catch up with as well."

He busied himself with a computer journal swarming with equations, and I turned to the book my aunt had most recently lent me, a novel by Bulgakov. While I wasn't sure I grasped every reference, let alone the whole of its explosion of ideas, I found its unbridled inventiveness exhilarating, and looked forward to the reappearance of Behemoth the cat, surely a demonic familiar. The edition used one of Thelma's paintings on the cover, a glade where the shape of every tree seemed mysteriously symbolic and the solitary androgynous figure in a robe decorated with sigils could just as well have been Margarita as the Master. I might have asked my aunt what she'd had in mind while painting, but I sensed she didn't want to talk. I could have thought she'd tried to use her research in the almanac as an excuse to shut herself in the studio upstairs.

Perhaps I shouldn't have read Bulgakov so close to bedtime. In bed I imagined Behemoth taking even more shapes than he did in the novel. The prospect kept me awake, and so did my uncle's inventive succession of snores. At some point I left all this behind, and wakened to hear my aunt and uncle murmuring in their room. No, the voice was just my aunt's, and my uncle's renewed snores weren't an answer. They weren't even in the same room. My aunt was talking in the studio, to herself or to her work, unless she was on the phone. I couldn't make out a word, and reverted to sleep.

The next time I awoke the house was quiet except for a snorting mutter from the other bedroom. I sneaked to the toilet for a discreet pee, having closed the door as quietly as I could. Embarrassment at being overheard made me aim my output at the porcelain above the pool. Having flushed the toilet, an action that didn't bother me as much, I was padding back to my room when I noticed that the door to the studio was open wide enough to let me see part of the view beyond the window. Distant treetops caught the dawn, and as the light advanced through the forest I glimpsed an odd illusion of a figure crouching among the highest branches of a tree as though it was poised to leap in the direction of the house. Surely it was composed of wood and foliage, but I was about to edge the door wider when I heard my aunt mumble and an equally protesting creak of the bed. I retreated to my room so fast that I couldn't be sure I hadn't seen the shape launch itself into the next tree like a squirrel.

I stayed in my room until I heard my aunt and uncle go downstairs, and then I had a shower. Although the bathroom window faced the forest, the frosted glass offered very little of a view. When I leaned towards it a generalised mass of foliage bulged at me, but that was the only movement. Soon I desisted, feeling inexplicably uneasy, as if I'd invited more than I could see. I was rubbing the mirror above the sink clear of condensation to aid my token shave when I had the unwelcome fancy that the hand imitating mine belonged to an intruder. It was flattened against mine like the underside of a snail, and felt as moist and chill as I imagined that would be. Of course all that was the glass, but I couldn't help feeling relieved once I was able to see my own face in the mirror. Perhaps my mother was right after all, and too much concentration on the likes of my aunt's paintings was inflaming my imagination. All the same, I wasn't about to give up my enthusiasm.

I took a question that had been nagging at me down to breakfast. "Do you have to talk to yourself when you're working?"

"It's been known. I don't think your parents would approve of some of my language."

Since my uncle was scrambling eggs, he hadn't realised I was talking to his wife. "Do you?" I asked her.

"I don't go in for curses, Patrick. Not that kind or any other."

"No, I mean do you talk when you're painting."

"I might." As she turned to find orange juice in the refrigerator she said "Why do you ask?"

"I thought I heard you last night while I was in bed."

"I'll have to keep my voice down. Your uncle was making rather a racket. I suppose you heard that too."

I contributed a laugh in case she expected one. "It was a bit thunderous."

"I decided since I was awake I might as well work."

"It's not like you to paint after dark," my uncle said.

"No need to apologise, Neville." Without waiting for an answer my aunt said "You'll be working all day, won't you? Patrick and I can have our walk."

She was making it sound like a ritual, and I thought my uncle didn't care too much for it – our outing or her choice of words. "Stay on the paths, won't you?" he said. "Don't let her go wandering off."

"If you don't go where other people won't," my aunt said, "you'll never see what's to be seen."

I made a youthfully enthusiastic bid to forestall an argument. "I expect that's what artists do."

"Some of us don't," my uncle retorted, which left me feeling I should have kept the comment inside my clumsy head.

He saw us off into Third Mile Wood from the back gate. A sun that looked shrunken white by its own heat stood above the trees, challenging breezes to cool the day down. The treetops flamed green, lending the foliage they shaded a secretive glow. Silhouettes of leaves crept back and forth on tree trunks, seeking crevices in the bark. On the forest floor, shadows passed over one another like a magician's hands, elaborating the patterns of fallen leaves. Perhaps some or all of this was why my aunt kept glancing away from the path, unless she was tempted by the shade. A long curve led to a further unshaded stretch, and my aunt said "Say whenever you've had enough, Patrick. So long as you can find your way back I can always go on by myself."

"Don't you want me to come with you?"

"Why in anybody's name wouldn't I want that?" Her laugh was as hasty as her answer. "I wouldn't like to be blamed for giving you sunstroke, that's all."

"I've never had it." Since she was equally hatless I said "Have you?"

"All right, I don't suppose we will," my aunt said more impatiently than I thought was called for. "I expect we're protected enough."

She looked as if she felt she'd either said too much or ought to say more, and I wondered if her concern about sunstroke had left me feeling vulnerable to the relentless heat. My uninvited sensitivity made a mass of agitated shadows seem to dodge from tree to tree beside the path as though keeping pace with us. Or perhaps my aunt's behaviour was affecting me, and eventually I said "What are you looking for?"

"Nothing I haven't found already, Patrick."

I thought this could mean she planned to show me aspects of the woods that had set off her imagination, like the inverted hooves and the log she'd said was waiting to be turned over, but she had yet to speak again by the time we heard voices ahead. They were high as birdsong, though I'd heard none of that for a while – so high that they'd left words behind. In a minute two giggling children appeared around a bend, and then a woman did. "Shush now," she kept saying, more forcefully as they approached us. "No more hide and seek for you," she declared as we met on the path.

"It wasn't just us," the little girl protested.

"Don't start fibbing as well or I'll never bring you here again."

"It wasn't," the little boy insisted. "There was someone and they wanted us to find them."

"That's it now. That's all." To my aunt the woman said "They won't be told these days, will they? Ran right off the path where I couldn't see them, and they know I can't run after them."

I might have suggested that the shadowy activity among the trees could have fooled if not enticed the children, since she appeared to be classing me with them, but that idea left me feeling too insulted to speak. In any case the illusion of company beside the path had vanished, though I was unsure when it had, and the boy was objecting "Well, we couldn't see them."

"We only heard them calling us," the girl said. "And they were a he."

"No, she was a she, and she knew our names."

"You're not impressing anyone. Come along at once," the woman said and came close to grabbing the children to urge them along the path.

We watched them scurry onwards while the woman called after them to slow down. "We ought to listen more to children," my aunt said.

I assumed she wasn't including me among them. "What do you think they were talking about?"

"Can you answer that yourself?"

Perhaps I wasn't being treated as an adult after all. In an attempt to demonstrate maturity I said "I expect they were making it up. That's what that lady thought, and she knows them."

"Patrick..." I couldn't tell what sort of disappointment this expressed, even when my aunt said "I suppose you're neither one thing nor the other."

"I don't know what that means."

"Let's say you're not a child any longer but trying too hard not to be."

If this involved a compliment of any kind, my resentment was in its way. "It sounded like the things you used to tell me in here," I retorted, "what they said."

By now we were alone on the path. I thought I heard a giggle somewhere in the trees, but it didn't sound like either of the children. Perhaps the shrill oddly liquid notes were a scrap of birdsong. My aunt glanced in that direction without turning her head. "Shall we leave it, Patrick? You were bound to grow out of my fairy tales. I'm sure your parents will be glad you have."

She'd raised her voice, presumably because she was walking faster, requiring me to keep up. There was no reason to imagine she wanted anybody besides me to hear. She didn't pause or speak again until we reached a junction where the red path crossed the blue. "I think that's enough for today," she said. "Let's get out of the sun."

I thought she was proposing to make for the shade, but apparently she meant to head for home. Despite her remark about the sunlight, she stayed in the middle of the gravelled track, well clear of the trees. I'd had enough of shadows myself, because the edge of my vision kept producing the illusion that a mass of them as tall as a man had solidified, slithering from tree to tree on my left, a swift indefinable shape scaly with bark. The impression vanished before we came in sight of the house, but as my aunt shut the gate in the fence I could have thought a tall flat intruder had slipped in, disappearing at once. Of course it was the shadow of the closing gate.

We had salad for lunch and then read in the garden. I finished the Bulgakov and started a Kafka. "He never reaches the castle," my uncle warned me when he came home. "Old Franz never got to the end of his book."

My aunt marked a location in her almanac as she said "All the more reason to keep on even if you don't know what you'll find."

"That's one way of working, dear. I'm afraid I'd get hopelessly lost."

"I know you have to calculate everything in advance." As she turned the page and poised her pen my aunt said "I wasn't just talking about work."

I waited for an explanation, but none came. I went back to the insidiously labyrinthine tale once I'd relished the cover again, my aunt's painting of a spiky fortress that appeared to have crystallised out of the peak of a mountain. After dinner, her defiantly fiery version of lasagne, we watched an Arthurian film in which each spell exhausted more of Merlin's power. "Tricky business, magic," my uncle said.

My aunt clearly found this facetious, and I think he was as surprised as I was that she took offence. "They've earned powers like those," she said. "You'd value them if you had them."

"I think I'm liable to have to do without."

She might not have heard him. "And you'd miss them if you lost them," she said.

She and my uncle said nothing more throughout the film, and not much once it was over. I went to bed wondering how much they were leaving unspoken until I was out of the way. By the time I fell asleep I'd heard no further conversation, but towards dawn my aunt's voice wakened me. "Wait till he's gone."

As I took this for a belated confirmation that they were delaying a discussion of some subject, my uncle emitted a snore stentorian even for him. I was muffling a laugh at his style of answer when I realised my aunt wasn't talking to him. She was in her studio, and so was another voice. "Not long," it said.

It was too muted to let me tell its gender. I strained my ears so hard they throbbed, but heard no more until a single set of footsteps crossed the landing to the bedroom. I lay as still as any of my aunt's paintings while the dawn started to revive colours all around me. Was someone hiding in the studio? I couldn't bear not knowing. Slipping out of bed, I eased my door open not much less silently than I was holding my breath.

The door to the studio was shut, although I hadn't heard that happen. Might my hearing have let me down in other ways? Perhaps I'd overheard just my aunt's voice. I crept across the landing and used both hands to turn the doorknob by fractions of an inch, and then I took as much care over easing the door open.

The dawn had just found the distant treetops, but the studio was light enough to show me that nobody was hidden among the paintings and easels and other items of my aunt's equipment, let alone behind them. I was about to close the door when a line of objects on the windowsill caught my eye – at least a dozen glass jars, and an open book resting against several. A page was settling into place as if someone had just consulted the book. Perhaps a draught had lifted the page, but the sight gave me an excuse to cross the room.

The jars and the book stood against the dark woods as if they were a secret the depths of the forest were offering. The entry on the page – a place name, I supposed, followed by an obscure annotation – meant nothing to me. Nor did the few inches of earth that were all each jar contained, never mind the initialled labels the jars bore. I picked up a jar in each hand, and the contents whispered as they shifted. They sounded like the start of a surreptitious chorus. I could have fancied that the noise wasn't in the jars at all, and I seemed to feel the room change at my back.

I might have imagined I was in a different room, with carvings on the cornices, in every corner and elsewhere. The house was too modern to have cornices, and it wasn't the room that had changed. The objects that I felt afraid of seeing if I turned around wouldn't be carved – the faces hovering behind me and above. I had a sense that their shapes would prove to be dismayingly unstable, and their sizes too. Perhaps they would swell to fill the room, or some would while their companions shrank. Perhaps just one would occupy the space, bloating like a malevolent balloon. I was barely able to focus on the window, to manage to distinguish that the reflection showed just the studio behind me, with no trace of the presence I sensed looming. Nevertheless I almost dropped the jars as I hastened to replace them on the sill. I swung around to confront the deserted room, and was afraid of making too much noise as I fled. Nobody came to find me – not my uncle or my aunt – but I begrudged every second I had to spend in silently closing the door. In my room I took refuge under the quilt, and as the day brightened I succeeded in believing I'd seen and heard nothing worth a mention. It was all explicable, and I'd behaved almost as oddly as my aunt did. My parents weren't always wrong, and I knew they would want me to put the incident out of my mind. For quite a while I did.

CHAPTER SEVEN

Old Words

Goodmanswood – fallen leaves make face. "You must turn the world over to reveal its truth."

Monks Cross – graffiti too prominent. "The world consists of symbols few can read."

Slatevale – eyes in cracks in rock. "If you would cease to be blind, descend into ultimate darkness."

Priory Ford – features gather on rocks in river. "Each of us is but a stream whose wholeness it is our sacred task to grasp."

Cloudhaven – cloud forms face. "Rise higher from the peak and breathe the atmosphere of space."

Drummer's Meadow – wild flowers sketch denizen. "Mistake not Spring for the season of growth, for the time of secret quickening is Winter, when Darkness comes into His kingdom."

Darkmarsh – tussocks crawl together. "The power of the swamp restores mutability to the world."

Dancers Oak – now housing estate – body formed of moss on trees. "Those who die on the oak may be caught and put to use."

Brightspring – pool mouths secrets. "Become one with silence, that you may hear the songs of streams beneath the earth."

Mountfoot – dew on grass takes restless shape. "To conquer time, contemplate the ghost that is the universe."

Plumb Mine – large face in entrance not on poster. "The deeper it is dug, the more ancient are the secrets which the excavation shall awaken."

Halfway Halt – trees reach for walkers in railway cutting. "Where man cracks the earth, beware the hatching of the egg."

The last entry in my aunt's journal was even more obscure, and hardly even legible. All I could decipher of the first word was the initial L, and the second appeared to begin as *Science* only to trail into a longer word. The scrawl was followed by a phrase that I eventually read as **MADE ABLE** but couldn't fathom. "Well," I said, and nothing else for some moments. "I hope you understand more of this than me."

"Do you know which paintings it's about?"

"I can't identify a single one."

"Maybe those are thoughts she had while she was painting and she didn't put them in. Did she often talk like that?"

"If you mean all the archaic language, my guess is she was quoting."

"Have you tried to find whichever book it was?"

"I'm afraid most of her library went to a charity shop, thanks to my mother. I only managed to salvage this and the books Thelma was involved in."

"You haven't searched," Roy said and typed one of the quotations into his phone, trying several before he desisted. "Looks like it's not online," he said.

"I can't recall ever seeing a book like that in her house. I've worked out what those jars she dropped off the roof were, though. Samples from places she listed in here."

Leafing through the journal had reminded me of initials on the jars – MC, DF, DM or just a single letter. "But why did she drop them?" Roy said.

"I'm afraid she took her reason with her."

"Maybe we'll get an idea when we go wherever you want to drive to." As though to give his eagerness a task Roy said "Shall I look up the distances for you?"

"The nearest one is pretty far."

"We'll still be going, won't we?" Not entirely without childishness Roy protested "You said we would."

"I just wonder if it's worth it when there may not be anything to see. I know what we can do today," I felt relieved to be able to suggest. "Why don't we take a closer look at Thelma's work."

Roy shrugged in the direction of the shelves where it was represented. "Already have."

"The actual paintings. We can see them at the Tate in Liverpool."

"I saw the exhibition when it was in Manchester."

"This will have a different curator and besides, you hadn't seen her book then."

I'd begun to feel unexpectedly if not inexplicably desperate when Roy said "Shall we bring it with us? No, I know. You hold it and I'll take the shots."

I thought I must resemble a criminal posing for an official record as I opened the journal for Roy to photograph the entries. Just my fingertips appeared in each shot, shifting as if troubled by holding the book. Roy even photographed the final entry before I returned the book to the shelf. "We'll take the train," I said.

Though the sun had been doing its job for hours, the heating was turned on throughout the train. Someone had opened every window, which didn't help much. When we sped underground the tunnel roared at us like a beast with no need of breath. Roy pored over his phone all the way to Liverpool, and on the escalator up to James Street too. As I and a number of commuters – not quite as many as I'd thought at first – followed him into the lift that would raise us to street level, I saw he was scrolling through the photographs of Thelma's journal.

Most of the pedestrians on the road that paralleled the waterfront were intent on their phones, like quite a few of the drivers speeding by. Some walkers were following maps or listening to them. As Roy and I made for the dockside, the relentlessly bright simulated voices issuing directions fell behind. We waited while a swing bridge let a barge painted with giant flowers into the Albert Dock. Reflections of visitors to dockland passed through the windows of the barge like film through the gate of a projector. There Roy and I went, and here we came again with somebody between us, so close that the figure appeared to have its arms around our shoulders. It must be a trick of perspective, not just because I could feel nothing of the kind but since our apparent companion's face, unlike ours, was an undefined blur. When I glanced around, nobody was even close behind us.

Across the bridge a colonnade with pillars painted redder than the converted sandstone warehouse brought us to the Tate. A lift carried us to the third floor of the gallery, which was occupied by the exhibition of my aunt's work, *Reaching Further*. Other canvases provided context – paintings by Laila Hallack, Frida Kahlo, Ithell Colquhoun and others, not least Leonora Carrington. Landscapes bristling with imminence were the work of Californian psychedelic artists – Gage Taylor, Bill Martin. I saw how these related to my aunt's vistas on the edge of revelation, but I was looking for an explanation of the entries in her journal. While Roy followed the chronology of the exhibition I made for the further room.

I felt as if I were encountering Thelma's late works for the first time once I set about examining them. I knew each painting contained a distant figure, an element one critic had called the imminent presence. My aunt had refused to say what the figure represented, which had led one hostile commentator to liken it to Wally, who lurked in a series of children's books – Wally, who adopted different identities around the world: Waldo in America, Charlie in France, Holger in Denmark, Van Lang in Vietnam... One analysis suggested that Thelma's motif was designed to entice the viewer to look deep into the image, and as I moved from canvas to canvas it felt like a secret key to each landscape it inhabited, if not the seed of some kind of transformation. I'd always taken the figure in a meadow to be far away, but now I wondered if it was much closer and no larger than a flower. As I went close enough to nuzzle the canvas and then backed away to take in the entire image, the elaborate patterns of grass and weeds appeared to shift until I could have fancied they were about to reveal a hidden form. None made itself plain, and I moved to the next painting, where a remote watcher stood at the far edge of a faintly luminous swamp. The treacherous ground was bordered by mist and trees, and there was no telling where solidity ended or began. As I peered at the painting it started to flicker, so that the traces of ground mist twitched as though eager to converge and take a shape. None of this helped me understand the entries in the journal. "The deeper it is dug, the more ancient are the secrets which the excavation shall awaken" – but I saw no sign of this in Thelma's painting of a slate mine almost indistinguishable from the depths of the night, in which a figure perched high above the jagged entrance became only very gradually visible. Though I couldn't distinguish a face, I felt as if one was implicit in the image. The yawning entrance to the apparently abandoned mine could be the mouth, an impression that led me to feel other features might be scattered through the stony landscape, eager to be gathered by the spectator. Might this be true of all of Thelma's final paintings? The spectacle of the slate walls around the entrance slowly forming from the blackness – the sense of a secret assembly – felt as though it was fastening on my mind. I didn't know how long the sight had held me motionless when Roy said "Dad."

Perhaps he was repeating it; his tone implied as much. I couldn't have said whether I resented the interruption or was glad to be released from the oppressive trance. I was about to ask how the picture looked to him when he said "Here's someone who wants to meet you."

He was with a girl something like his age. She was half a head shorter, slim with large pale blue eyes in a slightly chubby face. She had a small nose and a mouth my mother would have called petite. Long blond hair close to silver almost hid her ears, the tiny lobes of which were virtually invisible. She wore a black T-shirt and denim overalls too baggy to outline her shape, and sandals that left her long narrow feet not far from bare. "Bella," Roy said, "this is my dad."

She stepped forward swiftly and gracefully to clasp my hand. Her grasp was cool and light but firm, not to mention sufficiently brief that I wouldn't have minded a prolongation. I was instantly impressed by her confidence. "Very pleased to meet you," she said, "Mr…"

"Not Mister anything. Well, it's Semple like my son, but you needn't use it. The name's Patrick."

I wondered how unnecessary my babbling sounded, since Roy looked embarrassed. I thought I was doing my best to put the girl at her ease, but perhaps the attempt was more for myself. "Thank you for giving it to me," she said.

I found her turn of phrase charmingly odd. "So you'll be Bella."

"I will be." She smiled at my words or her own. "I am."

"Can I guess you're at school together?"

"You can guess," she said, and her smile widened as far as her small mouth would allow. "Go on."

I was disconcerted to feel she was flirting with me, not least because the notion seemed presumptuous on my part. "Then I'm guessing you've known each other for a while."

The laugh accompanying her smile came from my son. "We've only just met, dad."

"Well, you've certainly fooled me." This sounded rather too accusing, even if it was aimed at nobody in particular. "I expect it's your generation," I tried adding.

Bella gave me a gentle big-eyed look. "What is, Patrick?"

"If you want to know someone these days you go straight for them."

My suggestion left me feeling out of my depth if not out of place, but Bella stayed serene. "Maybe we just know who we like at once."

"That's the easy part. It was for me." I was addressing Roy as well now. "Getting to know your mother," I said, "that was more of a task."

"Maybe you never really did." Presumably this made him need to explain "My mum and dad split up."

"True enough," I said, not without pique. "You shouldn't be too ready to believe you know anyone."

"I hope I won't make anybody think they don't know me," Bella said.

"Then I'm sure you won't. Can I ask why you wanted to meet me?"

"Roy was saying you knew Thelma Turnbill."

"I stayed with her and my uncle quite a few times. I take it you're an admirer."

"It's lucky we were here when you came," Roy told her.

"I've been before. I was always interested in her work."

"What's the appeal for you?" I said.

"The mysteries. The things you aren't supposed to understand but let them come to you. They're what brings me back."

"And have they? Come, I mean."

"Maybe you need to know what she thought she was painting."

"That's what we think too, isn't it?" Roy said. "We know some of the places she did. I think that's Drummer's Meadow there, and that one's got to be Darkmarsh, and that'll be Slatevale or else it's Plumb Mine."

Bella looked impressed and eager to be more so. "How do you know all that?"

"We've got a book she wrote the places down in. I'll show you if you like."

"Roy," I said, "we haven't talked about making it public."

"Bella's not the public. Can't she see?"

"You mustn't show me if your father wouldn't like it. You've told me where she went."

"There's more in here than that," Roy said, flourishing his phone. "You'd like how Bella sees things, dad. It's the way your aunt would."

I thought he was trying to prolong their encounter. More urgently than he might have wanted her to notice he said "Tell him how some of the pictures look."

"Maybe that's the face the night has." It was the entrance to the mine, and Bella turned to the painting of the marsh. "The mist could be the swamp breathing," she said.

Though I found her views a little studied, I said "Are you an artist yourself?"

This prompted an appreciative smile. "I've never tried to be one."

"Sounds like you could be, though," Roy said.

I felt they'd reached a point where they could do without me, if indeed they weren't wishing me away. "I'll leave you to it, shall I? I'll be in the first room."

"Wait, dad. She's got a book. Show him."

Bella reached into her capacious shoulder-bag, which might have been plaited out of dried grass, and produced a history of polar expeditions, graced with Thelma's early painting of a thatched cottage halfway up a glacier. At the time the use of the image was criticised for being too narrowly English. "Is history your thing, then?" I said.

"We'd be nobody without the past and people who explore." As I took this for assent Bella said "I got it for the cover."

"It's the rarest of the books that use her work. They reprinted it without her cover. I don't even have it myself."

"Now you have," Bella said and held it out. "It's yours, Patrick."

"That's extremely kind." I was moved by her uninhibited instinctiveness. "But honestly," I said, "I wasn't asking."

"You don't have to ask me when it's what you need."

"Let me buy it from you at least."

"I won't. It has to be my gift to you." More gently still she said "It wasn't even new when I found it. It's been well owned."

She opened the front cover to display the underside, where an erasure pen had left a dull white patch. "That's a pity," I said.

Bella looked less than happy. "What don't you like?"

"Somebody hiding the inscription or the owner's name or whatever's under there. It's part of the history of the book."

"That's shops for you these days," Bella said like someone of an earlier generation. "Some people don't know what they've got, or they don't care."

As she handed me the volume Roy said "We can do a book for a book. I'll show Bella your aunt's journal."

It was barely a question, and I said "I expect we can."

Bella laid a hand on Roy's shoulder as he brought up the pages on his phone, and I was rather more than ashamed to feel envious. I remembered this kind of early stage of a relationship, if that was what I was witnessing, but I was past such experiences now. All the mistakes I'd made with Julia – most of them my fault or at any rate equally mine – were enough for one lifetime. Bella didn't move her hand until Roy finished swiping the pages aside, and then she blinked at me. "Your aunt never sounded like that," she said.

"That's what I told dad too. He thinks she was quoting someone."

"You haven't found out who." When I mimed empty-handed ignorance Bella said "Maybe she wanted the quotations to be displayed with the paintings."

"So why weren't they?" Roy apparently felt Bella ought to know.

"She didn't finish all her paintings, did she? Maybe she was going to put the mottos with them when she had."

Bella's observation sent me to Thelma's final uncompleted

canvas. As I recalled, the distant faceless shape that featured in her late work looked as simplified by winter in this painting as any of the trees in Third Mile Wood. The tree it stood beside was adorned with buds and foliage and blossoms – all the growth the seasons would engender – and now I saw the figure was more substantial than I remembered, as though some process separate from ordinary time had helped it take form. I was peering at the suggestion of a face when Roy said "Who do you think that's meant to be, Bella?"

"Someone she needed there, I should think," Bella said and turned to me. "Thank you for letting me read her journal."

"Well, thank you for completing my collection."

"And good to meet you."

As she gave my hand a swift polite shake I saw Roy hoping for a handshake if not a hug, but apparently neither was to be had. I couldn't help silently urging him not to let her go for good. If I tried to prevent this I would embarrass them both, but I was struggling against an impulse to nudge him or wink at him or even deliver a peremptory grimace when he spoke at last. "My dad's got some of his aunt's work almost nobody's seen."

"Which is that?"

"Just sketches of my unlovely mug." I was instantly afraid that deprecating myself had spoiled Roy's chance. "She made one every year for years," I said.

"I expect you treasure them," Bella said, adding only "See you then, Roy."

This sounded like a farewell, not an undertaking to meet again. She was turning away, which was surely my opportunity to send Roy some mute encouragement, when he made a noise that dislodged a word trailed by several. "Shall we swap numbers?"

I saw Bella hesitate, and held my breath on his behalf. "Let's," she said.

I was surprised by how venerable an iPhone she took out of her bag until I recalled that the early models were still popular, even sought after. She rested a hand on Roy's shoulder again while he copied her number into his contacts list, and typed his as he read it to her. The transaction was scarcely completed when she bagged her phone. "See you too probably, Patrick," she said.

I watched Roy watch her graceful progress to the exit from the room. As she crossed the linoleum I thought she displayed an old-fashioned discreetness, silent except for the faintest woody tapping of her sandals. The glass door on its metal arm might have belonged to an altogether different era. The doorway framed her distant figure, and then she was a blur beyond the glass. "Thanks for bringing me, dad," Roy said, and in case this was insufficiently enthusiastic "Thanks for making me come. It was worth the trip."

CHAPTER EIGHT
A Return

I looked up from the computer screen to find the workings of the world exposed. The cogs of the windmills were operating a diorama, advancing a procession of puffy pristine clouds along the horizon beneath an otherwise clear blue sky. For a moment the spectacle felt like an insight, and then like even less than one. While the clouds were progressing at a measured pace, the windmills weren't moving in unison, let alone at that speed. Any resemblance to my own task was emptily contrived. I was taking narratives apart to discuss them with my students next month. I had all day to myself, since my son was out with his girlfriend.

I was examining the presence of magic in contemporary mainstream fiction, an investigation prompted by my aunt's work. Here was a magus playing games with the narrator on a Greek island. Here was a headmaster's teenage daughter performing a rite designed to resolve her father's situation in an Iris Murdoch novel. I made notes on these and then set about interpreting Peter Ackroyd, not least the significance of the homunculus John Dee creates in a tale where the past seems eager for revival. My edition used one of Thelma's paintings for its cover, a mansion where all the windows showed an identical resident. The figures were increasingly remote, unless they were progressively approaching, and their faces were obscured by leafy shadows, though not a tree was to be seen. I was trying to put the image out of my mind – I couldn't even see why it had been chosen for the book – when my phone emitted its silvery trill. "Mother," it said.

I felt instantly guilty. When had I last seen my parents? Not since the beginning of the summer break, as if I'd wanted to get a duty done. However often I visited them, I had a sense that they were keeping quiet about the frequency of our encounters and wanted me to appreciate their discretion on the subject – very possibly about my remissness too. "Mother," I said rather more enthusiastically than the phone had, I hoped. "How are you both?"

"Still keeping them on their toes at the office. There's always something to improve."

Yet again I was glad I'd resisted their notion of following them into their accountancy firm. "Aren't you two ever going to retire? The world's out there. You should take the chance to explore it while you have the chance."

"My sister would have agreed with you, Patrick. You know we don't spend for the sake of spending. Money's for investment, not for squandering. I'm sure you'll be glad of it once we're gone."

"I don't need it, honestly, and I really think you and dad should have a break."

"We have those all the time. We only go in when we feel we're needed."

I was thinking that their staff might welcome a break or several from them when my mother said "I expect Roy will be grateful for what's coming to him."

I knew she would interpret any demurral as ingratitude on his behalf, and so I said only "He's staying with me at the moment. If you two want to come and see him I'll make dinner."

"He won't be with you just now."

I took this for a question. "He's with a lady friend in Liverpool."

"Perhaps you should keep an eye on them, Patrick."

"I don't know why you'd say that. She's rather more desirable than some of the friends he's been hanging round with. Desirable as in good for him, I mean."

"I've reason to believe they aren't in Liverpool."

"What reason could—" I interrupted myself with a wry laugh. "They've come to visit you, have they? You've been teasing all the time."

"I wish I were. I haven't seen Roy and I've never seen her."

"Then why would you say what you said?"

"I've just had a lady on the phone about them."

"You have. She phoned you." When my incredulity failed to change the situation I demanded "Which lady about what?"

"She lives opposite where Thelma fell."

"The woman in the cottage. I met her when Roy and I had a look at the place." Of the several questions clamouring for answers, the first to emerge was "Why on earth would she contact you?"

"She looked for Turnbill and found Turnbill and Semple, and the switchboard put her through to me. Would you rather we had no idea what Roy was up to?"

"Since you have, I'd appreciate it if you'd let me know."

"You should speak to Miss Derrison yourself. I didn't give her your number, but I said I'd do my best to put you in touch."

"Let me have hers and I will right now."

My mother enunciated the digits at a speed with which she might have favoured a trainee secretary, and then she said "I hope Roy isn't getting obsessed with Thelma. It can't be healthy at his age."

"It didn't harm me when I was."

"I wish we'd known you were obsessed. We'd have intervened sooner."

"Not obsessed, just intrigued, and I'm sure that's all Roy is."

In fact I was by no means certain. Why had he returned to Stonefield? I promised to see my parents soon and keyed the Stonefield number. It hesitated for some seconds before ringing and then found a rhythm that put me in mind of somebody plodding to retrieve the phone, unless it was measuring their search for it. I'd begun to expect a recorded message by the time a wearily impatient voice I seemed to recognise said "Who's that?"

"Miss Derrison?"

"No."

"I do apologise. I'm afraid my mother misheard the number."

"Who's she when she's at home?"

Rather than retort that she was at the office I said "Astrid Turnbill."

"Yes," the woman said like a challenge, "I rang her."

"Then I'm sorry, I don't understand why you said—"

"I hope she's not in charge of people's finances if that's how accurate she is. The name's not Derrison, it's Dennison."

"Then I expect I misheard. Apologies again." Feeling that I'd mollified the woman quite as much as she deserved, I said "My mother told you I'd give you a call, and here I am."

"It's a pity you weren't here."

"I was the other day. I didn't see any need to return." This only delayed what I had to ask. "Could you tell me what's happened now?"

"Your son went up the tower block with a girl. I've seen too many people going in there to buy drugs."

"I'm sure that can't have been why my son and his girlfriend were there."

"Perhaps you can explain what they were grubbing about for."

"I don't even know what you mean by that."

"After they came down they started crawling around outside. Tell me what anybody would expect to find there if you can."

"I'd say you should have asked them."

"I'm keeping my head down at my time of life. It's not advisable round here to get a reputation as a snitch."

"I don't think my son would have taken you for one."

"I'm talking about the people the rest of us have to live near. If I were you I'd make certain he isn't seen here again."

"I can't imagine you'll be seeing either of them."

I left it at that, feeling no need to apologise further if even so much as I had. I was ending the call when she spoke. "Aw," she said, or a word that sounded like it, unless it was just the first syllable. I didn't think she could tell me anything I'd want to hear or needed to, and in any case she would have my number now. Just the same, I was anxious to learn more about Roy's visit. I did my best to elucidate the Ackroyd and others of his novels that touched on the occult, until my ponderings grew too ponderous to bear. I was slouched like my teenage self against the kitchen sink, impatiently observing the birth of the first bubble in the percolator, when I heard Roy's key in the lock. "Where did you get to?" I said.

"You haven't been waiting for me, have you? It's not that late."

"I didn't say it was. I'm just asking where you went," I said, only to feel unreasonable. "No, I know that. I'm asking why you did."

"You know," Roy said from the kitchen doorway, and turned his stare along the hall. "He knows."

"What on earth do you think you're—" My protest faltered as Bella appeared beside him, and I didn't know whether I was apologising or complaining as I said "I didn't hear you come in."

"Sorry, Patrick. I didn't mean to intrude."

"You're doing nothing of the kind. You're involved."

As Bella risked a smile smaller than her mouth, Roy said "How do you know where we were? Have you been tracking my phone?"

"I wouldn't know how. The lady from the cottage was in touch."

"Who, that old bitch who didn't try and save your aunt?"

"Roy, even if that's fair I don't think you should—"

"She lives in one of those cottages you liked," Roy was already telling Bella. "The ones you said show you can't kill the past."

"Maybe that's why Thelma went there."

"Could have been," Roy said and turned on me. "So why was the old, why was she telling tales on us?"

"She didn't seem too pleased we were there, if you remember. She mustn't have liked you going back."

"Nothing to do with her. She doesn't own the place."

"Are you going to tell me why you were there? We'd already seen there was nothing worth the trip."

"It was my idea, Patrick."

"To do what, Bella?"

"To try and see what Thelma saw. She was always trying to see further."

"There's a lot that doesn't explain. She took some items from her studio with her."

"She must have meant to start work on something."

"Not that kind of item. Jars of nothing much." As Bella gave me an oddly remonstrative look I said "The lady from the cottage says Thelma dropped them off the roof and then went after them."

"I can't tell you anything about that, Patrick."

"I wouldn't expect it." I felt unhappy for catching them out as I said "The lady also says you and Roy were searching for something outside."

"Shit, was she spying on us the whole time?" As I let Roy's first word pass unrebuked, not that Julia would have, he said "Bell dropped it while we were looking over."

"Is it a secret?"

"I wouldn't keep that kind," Bella said. "It was my earring."

Though her hair was concealing her ears, I knew how small the lobes were. "I didn't know you wore them."

"I just can." She swept a blond lock back from her left ear. "It was one of these," she said. "Roy bought them for me."

I gazed at the tiny verdant metal flower, feeling grotesquely unreasonable if not irrational. "Did you find the other one?"

"This was it. It took a while to find." Bella gave her head a gentle shake, uncovering her other ear. "And here's its twin," she said.

I felt compelled to move us away from my gaffe. "I hope your trek was worth it," I said. "How did you get there?"

"There was a bus and Roy was on it. That was worth it by itself."

I tried not to be as embarrassed by her openness as I fancied Roy might feel. "Who's for coffee?" I said.

"I'll have one, dad."

"I've lived without it. I won't start now," Bella said in her curiously old-fashioned way. "I'll have water if it isn't from the tap."

I passed her a bottle of spring water from the refrigerator, and seemed to see her fingers grow pale on the far side of the chilly plastic, as if I were viewing them underwater. Roy was pouring coffee with his back to us, and I didn't think he heard her murmur "I hope you don't think I'm a bad influence."

"Not remotely." I patted her hand, which was as cold as the contents of the bottle. For a moment mine was too, and I restrained a shiver. "I'd say you were the opposite," I said under my breath, and she smiled as broadly as she could.

CHAPTER NINE

A Hint of the Familiar

That night I thought I heard them testing a message at the railway station. Was it an announcement about the first train? The repetition of a solitary syllable had wakened me: not first after all – closer to birth, perhaps, but not that either, nor worth or mirth. Now I recognised Roy's voice, muffled by a dream. In the year during which Julia and I argued so much that we could only agree our marriage had to end, Roy had started talking in his sleep. This had been another reason why we'd separated – that our behaviour was disturbing him – but what did his activity mean now? At least he didn't sound as if he was struggling to leave a dream or stay in one, as he'd sounded then. His mumbling subsided, and almost before I gathered he was sound asleep, I was myself.

At breakfast – coffee, juice, toast and eggs scrambled vigorously enough that my wrist ached as I imagined a scrivener's might have in the old days – Roy looked sufficiently rested. "Were you dreaming last night?" I risked asking.

"Some."

"You were quite vocal about it. Do you remember the subject?"

"Bell."

I thought discretion might need me to leave it at that, but decided it was safe to ask "Do you know what you were trying to say?"

"Didn't know I was."

"Could it have been earth? That's my best guess."

"That's not what I was dreaming."

It was plain I wasn't invited to enquire further. The silence this planted between us felt too cumbersome to shift, and the crunch of toast didn't help, any more than the scrape of utensils on china.

I was glad when my phone rang. "Father," it said before he spoke. "Not interrupting, am I, Patrick?"

"I wouldn't have said so. Why do you ask?"

"Just that you were so quick off the mark. Or were you wanting to be interrupted?"

"Not that either." In a bid to leave this succession of verbal hurdles behind I said "Let's talk."

"Your mother and I thought we'd buy you lunch in Liverpool today if you're free."

"I ought to be, but Roy's here too."

"He'll be just as welcome."

"Thanks, grandad, but I was going to meet someone."

"Would that be a lady friend?"

"Might." When I prompted him with a pointed look Roy admitted "Yes."

"Bring her by all means. Have you introduced her to your favourite cuisine?"

"We haven't eaten yet."

"Will noon suit everyone? We'll see you at the Szechuan unless we hear to the contrary."

Roy picked up his phone, and I saw he was making a video call. With unexpected directness he said "I like seeing her."

Bella's face appeared, only to vanish at once. It played the trick again before I grasped that shadows of leaves were swaying across it and then withdrawing their darkness. "Bell," Roy said, "can you meet for lunch in Liverpool?"

"I'll come to you wherever you like."

"It's Szechuan. Chinese with lots of chillies."

"I'm always up for new experiences."

"And it's being bought for us."

I gathered I was visible to Bella when she said "Thank you very much for including me, Patrick."

"Happy you'll be there, but I'm not the host. My parents are picking up the bill."

Another swarm of darkness almost put her face out before she ducked her head. She looked up through the shadows to ask "Is the food very hot?"

"Some of it's wicked," Roy said.

"Don't call me a weakling, but would you mind if I don't come after all? It sounds as if it might be too fierce for me."

"It isn't all like that. There's an ordinary menu as well."

"Say I'm sorry just the same, could you? Maybe I'm as delicate as I look."

"We can ring my grandad and we'll all go somewhere else."

"Don't let me spoil the arrangements. You all go where you like and I'll meet you afterwards. Call me when you've finished," Bella said and passed her hand over her face as though to brush shadows away, but with the opposite effect. "And look, no need for video if it costs you more."

"Like I was telling dad – " Roy said, by which point he was talking to himself.

I suspected Bella had been daunted by meeting more of the family so soon, unless she'd decided it was inappropriately premature. Sensing Roy was disappointed, I said nothing, and at length. He spent the morning with the book of expeditions Bella had given me, and then he took his Kindle – a birthday present from his mother – on the train. I saw he was reading a study of the magical in all the arts, and wondered whether he was seeking knowledge to impress his girlfriend. He continued reading all the way up the escalators to Central Station and leaned against the concourse wall to finish a paragraph.

Outside the station a Romanian in a headscarf was selling a magazine published to support the homeless. Her plaintive repetition of its name brought street cries of old to mind. Police were moving occupants of doorways onwards as a prelude to taping off a crime scene. Outside the restaurants and charity shops further up the slope, imported buskers were competing to perform. A back street glittering with shards of bottles, which reminded me of my aunt's fate, brought us to Well Reddened, where the display of a menu written in Chinese might have been designed to daunt the unadventurous. My mother waved to greet us through the pane, announcing "Here are the men."

She rose to her feet more swiftly than directly as we crossed the venerable carpet, while my father took his measured time over standing up. "How much more do you mean to grow, Roy?" she cried.

"I shouldn't think he has much say in the matter, Astrid."

"I'm only being silly, Jonathan. It doesn't hurt occasionally, you know. I'm just glad to see so much of him."

"You'd have seen more if I hadn't stopped him wearing shorts."

Perhaps my joke was too feeble to reach him except as a source of embarrassment, and I told myself my mother's mood might have abashed Bella. "Sit down before you make me dizzy," my mother urged and grabbed Roy's arm to speed up the process, unless she was aiding herself.

The round table left a man-sized gap between me and my father. He dealt it a slow weighty blink on the way to saying "Shall we have a tureen of hot and sour to be going on with? There'll be plenty left for the latecomer."

"Yes," my mother said, "where's the invisible girl?"

"She didn't want to risk the food," Roy said.

"A prudent lady, is she?" my father said. "You should have told us and we'd have gone somewhere everybody liked."

"I said you'd do that but she didn't want you bothered."

"Considerate as well," my mother said. "You tell her she was missed."

"Maybe you can. She might be meeting me here when we've finished."

A waiter was warning a young couple away from dishes he thought they wouldn't like, the standard approach to new customers here, but he knew us well enough to present us with authentic menus. While we selected items marked with bunches of chillies like flames, he brought a vast bowl of soup and ladled helpings out, leaving Bella's bowl emptily agape. Once we'd ordered my mother said "So what sort of mischief have you been up to, Roy?"

"Leave the chap a few secrets, old girl," my father protested.

"You know what I mean, Jonathan. Not that kind of mischief."

"Ah, that business. We hear you went where Patrick's aunt Thelma met her end."

Roy's grimace at me pinched most of his face. "Have you told mum as well?"

"Roy, I've told nobody. My mother told me. The lady at the cottage found her name from Thelma's, and please don't start calling her anything again."

He took a china spoonful of soup, visibly blocking a rejoinder, which gave my mother the chance to ask "What were you doing there?"

To relieve his obvious discomfort I said "Roy's friend is as interested in Thelma as he is."

"I'm surprised anyone of his age is. That's how old the girl is, I suppose. You don't think she could be saying it to get closer to you, Roy."

"She wouldn't do that. We're the same age, just about."

"I meant being interested in my sister." As though he'd accused her of incompetence, my mother shook her head at length. "Don't expect to understand her when I never really did," she said. "She liked keeping secrets even when she was your age."

"I think Bell understands her more than I do."

"We're even more anxious to meet the young lady, then."

"Did you say she'd be gracing us?" my father said. "You could call her to make sure."

Roy took his time over a laden spoonful before taking out his phone. Bella's onscreen number brought her icon with it, so miniature an image that I could scarcely distinguish her face. My mother leaned over to look and then peered closer. "Well, that's…"

"What, gran?"

She squeezed her lips thin as if to lock in a remark and sat back. "Just my brain wanting me to know how old I'm getting."

Before anyone could follow this up, Bella said "Where are you?"

"Just started eating. Come here so you can meet dad's parents."

"I could be a while yet. Meet me here instead, where we met the first time."

"She's at the Tate," I told my parents, and had to raise my voice as an ambulance sped wailing past the restaurant. Roy's phone joined in so enthusiastically that for a moment its version of a siren sounded just as loud. "There must be an accident somewhere," I felt it necessary to establish. "They're going from all over town."

"That's right," Bella said, "I'm at the gallery. I'm just going in."

"You must think a lot of Thelma," my mother said.

"I expect you do. Wasn't she your sister?"

"She was that," my mother said but looked silenced.

"Before you go, Bella," my father said, "we can see you."

Presumably he meant to satisfy my mother's eagerness to do so, but Bella sounded disconcerted. "How?"

"If Roy turns on his video and you do."

"I don't think they let you use cameras in here. I don't want to get thrown out."

"I can't believe they'd do that," my father said, but my mother intervened. "Don't harass the poor girl, Jonathan. We're already seeing her."

This time Bella's question sounded terser still. "How?"

"Roy has your picture on his phone."

"I should have known he would," Bella said. "I'll look forward to meeting you both properly. Goodbye as well, Patrick."

"She sounds like an old-fashioned girl." More reproachfully my mother said to Roy "You should have told us she was shy."

"She's not."

"I just thought she didn't want to be seen. I suppose a lot of people your age are bothered how they look when there's absolutely no reason."

As she frowned at his phone Roy said "What's wrong, gran? What did you stop saying before?"

"It was just that something seemed familiar. I couldn't even tell you what." With a weariness I gathered was directed at herself she said "Let me have another look."

"You mean at Bell?"

I should have thought my mother could hear how this troubled him, but she only squinted at his phone and shook her head slowly as though to reorganise her thoughts. Far too eventually for my taste she said "I really don't know."

"What don't you, gran?"

When her only answer was an even slower oscillation of her head, I couldn't keep quiet any longer. "Don't you think you're making a mistake?"

"Have you noticed me doing that much, Patrick?"

"You did get somebody's name wrong."

"I don't think I've used it once, and it's there for anyone to read. It's Bella."

"Not her," I said and tried to make it clear that my laugh was at myself. "The lady by the tower block. You told me her name was Derrison but it turned out to be Dennison."

"Well, I hope I haven't embarrassed anybody," my mother said with imperfectly concealed pique. "Just ignore me, Roy. I don't want to spoil whatever you have." By now she had rediscovered gentleness, and slid the phone towards him as waiters with dishes of fiery delights converged on our table. "Here's to meeting your girlfriend in the flesh," she said.

CHAPTER TEN

A Source of Visions

Hunter was in the throes of a vision as he crossed the desert when I heard a car draw up outside my aunt's house, and I slipped a tasselled marker into the book. My parents would be staying overnight before they took me home. I let them in, and my mother peered along the hall. "Isn't Thelma here?"

"She's upstairs painting."

"I thought she'd be looking after you."

"I'm sure he's old enough to do that for himself, dear," my father said.

"I've been reading, mum."

As my father pushed down the handle of their dwarfish two-wheeled suitcase, my mother glanced into the front room and caught sight of *Fear and Loathing in Las Vegas*, which I'd left on my chair. "Is that what you're reading?"

While her tone made me wary, I couldn't lie too much. "Looking at it," I said.

"Isn't it about—" She turned it over as if she thought insects might be lurking underneath. Having scowled at the blurb, she brandished the book at me and my father. "This is all about drugs, Jonathan."

"He isn't taking them, is he? Just learning about them."

"We don't want him doing that either. There's absolutely no need."

"Mum, Aunt Thelma didn't know I was."

"She ought to have known. We put her in charge. Has she told you there's anything you can't read?" When I had to deny it my mother said "Then she should be watching what you do."

"She has her job as well, dear, just like us."

"Not like ours at all." Although this didn't end the argument, the sound of a door upstairs did. As light footsteps crossed the landing my mother called "Is that you, Thelma?"

"Who else is it going to be?" my father murmured.

"I'm hoping Neville may be back," my mother said by no means as low.

The answer – perhaps to her original question – came from the top of the stairs. "No."

It was a man's voice, not one I thought I recognised, unless I'd heard it once before. My mother stared at me before saying fiercely but just audibly "Why didn't you tell us someone else was here?"

"Mum, I didn't know."

I was at least as disconcerted as my parents had to be. How engrossed in reading must I have been not to notice a visitor? My aunt had been in her studio for hours, and I'd finished a book in the garden before retiring to the front room. My mother gave me a look no less unconvinced than reproachful as we trooped into the hall. The man was descending the stairs, resting his fingertips above each upright of the banister like a mountain climber wielding a stick he didn't need. "You'll be the Semples," he said.

He was tall and imposingly broad, with a wide nose and mouth and large pale blue eyes, but he conveyed an odd impression of withholding some of himself. His long ears were big enough to border on a joke, but presumably he didn't mind, since his blond hair was cropped well short of them. He wore black: T-shirt, slacks, socks and shoes. "And you'll be…" my mother said, despite knowing perfectly well.

"Call me Abel. Thelma does."

He leaned down from the third stair to offer a hand, which my father accepted. "Jonathan," he said.

He shook the hand, and then my mother barely did. "Astrid," she said with no tone at all. "Thelma's sister."

"And I've been seeing this young man. I believe his name's Patrick."

The firmness of his handshake gave a sense that it could easily turn firmer. He was still on the stair, which made me feel he was reaching down from a height to indulge my status. "What do you mean," my mother said, "you've been seeing him?"

"I was in the studio while he was down below."

As my mother's lips parted with a dry determined sound, my aunt appeared on the landing. "Oh, you've met," she said.

"Would you rather we hadn't?" my mother retorted.

"I should say not." This came from Abel, who released my hand and rose to his full height on the stairs. "Whyever would she?" he said.

"Pardon me," my mother said, though not as if she wanted it, "I was talking to my sister."

"I just wanted to introduce you myself, Astrid," my aunt said.

"Why, what would you have said to clear things up?"

"Just this is Abel," my aunt said as she came downstairs, "and now you know it twice. Is everyone ready for dinner?"

"Will you be staying, Abel?" my mother said.

She plainly didn't care whether he found this uninviting. His stance put me in mind of a guard, presumably protecting my aunt if she needed it rather than barring her way. As she reached him he poised his fingertips on the banister once more and descended into the hall with a single lithe movement that made my mother retreat a step. "I believe I'm invited," he said.

"You don't need to be," my aunt assured him, "but you are."

"That's so. There's no longer the need."

I saw my mother took this for a gibe at her, but he turned to my aunt at once. "You know what I'll have."

"How would she know that?" my mother objected.

"I'm a creature of simple tastes. Just a salad with no dressing."

"Are you a vegan, Abel?" my father said as if to pacify the conversation.

"From the star, do you mean?" Abel's eyes widened at me, though I couldn't tell whether he meant to absorb or convey the idea. "You come from those, Patrick," he said. "You're made of the same material. You're closer to it while you're young."

My mother visibly resented some or all of this. "Jonathan was asking if your tastes are vegan."

"Of course, that's another meaning now. Yes, I'm nourished from the earth."

When he and my aunt shared a glance my mother said "Have you gone that way too, Thelma?"

"I'm the omnivore I've always been. You know me, eager for experience." No doubt she sensed the disapproval this roused, because she said "It's cold meats and salads for the family."

"I'm glad to hear it," my mother said heavily enough to squeeze an extra meaning forth. "Would you like some help?"

"Abel will be. That's why he's here."

"He's brought you inspiration, has he?" my father said.

"We've helped each other grow," Abel said and waited for my aunt to follow him to the kitchen.

My mother rested her gaze on their backs before leading the way into the front room. "Find something to read, Patrick," she said. "Not that book."

I leafed through a study of surrealism, more hastily whenever nude women made an appearance. My parents stared out at the sky, which was growing prematurely dark with the omen of a summer storm, but neither of them spoke until Abel came to fetch us. "We're ready for you," he said.

"We're on our way," my father told him, so immediately that I suspected he was forestalling whatever his wife might have said.

Abel bowed us into the dining-room, even giving me the salutation, which made me wonder if all the gestures were ironic. The floor-length windows displayed the back garden, beyond which the sky above Third Mile Wood resembled a midnight too solid for stars. My aunt was tossing salad in a wooden bowl as wide as her forearm was long, and a smaller bowl of unembellished leaves stood at the head of the table. Unnecessarily in at least one sense my mother said "Is that your place, Abel?"

"That's for our host to say. I'm at her disposal." When my mother raised her eyebrows so high they appeared to tug her lips thin, he said "I expect people do your bidding where you work."

"That's how you operate, is it?" my mother said more meaningfully than I understood.

"It's how I'm made."

"Then sit where I've put you," my aunt said, "and the rest of you sit where you like."

She dealt portions of dinner until the recipients cried enough. "That's for a growing boy," she said as she loaded my plate, and gave Abel a glance which I saw my mother take for an indelicate reference. When he set about his meal he began by lowering his head towards it, so that I wondered if he mightn't use his utensils or his hands. Perhaps he was simply scenting the ingredients, but I was glad he didn't play the joke he appeared to be threatening. Even the morsels into which he cut the salad suggested one. My mother watched the process as she might have viewed an exhibit in a zoo, a creature presenting some trait more unusual than attractive. As he raised a dinky forkful to his mouth, revealing small uncommonly even teeth, she said "So may we ask what you are, Abel?"

He shut his lips on a discreet crunch no louder than the shattering of shells and swallowed before answering. I was surprised to notice how smooth his throat was, not lumpy like my father's and mine. "I'm what you see," he said.

"I see somebody playing with words." As if she was indulging him, though only barely, my mother said "I was asking what you do."

"Whatever I need," my aunt said.

My mother jerked her hands up, flinging any further questions heavenwards. Abel took another muted meatless bite and dabbed at his faintly glistening lips with a finger. "Your turn now, Astrid."

"I've had it." When his wide eyes didn't blink she said "For what?"

"What do you bring to the world?"

"My son, for a start."

"There's one gift I can't provide," Abel said and shifted his gaze to my father. "Children."

"I'm sorry to hear that." The unwavering gaze prompted my father to add "If I should be."

"Some creations abide longer."

"We wouldn't know," my mother said. "Other than parents we're just dull accountants, both of us."

"Don't undersell yourself, Astrid," my aunt protested. "You've never been just anything, and I'll say the same for Jonathan."

"Just a bit out of our depth with all the arty conversation," my father said.

My mother gave this a decidedly unappreciative look, and I

felt compelled to contribute if not to rescue everyone from further confrontation. I asked Abel the first question that came to my mind, having found it oddly bothersome. "How old are you?"

"Patrick," my aunt said, manufacturing a laugh. "No need to be quite so uninhibited."

"Perhaps he feels encouraged when he's here," my mother said.

As I regretted speaking Abel said "It's never wrong to learn all you can. That's what life is for."

"Point proved," my mother said.

"How old would you say I am, Patrick? Be as honest as you can."

"Older than my aunt."

"You wouldn't care to put a figure to it."

I saw he was amused, perhaps encouraging the rest of the adults to be, but I muttered "Can't."

"He hasn't inherited your calculating mind, then. Perhaps he'll follow Thelma's path instead."

As my mother made to retort, my father intervened. "How did you two meet, if you don't mind my asking?"

"Thelma brought me home from her woods."

My mother spoke at once. "And how long have you known each other?"

"I'd often seen her. Your son too."

"You're local, then," my father said.

"Just now I am."

"You didn't answer my question," my mother said.

Abel widened his eyes as though to stretch all expression out of them, but it was my aunt who answered. "It feels like years."

As I saw this fail to satisfy my mother I heard a moist whisper at the windows. Above the fence the treetops had begun to twitch as though Abel's mention of the woods had roused them. A stain like a trailing hem of the sky spread down the fence, and the panes resounded as rain blundered against the glass. "The night's upon us," Abel said.

Apparently my mother didn't relish such a fancy. "Just a storm."

"The night's always eager to be here. Can't you feel it, Patrick? It's all around you every moment of your life."

"I hope you'll forgive me," my father said, "but I'm not sure that makes sense."

"The sky is the illusion. The night is waiting all the time. If you don't embrace the night you'll never see the stars."

Abel was still addressing me. I saw this had begun to antagonise my father, but it was my mother who spoke. "Let's hope this ends soon."

"We're all safe in here," my aunt said, "however fierce it gets."

"I was only thinking your friend won't want to be walking home in it."

This produced a pause that I imagined swarming with unspoken thoughts as well as rain. Abel ended it by saying "I know my course well enough."

This sounded ominously formal, and made the dinner feel that way. My father strove to start a conversation aimed at nobody in particular, but it soon ran out of breath. Even prompting my aunt to talk about her latest work didn't find much life, since she wanted her paintings to speak for themselves. Rather than meet anybody's eyes I watched skeins of rain writhe and merge and unravel on the windows. The downpour was still tousling the forest when dinner ended. I was relieved that it was time to clear away and start the washing-up. "Shall I join you, Patrick?" Abel said.

My mother hastened after him into the kitchen. "He's fine by himself, thank you."

"Then I don't think I can be any further use just now. I expect you'll have family matters to discuss."

My aunt had caught up with my mother. "There won't be anything Abel can't hear, will there, Astrid?"

"I wouldn't like to say."

"I'm sure I'll hear it in due course." Abel gave the women a look too brief to read and moved to the back door. "I'll bid you all a good night, then," he said, turning the key in the lock. "Remember, Patrick, night is good."

As Abel opened the door, admitting an extensive hiss of rain on leaves, my father wandered into the kitchen. "You're leaving us already," he said, rather less than half a question.

"You can't go out like that," my aunt protested.

She might have meant the weather or the situation, but Abel seemed unbothered by either. "I've experienced far worse in my time."

"I haven't even got an umbrella you can borrow. Have you, Jonathan?"

"I fear we didn't come prepared."

"That's an understatement," my mother said.

As my aunt's lips emitted a sharp prefatory sound, Abel stepped into the rain. "I'll see you before you know it," he said, presumably just to her, and made for the gate in the fence. Rain and the light from the kitchen surrounded him with a luminous aura all the way along the path. He opened the gate, revealing restless darkness striped with hints of trees, and at once he and the glimpse were gone. My aunt dashed to bolt the gate and sprinted back to the kitchen, where she shook her head like a sodden animal, a gesture expressing violent emotion as well. "I hope you're satisfied, Astrid," she said.

"To tell you the truth, I'm nowhere near. Would you like to read upstairs for a while, Patrick?"

"I'm helping Aunt Thelma."

"We don't need any more helpers. Your father and I will wash up. You go and read whatever you're reading."

This sounded almost permissive enough to let me risk retrieving the Las Vegas book, but I didn't want to attract any of her suppressed displeasure. Instead I took the surrealist volume upstairs, where I saw my aunt had left the studio door open. Activity beyond the window caught my eye, and I tiptoed across the unlit room to look. Surely the fluid movement in the dark beneath the trees belonged to rain, yet for a moment I thought I was seeing a figure faintly outlined by a glow. It reminded me of how Abel had looked on his way to the gate. Before I could focus on the shape, it disappeared among the trees. As I strained to locate it the dimness appeared to take on more substance and loom at me, not just beyond the window. I'd forgotten the impression I'd once had of faces at my back, but now they felt imminent again, hovering before they descended or swelled towards me. I could easily have thought not all the whispers in the studio came from rain. When I twisted around I saw no intruders, and told myself the faces lying in wait in the dark around me were on canvases, every one. I was making fast for the lit doorway when my mother called "Patrick, are you in your room?"

"I am now," I shouted, and sneaked across the landing to slam the door.

I was about to lie on the bed with the book when I heard the door of the front room shut beneath me. For a minute or more there was silence, no doubt while my aunt and my parents sat down and perhaps while they gazed at one another, and then my mother said "What's been going on while Patrick was here, Thelma?"

I could only just make out her words. If she hadn't brought me into it I mightn't have eavesdropped, but I felt she'd given me the excuse if not the right. I lay on the floor, pressing my ear against the carpet just in time to hear my aunt's response. "Nothing he knows about, Astrid."

"He does now."

"I really don't think you can blame me for that. You did rather make an issue out of it in front of him."

"There'd have been no issue if it weren't for your behaviour, and please don't tell me Patrick wasn't aware of that."

"I don't believe he even knew Abel was here till you all met him."

Should I have known? Had I heard him in the studio one night when my aunt and uncle were still together? I thought my aunt's contention might placate my mother, but it seemed to displease her all the more. "He's your latest secret, is he? How long were you seeing him before Neville knew about him?"

"Not too long. At first he thought Abel was my model."

"And when did he find out the truth?"

"How do you know that isn't, Astrid?" This earned a silence I imagined coming with a stare, and my aunt said "When I told him how much Abel means to me."

"More than Neville after everything he did for you? You'd never have had your career if he hadn't kept you both for years."

"It isn't all about money, Astrid. Sometimes I think that's all you think there is to life."

"That's a shade unfair, isn't it?" my father said. "It's no more true of her than me."

"I'll apologise to both of you, and I did to Neville. He knows how much I appreciated his support and a good deal else about him. I just need more than he can give, and I think I made him understand."

"I don't suppose he had much choice, had he? Were you tired of him in bed?"

"Really, Astrid," my father said, and my aunt retorted "I do wish sometimes you could be a little less..."

"Less what, Thelma? If you didn't spare your husband's feelings there's no need to spare mine."

"I was about to say banal. Let's say mundane instead, shall we? My relationship with Abel isn't so much about sex."

"Not so much, but you aren't saying not at all."

"Astrid, you'll have me thinking you've got a calculator for a brain. I'm saying Abel brings me things nobody else could. Look at my new work and perhaps you'll understand."

"I never have and I don't imagine I'll be starting now."

"That nonsense he was telling Patrick," my father said. "Is that the kind of thing?"

"It isn't nonsense, and I think you've just proved my point about you both."

"Whatever you call it," my father said, angered at last, "we don't want it anywhere near our son."

"Or your friend either," my mother said.

"I'm not sure how that can be achieved," my aunt said.

"You'd better find a way," my mother warned her, "or we will."

This led to a silence, and I was wondering what it might signify when my father called "You can come down now, Patrick." He sounded as if he was at least halfway up the stairs, and I stumbled to my feet in case he discovered my behaviour. In the front room I found everyone pretending either that there'd been no argument or that it was resolved. The card games we played at the dining-table felt like a postponement of further discussion or of worse.

As I lay in bed that night I heard low voices nearby. They belonged to a man and a woman, but without venturing out of my room I couldn't identify them, let alone distinguish any words. I assumed I was hearing my parents, but I would never be sure. In any case I didn't learn their decision until we were on our way home.

CHAPTER ELEVEN

Farewells

"Say goodbye to your aunt, Patrick," my mother said.

"Bye, and I'll see you next time."

"Goodbye, Patrick," my aunt said, and to my parents "Goodbye. Goodbye."

This sounded far more final than I hoped it would be. As the car left my aunt behind I looked back. She was resting both hands on the garden gate, and its metal bars put me in mind of a cage. Beyond her I could see through the front doorway into the house. Was the back door open, and the gate into Third Mile Wood as well? For an instant I seemed to see someone approaching down a corridor that consisted not just of the hall in the house but of an avenue that had opened at considerable length between the trees. The car turned a corner, and the sight vanished like the illusion I told myself it must have been. "Did you enjoy your stay, Patrick?" my father said.

"Yes." I wanted to leave it at that on my aunt's behalf, but his glance at me in the mirror expected more. "Most of it," I admitted.

"Then make the most," my mother said.

This sounded somehow worse than simply incomplete. I saw my father wait for more from either of his passengers, but eventually he said "What did you think of your aunt's new friend?"

I sensed how tense this made my mother. "I liked him," I risked saying.

Her retort posed as a question. "What did you like?"

"He was interesting."

"Not like your parents, you mean."

"I didn't say that, mum. I meant more like Aunt Thelma." At once I grasped how this might endorse my mother's grievance. "Arty," I said like my father.

"More so than Thelma," he said.

"More and a lot worse." My mother twisted in her seat to gaze at me. "How long have you known about him, Patrick?"

I had to remind myself how much I wasn't supposed to have overheard, and it seemed best to ask "Known what, mum?"

"Anything." This appeared to sum up issues she preferred to leave unvoiced, and she said "How long have you been aware of his existence?"

"The same as you and dad have."

"She's better at keeping her secrets than ever, then." As if this provoked her my mother said "I don't care for him at all."

"Why not, mum?"

"I don't like his look."

"I shouldn't think he can help that, Astrid. I saw nothing wrong with him on that front."

"Then perhaps you need to use a little more imagination like my sister says."

"I believe she was talking about us both."

"Now her friend's got us falling out as well, and that's enough of him." My mother turned to stare at me again as if I was somehow implicated. "Unless he goes away," she said, "you won't be seeing Thelma again without us."

"You'll come and stay when I do, you mean."

"No." She paused long enough to let me feel I'd had all the response my suggestion deserved. "You won't be seeing her again," she said, "while there's any chance her friend's around."

I was about to appeal to my father when he said "I'm afraid that's our decision, son."

"But if it's only what he looks like…"

"I didn't say that," my mother said, "and there's a great deal else I don't care for. Now I won't discuss it any more, especially not with you, Patrick."

I slumped into a frustrated sulk as only a teenager could, and we never mentioned Abel again. After that I saw my aunt just once more, when she came to stay with us at Christmas, an occasion that felt laden with the undiscussed. Even the festive meal and the seasonal game of Monopoly seemed somehow inhibited, driving the adults to manufacture jollity to compensate. If this was for my benefit, I wished they hadn't bothered, but perhaps they were anxious to convince one another that nothing had changed, at least between them.

I remembered all this as I sat at my desk, making notes on *The Master and Margarita* in preparation for next term. I was trying to restrict my thoughts to the novel – the memories of visiting my aunt had begun to feel as if I hadn't fully understood some part of them that needed to be grasped – when the phone rang and announced my mother. I could almost have imagined my memories had functioned as a summons. "How are you both?" she said.

"All doing well, I think."

"Are Roy and his friend with you just now?"

"No, I'm on my own. Busy, though."

"Can you organise your party?" my father said at a little distance. "We're on our way to buy everybody dinner."

"Really, you shouldn't. You've already bought lunch."

"That wasn't all of you," my mother said. "We'd like it to be this time. What's Roy's friend called again?"

I wondered if my mother's memory had begun to let her down. "Bella," I said.

"Bella, of course, Bella. Bella, Jonathan."

Was it his memory that had developed a lapse? "Yes," he said tonelessly enough to suggest the possibility.

"Will she be coming home with Roy, Patrick?"

"I shouldn't be surprised."

"Do your best to see she does, could you? We want to meet her properly. Where are they both?"

"In Manchester, apparently. A gallery with some of Thelma's work and then the library."

"They'll be seeing Roy's mother there, I suppose."

"They won't. She's still at her conference."

"Just one more thing before we go. When you spoke to Miss Derrison—"

"It's Dennison, my love, if you recall."

"There's nothing wrong with my memory, Jonathan, or anything else up here. What did she say to you, Patrick?"

"Not really very much. She thought Roy and Bella might have

been there for drugs, which you'll appreciate is nonsense. And she was suspicious because they were searching near her house, but it was just for an earring Bella dropped."

"Would you say the lady was delusional?"

"I wouldn't go that far. More like constantly on the alert."

"I'm glad to hear you say that, Patrick."

"Glad because…"

"When she called about the trespassing, I'm saying that's how she saw it, she said she thought she knew them."

"Nothing odd about that." It didn't even seem worth mentioning. "Roy was with me when I went there," I reminded her, "and she saw us."

I heard a faint drone suggestive of speed on a road, and then my father said "Astrid thinks—"

"I'll tell him myself, thank you, Jonathan. I will when we're face to face."

I tried not to sound harassed while asking "How soon will that be?"

"Half an hour or so," my father said. "Longer if you prefer."

"I'll try to be finished by then."

"Don't look at me like that, Jonathan. This needs to be settled." Even more stubbornly my mother said "Those eyes."

I assumed this referred to his look, no doubt reproachful, and I came close to telling him to keep his eyes on the road. I was opening my mouth when he spoke, so nearly inaudibly that I couldn't judge his tone. "My God, she's—"

If he meant to acknowledge my mother was right, I had no chance to hear. My parents had gone, along with the sound of their car. I supposed they didn't want to distract me any further, but I found it hard to return to my work. I watched windmills twirl at the edge of the world, so variously that their antics resembled a mime of chaos, and heard a train listing the destinations it was required to visit. I ought to call Roy about dining with my parents. He or Bella might have plans of their own.

I was anticipating the doggedly adolescent message he'd recorded, but the phone rang just once before he spoke. "Bell?"

"No, it's your father. Hasn't she shown up?"

"Of course she has. We've been together hours."

"But you aren't now."

"She's just gone back in the library to check something. I'm out in the sun."

"Have you finished whatever you're there for?"

"Think so. Why?"

"My parents are offering everyone dinner."

"I'll have to ask Bell."

"Can you call me as soon as you know?"

"I won't have to. What did you find out?"

I wondered why he would ask me such a question — it left me uneasier than I could grasp — and then I realised it wasn't aimed at me. "He mustn't have written any of that down," Bella said.

"Then dad's aunt couldn't have seen it, could she?" Any answer Bella gave was obscured as Roy said "My dad wants to know if we'll be there for dinner."

"I don't see why not, do you? It won't take us even two hours."

"My grandparents will be there as well. They're saying they'll get us all dinner."

"That's very kind of them."

"I think they just want to meet you, Bell."

As I wished Roy had kept this to himself in case it roused her shyness, Bella said "I've been feeling I should meet them."

"We'll go then, shall we? I expect they'll let you say where."

"I'll let them know," I said. "Don't let me keep you from your train."

I thought my parents must be imminent, and tried to work on the Bulgakov while I could. Was the feline familiar a Russian tradition? No doubt this kind of ambiguously helpful presence differed from culture to culture, and I was searching online for Russian variations when my phone vibrated wakefully. I answered it before it had a chance to ring. "Semple," I said.

"Mr Semple?"

The man's voice sounded consciously official, and the background noise — activity muffled beyond definition — put me on my guard as well. "That's what I said."

"Can you confirm your address?"

"I can, yes."

I assumed the pause meant we were both waiting for the other to make the next move in the game. "Then could you do that, sir?"

"Certainly, when you give me the chance."

I thought this might throw him off his script, but heard him carry on performing. "If you could just confirm where you live, sir."

"I'll confirm it when you say it. I can't confirm a thing until I know what you've got on me."

I was hoping to have undermined his pretence when he said "Can you just give me the address, sir? Do you live in New Brighton?"

"You've found out that much, have you? Would you like my bank details as well?"

"We have those." With a hint of uncertainty he said "Sir, if you think—"

"I think exactly what you think I'm thinking, and now you've wasted enough of my time when I shouldn't have let you have any. Take my number off your database and try finding yourself an honest job."

Before I'd finished he tried to make himself heard, but I was determined to fend that off. I ended the call and brought up the last number so that it could be blocked, and then I stared at the screen. According to the list, the most recent call was from my mother's number.

Were scammers able to conceal not just their number but any evidence they'd even called? I laid the mobile on the desk and was turning to my notes on the computer when the phone rang again. I didn't bother looking until it announced my mother, and then I dabbed it with my thumb to take the call. "Where are you?" I said as gently as I could.

"Mr Semple, could you just listen to me for a moment?"

I nearly did, having been silenced by outrage. So they'd hacked into my mother's phone somehow or at any rate stolen or copied her number. "You're the supervisor, are you?" I said with another version of gentleness. "You think you can convince me when your man didn't get to me."

"Mr Semple, we just need your address so we—"

"You're admitting you haven't got it now, are you? So much for confirmation. I hope you don't think I'll be more receptive to a lady. Believe me, I wouldn't call you one."

"Mr Semple—"

"Go on, try and persuade me this is all legitimate. Your helper or whatever he is said you have my bank details. Let's hear them."

I heard muffled offstage noises again – voices and traffic, hardly the sounds of an office. In a few seconds the woman came back. "These are the last four digits of your account," she said, "and I'll give you the sort code as well."

The figures were correct, which enraged me more than ever. I knew my mother kept the details in her contacts list in case she needed to make a bank transfer. I'd always found it more careless than professional, though I'd never seriously thought it could put my finances at risk, but just now I hadn't time to blame my mother. "Do tell me how you know all that," I said with so much restraint my head began to throb.

"It's stored on the phone, Mr Semple, and—"

"My God, you're admitting it. Since you're so happy to be blatant, why don't you tell it to the police."

"We are the police, Mr Semple. Now if I could—"

"I haven't heard that one before. You people never give up, do you?" With mounting rage I said "My mother authorised you to use her phone, did she? She'll be here very shortly and you can tell her that yourself."

"Sir, she won't be."

"What the f'' – I rescinded the rest of the word so as not to be delayed by any objection the woman might raise – "what do you mean by that?"

"Mr Semple, this kind of situation is best handled face to face. That's why we've been trying to ascertain your address, which doesn't seem to be on here."

My rage was growing nervous. "Which situation? Just tell me what you mean."

"I'm sincerely sorry. I'm afraid there's been an accident."

"An accident." When this prompted no expansion I said louder "Yes, go on."

"The car the lady was travelling in."

"With my father. He's driving today." If I thought this would bring more information or at least speed us past a delay, it appeared I was mistaken. "What about it?" I demanded.

"I'm afraid it was involved in a collision."

"Oh God," I heard myself say so conversationally that it sounded horribly uncaring. Had I witnessed the moment of the accident, when the phone had gone dead? Could I have been even slightly responsible for distracting my father? These thoughts were among the reasons why I found it suddenly so hard to speak. "How are they both?" I said.

Although the woman's pause was brief, it left her words close to redundant. "I'm very sorry to have to tell you they're gone."

"Gone." I didn't want this expanded; my repetition felt like a pitiful bid to change its meaning. "Where are they?" I was scarcely aware of saying.

"Where you leave the motorway for New Brighton." As though to head me off she said "We'll send someone to you if you'll give us your address."

I did before covering my face with my hands. I felt as if the fingers clamped to my forehead were caging my brain, locking up its function. I couldn't think what to do next, even to the extent of finishing the call, and so I heard a man in the background. "There were three of them," he was insisting. "I don't know if it was a man or a woman, but there was somebody else in that car."

CHAPTER TWELVE

Out of the Background

"At least they'll be peaceful now, won't they, dad? It's all they can be."

"Roy, perhaps we ought to be a little bit more careful of your father's feelings."

"Don't worry, Julia. I mostly feel as if they haven't quite caught up with me."

"Do you think it will help to talk?"

Once upon a time I would have known if she meant this as an invitation. Not knowing whether she was telling me I shouldn't talk about my parents reminded me how far apart we'd grown. "It might," I said.

"Say whatever you need to say, Patrick," Bella said. "We're listening."

She was perched on one arm of the chair she was sharing with Roy. Julia had the other chair while I sat at my desk, with my back to it and the world beyond. I wondered if Julia might find Bella's contribution intrusive, but she seemed not to. "I feel as if they won't catch up until I understand what happened," I said.

"What do you think did?" Bella said.

"Supposedly they came off the motorway too fast, straight in front of a lorry." I pictured the juggernaut bearing down on them, and did my best not to imagine further. "My father must have been distracted," I said. "I never knew him to be less than absolutely careful."

"You won't know what distracted him," Bella said.

"I think I may have heard it happen."

She sat forward, gripping her knees. "What do you think you heard?"

"I think he was looking at my mother when he should have been concentrating on the road. There was something she wanted to tell me or show me. Maybe he saw it and that was the distraction. I heard how it surprised him, and then they were cut off."

"Cut off by a truck," Roy muttered.

"There's no need for that," Julia said.

"Only the phone wasn't quite." Establishing this let me feel a little more informed. "The window must have been open, and it ended up by the road. Someone rescued it before it locked itself and gave it to the police."

"That's how they found you," Bella said, "with the phone."

"When they did I thought they were a scam." I was hoping my audience would find this comical, but perhaps nobody wanted to take the risk. "I did hear one odd thing," I said.

The arm of Roy's chair gave a faint squeak. "What was that?" Bella said, though not about the sound.

"Someone was telling somebody there'd been three people in the car. Of course there were just my parents. The police who came to see me didn't even know who'd said otherwise. They couldn't have thought it was worth putting on the record."

"I shouldn't think you do either," Julia said.

"It's weird like dad says, though."

"I think the situation's bad enough without bringing mysteries into it." As if she'd realised the comment could home in on me, Julia said "Sorry, Patrick, did you have more to say?"

"Nothing comes to mind just now."

"Then dinner's ready when everyone is. You can thank Bella as much as me."

I wasn't sure how hungry I might feel, especially when I saw the offerings laid out on the kitchen table – bowls of salad composed of leaves or nuts or pulses. "When did you turn vegetarian, Julia?"

"It's all vegan, and that's Bella. You've cold meat in the fridge if you feel the need."

I supposed she meant to help Bella feel welcome, and so I tried as well. "How long have you been vegan, Bella?"

"As long as I can remember." As she served salad with a giant's wooden fork and spoon she said "I think the earth gives more than people know."

"That's funny," I said.

"No need to scoff at her beliefs, Patrick."

I was reminded how misunderstanding each other's words had helped to end our marriage. "I'm not," I protested. "It's just the man my aunt was seeing said something of the kind. He was vegan as well."

"More and more people are," Julia said and turned to Bella. "So you've fallen under her spell too."

"You think she had one."

"I'm saying you're as taken with her as Roy is."

"We wouldn't have met otherwise."

"I think someone's under someone's spell," I said, only to feel I'd embarrassed everybody. "I mean we're glad you met that way."

As Roy planted a platter spread with meats between the two of us, Julia said "If that's how it had to happen."

Bella gave this a large but neutral look. "Don't you care for Thelma's work?"

"I find it a bit sly. I'm not the only person who did. Sorry, Patrick."

"Honestly, don't avoid talking about my parents. It won't stop me thinking of them."

"They weren't fond of Thelma either, then," Bella said. "They weren't ready for her secrets."

"I think if you have to keep secrets you must know they're better kept hidden."

"Unless they're meant to be seen by anyone who can."

"I like people who make themselves clear." As though to avert further argument Julia said "I don't care for the occult, if that's what she was playing with."

"You've got books like that in your library, mum."

"We don't censor anything that's not against the law." With not much of a pause Julia said "Books like what?"

"Witchcraft books. You've even got someone's diary of his magic."

"How do you know about that?"

When he hesitated Bella said "We went to look."

"While I was away, you mean." Julia made this sound like another example of slyness. "Were you involved too, Patrick?"

"No, I was here waiting for my parents to show up, the day they never did."

"Forgive me." In not much of the same tone she said "Why were you reading it, Roy?"

"Bell thought dad's aunt might have mentioned it in her journal."

Julia laid her weighty gaze on me. "You've been reading that as well."

"I found it here at dad's, and I showed Bell."

I doubted Julia would have let me off except for my bereavement. "And did you get anything out of the book in the archive?" she said.

"It's hard to read. It's all handwritten. Bell read more than me, but we couldn't find anything to do with dad's aunt, could we?"

"That's what we said."

"I hope you've finished with it," Julia said. "I'm back in the archive if you come looking for anything else."

"Roy was saying you don't care much for books."

"I most certainly take care of our stock. Why would you say such a thing, Roy?"

"No, he says you think they're out of date."

"I think they may be in my lifetime. Certainly in yours." As if she shouldn't have evoked mortality just now Julia said "They'll still exist if people want them, but I think they'll be electronic."

"That's the way with old things. They come back in another form."

Perhaps Julia meant to leave the past behind by asking "So how do you see your future, Bella?"

"I'll know soon what I'll be."

"Roy isn't too sure either, are you?" As he shut his eyes while he shook his head, Julia returned to Bella. "Have your parents any plans for you?"

"Less than I have."

"What do they do themselves?"

"My father." A pause left the phrase oddly isolated, as if Bella had displayed it for examination, until she said "You could say he was in research."

"And your mother?"

"Mum, you're interrogating her."

"I hope you don't think I am, Bella." When the girl smiled rather than speak Julia said "You've met Roy's parents, after all."

"I'm happy to."

"We should never undervalue parents." Even less to anybody specific I said "Let them know they're valued while you can."

This appeared to inhibit the conversation, though I wasn't sure who I'd left wary of speaking. After that we ate mostly in silence, Bella in particular making hardly even the discreetest sound. As she and Roy cleared away at the end of the meal, Julia said "I really should be going, Patrick. I'm in work early tomorrow."

"Thanks for dinner and just being here for me. You too for dinner, Bella."

"Anything I can do to atone for your loss," Bella said.

I found this oddly awkward, unless that was how it made me feel. "Would you like anyone to stay tonight, dad?" Roy said.

"I'll be fine. I need to catch up with my work."

"Roy, why don't you show Bella the sea," Julia said, "and I'll drive down and find you. Your father and I will wash up."

"I like seeing it," Bella told Roy. "It's the oldest thing and it's never the same."

On her way out she lingered in front of my aunt's annual portraits of me. "It's like watching you for all those years," she said, "seeing what Thelma saw."

"I prefer them to her others," Julia said. "She didn't hide anything in them."

"You wanted dad to sell them, didn't you?"

"No need to make me sound so mercenary, Roy. More people would have had a chance to see them."

"Suppose they were messages meant just for Patrick?" Bella said.

I blinked at them but saw none. Roy held the door open for Bella, and I heard their footsteps go downstairs, largely his. We were in the kitchen, where I scraped plates above the bin before Julia filed them with considered precision in the dishwasher, when she said not entirely to herself "A bit fey."

"Young Bella, you mean."

"Young in some ways."

She said this so ruminatively that I felt compelled to wait for more, but eventually I had to say "So your overall impression..."

"He could do a lot worse for his first real girlfriend, and I wonder if she'll be more than that. I just hope they grow out of your aunt and what she left behind."

"You'll remember you know somebody who hasn't."

"There's more than that you haven't outgrown, Patrick."

This could have revived an argument that neither of us wanted. Silence seemed wisest, and we didn't speak again until we left the kitchen. "You just wanted that word about Bella," I said.

"If we're agreed that she ought to be good for him."

"I should think so. You saw him being a gentleman on their way out, didn't you? We've brought him up right after all."

"I don't know what you mean by after all."

I could have cited her doubts about Thelma's influence, but thought it best to restrain even a shrug. "Thank you again for caring," I said.

"I hope you don't think I'd do anything else."

I avoided taking this one way it could be interpreted. "Still, you're very kind."

"Let me know if there's anything more I can do, and of course when the funeral will be."

"I will, of course."

This seemed to use our words up. I held the door open for Julia, only to feel as though I was demonstrating I'd been Roy's model. "Don't bother coming down," she said and turned her face aside to save her mouth from my approaching kiss, which landed none too firmly on her cheek. "Look after yourself, Patrick," she said.

I shut the door once she was no longer to be seen and wondered why I'd loitered to watch, so little had the sight of her descent conveyed. My aunt's portraits in the corridor weren't too communicative either. I found no message in the spectacle of my sketched face growing older – certainly nothing remotely mysterious. The impression of the forest in the background did change, growing a little more detailed each year, though even in the last picture the tangles of branches looked hardly more substantial than cobweb. I could have fancied that they either hid or formed a figure that progressively took shape, though not much. Even in the final portrait the distant figure wasn't much less thin than the branches, if it was there at all. Striving to distinguish it made me feel as though the web of a forest was fastening on my mind.

That night I dreamed of an enormous web that was also a maze. My son was caught somewhere in it, and I had to find him without becoming lost to the web myself. Whatever had constructed the elaborate apparently endless trap was not just its denizen but its essence. The creature was itself the web, hiding in plain sight all around me while it waited for my fatal move. The insight drew me deeper into the labyrinth, and the only way out was to waken, though I thought years passed before I struggled free. I lay in the dark, feeling appalled that I'd left Roy in the web, and took some time over convincing myself it was simply a dream.

In the morning I left the portraits alone, and went to my desk as soon as the bathroom and a token breakfast were out of the way. Having checked my emails – offers with nothing to offer – I glanced at Facebook. Roy had posted photographs of his excursion with Bella two days ago, showing a field surrounded by a spiky hedge. Although the sun was at the zenith, some quirk of the image extended what appeared to be shadows of the hedges into all four sides of the field. Hadn't I once seen something of the kind? Yes, in one of Thelma's paintings – and then I read the name of the location. It was Drummer's Meadow, which was listed in her journal.

CHAPTER THIRTEEN

The Next Step

"It's Roy. Don't know who you are or what you want, so say. Your number would be good as well."

He'd recorded this at least a year ago, and I felt I was hearing an immature version of my son, someone less than Bella had begun to make him. I wondered when he might change the message and what the change would say about him. "Just me," I said. "Call me when you've a moment, could you? There's something I'd like to check."

I waited in the hope I'd prompted him to answer, but when the phone stayed as quiet as a slab I went back to work. I was looking at books by Colin Wilson, a philosopher and novelist who'd concluded magic was essential to living a complete life. He'd felt humanity had to rediscover ancient occult powers so as to see beyond the trap of the mundane and develop the next stage of evolution. I took him to believe truths could be found in grimoires and in other legacies left by practitioners of witchcraft. I wondered if my aunt had read him, and why Roy was following her trail. I urged my phone to ring, and when the only messages came from the railway station – every train with the same voice, prophesying the same route, which defined the train – I gave in to making another call.

"It's Roy..." Though some of the brashness must be manufactured or at the very least studied, this failed to prevent the inhospitality from feeling aimed at me. Could he have seen my name on the screen and decided for some reason not to answer? If he was simply too occupied with his girlfriend then I supposed I had to understand, even if it seemed unsympathetic to my situation. My grief at the loss of my parents was still keeping its distance, but

Roy didn't know this, and I tried not to feel I would be trading on his misapprehension. "Me again," I said once his routine finished confronting the caller. "Forgive me for badgering you, but—"

"Dad, I'm sorry. I was going to get back to you. There wasn't any coverage when you called."

"I thought that might have been it," I felt able to say. "Where were you?"

"Nowhere special. Just somewhere the phone didn't work."

"You were somewhere special the other day, I believe."

"Anywhere with Bell is pretty special." As I imagined him presenting her with a look that went with this he said "Do you need me to come over?"

"If you're in the neighbourhood you know you're very welcome. Bella too."

"Thing is, we're not. Near you, I mean. You can talk if it helps."

"No need to worry about me, but yes, let's talk. I saw where you went the other day."

"What was that?" Bella said at some distance but with force to compensate. "Did Patrick say he saw us?"

"Yes," I said, "online."

"Who put us there?"

"I did, Bell. My pics on Facebook."

"Oh, just those. I wasn't even in them."

"I'll put you in next time."

"Don't even try, Roy. I've told you I don't photograph well."

I wondered if I was about to overhear their first argument, but Roy said "What about it anyway, dad?"

"Why did you go to Drummer's Meadow?"

"To see if we could see what your aunt saw."

"And did you?"

"Don't know." With obstinacy that sounded like reverting to the adolescence he'd begun to leave behind he said "Maybe we will."

"Was it worth the journey? Quite a way without a car."

"I'd say it was." At once he added "Worth it. Bell does."

I suspected those two statements were inseparable. "Whose idea was it?"

"Both of ours."

"And what was the place like?"

"It just looked like a field to me. Felt colder, though."

"Colder than what?"

"Than walking to it, and when we walked back to the station. The sun was up above us all the time." After a pause he said "And you couldn't see the far side."

"I don't understand. It was in your photograph."

"Maybe I started seeing like your aunt did after all."

Other than uneasy, I was unsure how this made me feel. I was reaching for another question when I heard a man's voice. "Excuse me, what are you doing there?"

A silence left me wondering as well, and with increasing nervousness. Perhaps it simply meant the activity was being completed, since Bella ended the silence by saying "Just taking a sample."

She'd given the voice time to approach. "Who gave you permission?"

"I don't think we need that, do we? Look, I haven't taken much."

"You don't remove other people's property without asking first."

"Come on," Roy protested. "It isn't anybody's property, or it's everyone's."

"I wasn't talking to you, son."

"You are now." As I willed him not to become embroiled in an argument, especially when I had no chance to intervene, Roy said "It's for a project at our school. We have to take them from all over."

Even if he was lying on Bella's behalf, I was disconcerted by his glibness, which I'd never known him to show. "Which school?" the man said.

"The earthen college," Bella said.

"Never heard of it."

"Unearthing knowledge, that's the slogan."

"Never heard that either."

"The school isn't round here," Roy said.

I could tell the man was growing more suspicious. "Then don't you be."

"We're going now. No need to watch."

I would have spoken except for listening to reassure myself they'd left the altercation behind. I heard nothing for some moments, and then Roy said "Sorry, dad."

"For what?"

"Leaving you like that. I expect you wondered what was going on."

"You didn't leave me. I could hear the whole thing." When this brought no audible response I said "Just where are you?"

"On our way to the station."

"You know exactly what I mean. You may have played a game just now, but please don't try it on with me."

"All right, we're in Dancers Oak. I was going to tell you." Before I could decide whether this was as true as I would have hoped, he said "It's like your aunt wrote, just a housing estate with an old tree in the middle."

"And what are you doing there?"

"You said you heard."

I tried not to think Bella was changing him in ways I might dislike. "Tell me precisely."

"What your aunt did."

"And why, Roy, why."

"Didn't you ever want to see what she saw? I thought that was why you kept her journal."

"I think we can see it in her paintings if it's to be seen at all, and I wouldn't—"

"We want to try going back to her way. It means a lot to Bell."

"Going back how? What do you think digging up the place is likely to achieve?"

"We didn't dig much. I shouldn't think your aunt did."

"I'm still asking what it's supposed to do."

"It kind of helps you meditate, doesn't it, Bell?" However she responded, Roy said "You ought to try it, dad."

"Did you dig up Drummer's Meadow as well?"

"A little bit. There wasn't anyone to mind, was there, Bell?"

"You didn't see them, did you?"

"That's because there wasn't anyone to see."

I had an odd sense of an embryonic argument, but I was more concerned to discover "How are you keeping these souvenirs of yours?"

"We've got jars for them. Bell calls them relics."

I found this less important than establishing "What's your mother going to think of all this?"

"Do you have to tell her?"

"You know I'm happy that you're interested in Thelma and her work, but this is going further. Have you considered your mother at all?"

"She wouldn't understand like you ought to. She might even try and stop me seeing Bell."

I shouldn't have let this influence me, but it did. "How much longer do you mean to carry on with this?"

"Seeing each other, do you mean?" Bella said.

"I've no problem with that. I'm not sure it's up to me to have one. I'm asking how long you mean to visit places Thelma mentioned."

"As long as it takes," Roy said. "We've got weeks yet off school."

"You're saying you intend to go to all of them."

"Just the ones we haven't been to yet."

"And when you reach the end—"

"Roy, there's our train."

I heard wheels whining distantly along a line. "We've got to run. Speak soon," Roy said and left me with the progress of the train.

It wasn't on the phone. It was on the track beyond my window. Of course this needn't mean I hadn't heard one in Dancers Oak as well. I laid the phone on its back on my desk, and its face turned as blank as my mind. I stared at the observations I'd typed on the computer – thoughts about books for next term – and then I fetched Thelma's journal. Soon I was consulting the map on my phone before heading for my car. If only so as to be prepared in case I had to discuss Roy and Bella's expeditions with his mother, I wanted to see some of the places in the journal for myself.

CHAPTER FOURTEEN

It Speaks

"In half a mile leave the motorway by the first exit."

The navigator on my phone had the voice of a butler out of Hollywood, and sounded surer of itself than I felt. All around me the flat land that stretched to the horizon beneath an undecided whitish August sky was strewn with clumps of grey stone houses, and I wondered how it had looked to my aunt. What could have brought her here? Perhaps she had already known more about Halfway Halt than I'd managed to discover, which might as well have been nothing at all.

"At the top of the ramp take the first exit onto Sunward Way..." The broad road – four lanes divided in half by a protracted sliver of verge – wound east through grey Yorkshire villages that appeared to be staining the sky beyond them. Each one had a pub and a church, and the succession of ecclesiastical towers put me in mind of a painting of Thelma's, an early work in which all the spires of an English countryside were linked by horizontal lightning, the bearer of some unspecified mystical message. Had she subsequently found this inspiration too conventional? That didn't explain how she'd learned about Halfway Halt or anywhere else in her journal.

"In five miles take the second exit onto Northerly Lane..." This was a road just wide enough for two large vehicles to pass each other. Hedges barbed with outsize thorns fended trespassers away from fields and obscured bends that grew progressively sharper. At least I met no traffic, in fact no signs of life on the move except for the delicately jagged flights of butterflies, and once a head that rose over a gate to watch me as best it could while its eyes crawled with insects. It was a cow, but I was glad to leave the spectacle behind, especially when it poked out a considerable tongue onto which flies swarmed at once.

"In three miles turn left on Old Station Road..." Without my artificial helper I might have passed the sign, which was almost engulfed by a hedge. I was just able to distinguish that the first word had been added, although the appended plaque was pretty well as rusty and lichenous as the original pointer. The road it identified was barely wide enough for my car to pass another, and ran straight for no more than a couple of hundred yards at a stretch. Where attempts had been made to create passing places, unrestrained hedges had invaded the space. Once again I saw little evidence of life, though I caught sight of a bovine head beyond a gate. I thought it was watching me until I realised the movement I'd taken for eyes belonged to creatures teeming in the sockets. The head was a cow's skull on a pole, presumably erected to deter intruders of any kind. Certainly it didn't leave me anxious to linger.

"In half a mile arrive at your destination..." I thought I would be relieved to see the end of the devious route, but I was wondering how close public transport could bring anybody to the site. How far would Roy and Bella have to walk? Perhaps I should have offered them a lift, but however excessively wary my behaviour might be, I'd wanted to view the place before they did. Perhaps I could drive them there if that wouldn't risk inhibiting their relationship.

"Arrive at your destination..." My helper couldn't change his tone – its tone, to be accurate – and yet the direction felt peremptory, an assumption of obedience or of the lack of any choice. Ahead the road ended at a towering metal fence encrusted with rust and quilted with ivy, and I thought the phone had misdirected me until I noticed a gap in the hedge to the left. Though branches bound with ivy were well on their way to closing the gap, it was the entrance to a car park.

The deserted expanse was spread with ragged rugs of moss. Weeds sprouting from cracks in the concrete gestured in a wind that rattled scales of dead ivy on the outer wall of the abandoned railway station, which resembled an elongated single-storey cottage with a steep roof. Holes left by fallen slates honeycombed the roof, which poked three lanky chimneys and their blackened pots at a sky like a reminiscence of their sooty past. I parked near the station entrance, where double doors had lost their hold on the frame, sprawling face down on the concrete. As I slipped my phone into a pocket, having climbed out of the car, I appeared to rouse the navigator. "Arrived," it said.

"I know that," I retorted, despite feeling less confident than I tried to sound. Through the exit from the waiting-room beyond the doorless entrance I could see a sign on the further platform. Black lichen or a vandal's paint spray had covered the name of the station except for the first two letters of each word, so that the sign resembled a joke at the expense of any visitor. I wondered how my aunt had read it, although would it have been in this state when she was here? I didn't even know how long ago that was. Perhaps I would find some insight in the waiting-room.

The doors to the platform had collapsed, and the windows overlooking it had been thoroughly smashed. At least this let in the daylight, such as it was, enabling me to pick my way around the rubble strewn across the floorboards. Tattered posters clung to the walls, portions of them groping at the shadows as a chilly wind enlivened them. The vintage images advertised holiday resorts, bygone or certainly transformed since. One poster showed a family on a seafront while the other placed a couple with their son and daughter on a beach. Of course they must be different families, but somebody had gouged out every face and the plaster behind them, filling their outlines with wet red brick. The tattered silhouettes were growing restless with a wind, and I was reminded of the kind of seaside sideshow where customers paid to thrust their faces through the holes that grotesque figures had above their necks. Why should I imagine that all the holes in the posters were about to produce the same face? Just now I preferred to leave that kind of fancy to my aunt, and I made my way over to the booking office.

At the foot of the grimy window a low arch gaped in the glass. Heavy wire mesh protected the aperture, putting me in mind of a church confessional I'd once seen in a film, but left a narrow gap above the sill for hands to reach through. Items encased in dusty cobwebs – a ledger, a pen and a chewed stub of pencil, obsolete little machines – lay on the extended sill beyond the window. A fireplace stood in so much gloom that it appeared to lead into a deeper darkness than it should. Between the hearth and the ticket window, a small table bore a teapot divested of its lid. Weeds occupied the pot, though in the dimness they could have been taken for a version of a genie emerging from a lamp. Some sort of growth poked out from the lid beside the pot, as if a hermit creature had appropriated it for a home. I was about to move on when I glimpsed activity around an office chair lying on its back near the hearth. Several thin fingers were fumbling out from underneath, as if an occupant had been squashed flat but was determined to return. The scrawny digits began to crumble, sending particles to swarm in all directions, and even when I realised that spiders were hatching under the chair I found no reason to linger.

I stepped onto the platform under the threat of a storm. Grass grew between the flagstones, twitching in the wind. Rotten lopsided benches stood about in remembrance of commuters, and one knelt on its solitary left leg like a beast about to die. On the opposite platform more than one flagstone had been heaved up by the knotted limbs of an intruder, the roots of trees beyond an insecure brick wall, which the trunks and branches were urging towards collapse. Apart from the sign that suggested a burst of silent mirth, one remnant said WAY ALT, another just A WAY. Perhaps this was the work of vandals, like the words sprayed or scraped on the mossy wall, MAG and GIST and TELL and RUM scattered along its length. No doubt the words meant more to their author than they did to the rest of the world, often the case with graffiti. They only helped to leave me increasingly unsure why I was there at all.

The railway tracks had been removed. If anyone had planned to turn the route into a nature walk, the scheme had been abandoned before they'd taken up the sleepers. The overgrown boards suggested stepping-stones over a medium less solid than the ground they were embedded in. To my right they climbed between grassy banks to follow a ridge that was eventually blocked by fallen trees, while on my left the route descended into a cutting. My aunt had written something about the latter in her journal, and if I was to gain any insight from my visit, presumably it would be there. I made for that end of the platform, where a slippery ramp led down to the remains of the track.

While the sleepers were spaced closely enough to invite my stride, they looked precarious with lichen, and I walked beside the vanished tracks instead. In a few hundred yards the ruddy sandstone walls were higher than my head. I could have fancied I was descending into a past embodied in the strata of the exposed rock, or at least my aunt might have had such an impression. Trees perched on the edges above me, their contorted roots gripping the cracked stone. Patches of the walls bulged with lurid fungi, and other stretches were mottled with moss. About a quarter of a mile ahead a road bridge crossed the cutting, and I was halfway to it when a voice spoke close to me. "In three hundred yards," it said, "turn left onto Riders Lane."

The walls must be distorting it, because it sounded untypically shrill. I thought I'd switched it off before pocketing the phone, but I made doubly certain now. Having stowed the phone again, I advanced to the bridge, where the arch was toothed with loose bricks. Its darkness closed over me as I glanced back. There was no sign of the station – just the artificial valley tapering into the distance. Of course the perspective was hiding the platforms, not to mention narrowing the gap between the walls, as if the perilously tilted trees were urging them together. Was this what my aunt had seen? She'd written something of the kind. I should have copied her journal onto my phone, as Roy had. If he and Bella came here they might venture further, and so I should. I was still under the bridge when my companion said "In a quarter of a mile turn left to your destination."

He sounded shriller than before, no doubt because of the acoustic, and I had the grotesque notion that he was about to change gender. "I'm there already," I informed him, and a voice that wasn't his said "Ready" – my echo from the arch. I muted the phone and shoved it in my pocket, and then I set out from the bridge.

Trees leaned out further overhead as the downward slope grew steeper. Would my aunt have seen the blackened sky weighing them down? She might have thought the past represented by the multiplying strata of the walls was drawing us lower still. No doubt she would have appreciated how some of the sets of bracket fungus on the walls resembled pairs of fleshy lips. She could have envisioned the large beads of moisture that clung to the lichen as lidless eyes, their blank stares following me through the gloom. Had I undergone enough of her kind of fancies yet? Although the wind seemed not to reach down here, I kept feeling colder. The trouble was that I had no real idea of how she might have viewed the place or how it might appear to my son. Surely there was nothing he ought to avoid, and why should I have imagined there might be? That was Julia's attitude, not mine. I was still trudging down the slope when the land above the cutting emitted a moist whisper that progressed into a hiss as it closed in, and the branches overhead began to writhe as if they were struggling to fend off the storm.

The nearest shelter was the bridge I'd left behind. As I sprinted for it, the ground underfoot grew treacherous. It must be soaking up the rain, even if I didn't yet feel drenched. It felt no more stable than a marsh, and I dodged onto the nearest sleeper and then the next one up. They weren't quite as close together as I'd assumed, and the slope was steeper than I was anticipating. Wasn't this often the case when you had to return uphill? I told myself so while deploring the incompetence of the workmen who had laid the line, since the sleepers weren't evenly spaced – indeed, each pair was a little further apart, and I was having to stride wider. I felt as if I were striving to climb a ladder without being able to use my hands to clamber, and soon I had to jump from board to increasingly slippery board as outsize raindrops plummeted from the trees to thump my scalp. I tried walking on the ground instead, only to slither backwards. I could easily have fancied that I felt the ground shift underfoot, and I retreated onto the sleepers, lurching from one insecure foothold to the next. I'd missed my footing more than once, landing on the restlessly insecure earth, by the time I stumbled under the bridge.

I did my best not to think the shelter felt even slightly like a trap. The downpour must be weighing on the trees, which looked bent on dragging the rock walls together. The prematurely nighted sky appeared to have narrowed the cutting and blocked it in both directions with blackness, closer than the railway station. I stood under the middle of the arch beneath the untravelled road and tried to be soothed by the incessant liquid murmur of the rain, rendered stereophonic by the bridge. I was finding reassurance in the inability of the storm to touch me when I began to hear a voice.

I snatched out my phone, but it stayed mute. For a distracted moment I wondered if I could be hearing an announcement at the railway station. Might someone be listening to a car radio nearby?

I strained my ears to make out the voice through the downpour. It sounded almost as thin and as randomly shaped as the rain. Was it whispering "Must" or "Master"? No, there were more than two syllables, although not quite either of those. "Mist tells"? Not that, and I peered down the slope, where the sounds almost indistinguishable from the rush of rain appeared to come from. Perhaps they were just part of the downpour, like the twin globules of water that swarmed down a patch of lichen to lodge above an especially prominent outcrop of fungus, two thick piebald ledges pressed together. The rain was rousing the plump fungoid strips, causing them to twitch apart and extrude a swollen greyish tendril like a relic of a tongue. The spectacle appeared to locate the whisper and lend it substance. "Magister," I was almost sure it said. "Magister Stellarum."

I tried to believe that only the rain was shifting the fungus, however allied to the syllables the movements seemed to be. Perhaps the movements were making me hear words where none were to be found. I couldn't help recoiling when the left-hand globule either lost its hold or burst, streaming down the wall, to be followed at once by its twin. The fungus drooped as though exhausted by its efforts, and then I caught sight of another pair of globules that had come to rest above two lips of fungus, much closer to the bridge. Moisture eased the protrusions apart, and I heard the simulation of a voice. "Magister Stellarum."

The downpour was abating, and I could no longer mistake the voice for rain. It sounded soft as rotten fungus and similarly liable to collapse. Although the wind had dropped, I was seized by a fierce chill. I couldn't move or look away from the unnatural activity on the wall until it fell apart, the watchful globules drooling down the lichen as the strips of fungus sagged. Ought I to have felt reassured? Not when I feared the presence was simply moving on and about to reappear.

I held my breath until I had to gasp, but heard nothing beyond belated rainfall from the trees. The cutting had grown almost silent when I sensed movement overhead. My eyes were aching by the time I made out a swollen shape like a bag stuck to the underside of the bridge. I thought its eyes were glinting darkly in the gloom, and other restless parts of it bore some resemblance to lips. Certainly I heard the whisper, amplified by the echo until it sounded as though the bridge was pronouncing the words like a great stone mouth. It paralysed me and my thoughts until a dreadful notion overtook me – that the ill-defined object was about to relinquish its hold on the arch and drop on me like a huge swollen spider. Almost before grasping I'd regained the ability to move, I fled.

The whisper ceased at once, which only left me dreading where it might reappear. I thought I glimpsed unwelcome features starting to take shape here and there on the lichenous walls, which were streaming with the aftermath of the downpour. I fancied I heard attempts to pronounce syllables that had grown entirely too familiar, however meaningless – tentative almost liquid whispering behind if not beside me and once, far worse, ahead. The slope was gentler on this side of the bridge, but whenever I sensed a presence beginning to form close to me I was overcome by a renewed chill, which drained my energy so much that I almost couldn't lurch from sleeper to uphill sleeper. I had a wholly nightmarish fear that I might never reach the railway station – that somehow there was no longer one at Halfway Halt to reach. Far too belatedly the walls of the cutting gave way to the platforms, and at last I stumbled up the ramp towards the waiting-room.

My footsteps on the bare boards resounded so much that I doubted I would hear a whisper, and the room was too dark for me to make sure it was as empty as it had been. I was heading for the exit to the car park – just a few more determined strides and I would be out beneath the relentlessly black sky – when I hesitated, having been drained of momentum by another sudden chill. In the silence I heard surreptitious movement above me, where I could just make out a discoloured bulge in the plaster of the ceiling. It reminded me far too much of a cocoon even before I heard its contents stir again. They weren't merely restless, they were mumbling blurred syllables, which I felt helplessly compelled to distinguish. As I peered at the wakeful shape I saw the plaster start to crack, and was terrified that the contents would fall on my face. A convulsive shiver released me from my paralysis, and I dashed close to blindly into the car park.

I didn't look back even once I was locked in my car. As I swung it around, crushing weeds beneath the wheels, I wasn't sure whether

I saw two outsize raindrops swell bigger still on a patch of moss on the concrete while a thick-ridged slit parted in the vegetation. I drove out of the car park almost faster than I dared, and barely managed to take all the bends of Old Station Road without straying off the greasy rain-washed tarmac into a ditch. I felt close to hysteria, both at having escaped and about the grotesque experience I'd had. If I started laughing it wouldn't denote mirth, and I suspected I would find it hard to stop. Besides, there was nothing comical in the possibility that my son and his girlfriend might have a similar experience. I ought to prevent it, and I pulled over at once.

As I found my phone it spoke. "Messages," it seemed to say, and "Tell all them." Perhaps the mumble sounded so unlike its usual voice because it was still in my pocket, and I might have concluded that I'd inadvertently activated it to pronounce random words on the screen. Just the same, its behaviour revived a chill that made me shake, and I couldn't help feeling I hadn't left Halfway Halt far enough behind. I let go of the phone and didn't stop the car again until I reached Northerly Lane, where I parked on the verge of a straight stretch. The phone kept its peace while I fumbled it out of my pocket, and Roy spoke almost as soon as his phone began to ring. "Dad, we're a bit busy right now."

"I won't keep you. I just wanted to tell you not to bother with Halfway Halt, if you meant to."

"Why not?"

"I don't know how you'd get there, but it isn't worth the effort."

"We already have."

This made me uneasier than ever. "What did you find?"

"I think Bell's getting more out of all this than me. If she does that's what matters."

"Where are you now?" I had to ask.

"Just walking."

"Yes, but where?"

As though he shouldn't have withheld the information Bella said "Darkmarsh."

"And what are you expecting to turn up there?"

I meant this for Roy, but Bella answered. "We'll know it when we meet it, Patrick."

"Talk more soon, dad, okay? It's getting a bit cold just standing round."

"I may know what you mean," I said and was preparing to explain when I realised they'd already gone. I had to resist the urge to call Roy back; at the very least it would irritate him, and I wasn't even sure he would answer. No doubt they would take a sample from Darkmarsh and had collected one from Halfway Halt. Could their souvenir do any harm? I might have been more qualified to judge if I'd taken one myself, but I was considerably less than eager to go back.

Perhaps I had a source of insight in my hand. I told the phone to search for Magister Stellarum. I thought it might inform me that it didn't understand, a response that always sounded like a polite rebuke, but a link to a site appeared within seconds – the Sorcerous Atlas of Britain. The link brought up an outline map swarming with tags. One tag was enlarged, and its pointer rested somewhere in the middle of the country, uncomfortably close to my location. The tag said **Magister Stellarum**.

When I touched it, the tag expanded. **Victorian occultist**, it added. **Real name Harold Lambkin**. I tried to find this laughable if not pathetic, but was troubled by the last phrase on the marker: **His domain**. I used a thumb and forefinger to zoom in on the map, and a border swelled up like a stain around the pointer. As the circle spread from Halfway Halt it appeared to be creeping to catch up with me. I didn't need to see how close it might come, and I dropped the phone on the seat beside me before starting the car. I'd already seen more places I recognised by name on the map, and one I knew very well indeed.

CHAPTER FIFTEEN

Burials

"You never met them, Bell."

"I don't believe I ever said I had."

"No, I mean you should have."

Bella glanced at me, presumably to ascertain how Roy's comments were affecting me. "Why do you say that?"

"I expect you'd have liked them and they'd have liked you."

"Then I'm sorry. I am anyway, Patrick. What do you think I'd have liked?"

"I used to like how they never tried to be like me."

"Who do you know that does?" When he shook his head as if to dislodge a quick grimace Bella said "Unless you mean Patrick."

Julia offered this a laugh that sounded tentative or just polite. "Don't take this the wrong way, Patrick, but I wouldn't exactly call you trendy. What are you thinking of, Bella?"

"Roy knows." Since his face betrayed no knowledge Bella said "Following our search."

"I'm afraid you've left me behind," Julia said.

We were in the pub – the Green Female, apparently formerly a man – where the wake had been held after my parents' funeral. The last of the other mourners had left a few minutes ago, probably concluding I might want to be alone with my feelings and my family, however temporarily reconstituted. In fact my emotions felt as if they'd been embalmed before I'd had a chance to experience them properly, and the spectacle of my parents packed in plush at the undertaker's had only helped freeze my response. They had both looked so rejuvenated that I could almost have imagined someone had substituted flattering waxworks. Even their calm seemed unreal, a denial of the shock and injuries they must have suffered in the car crash. When I'd spoken from the lectern at the funeral I'd felt as though I was enumerating their merits rather than truly remembering my parents as they'd been while they had breath. I'd heard myself talking like a candidate for a job at Turnbill and Semple, exhibiting the qualities my parents would have wanted from a potential partner in their firm.

Perhaps my eulogy had grown arid because I was striving to be rational about other events in my life. What had I really experienced at Halfway Halt? Had I been so bent on seeing things from my aunt's viewpoint that I'd turned the place into a deranged cartoon of itself? Perhaps at some time in my childhood I'd overheard her mentioning Magister Stellarum in connection with Halfway Halt. The notion seemed not too far from desperate, and there was too much that it failed to explain. Now I was additionally disconcerted by Bella's comment – by feeling I'd been used as a defence, though I had no idea why she should feel defensive. "So," Julia said, "is anybody going to let me into the secret?"

"It isn't much of one," Roy said.

"Then it shouldn't take much keeping."

Resentfully enough to be blaming me Roy said "Dad can say."

I thought he should be blaming Bella for alerting Julia, but no doubt his girlfriend was exempt. "We've been visiting places that gave my aunt ideas," I said.

"Are you trying to recapture memories?" Julia said.

"These aren't memories."

"Things to do with your family, then." As though I'd rebuffed her sympathy she said "Trying to hold on to anything you can."

"Anybody would," Bella said. "It's only human."

We were letting Julia assume too much that wasn't true, but I preferred this to arguing. When I didn't speak she said "Where have you visited?"

"Places Thelma wrote down. I think she started after she met the character who took my uncle's place."

"You think that's what he did," Bella said.

"Gave my aunt ideas or helped to, yes, I believe so."

"He didn't try to be like your uncle, then."

As though she found the digression at the very best irrelevant Julia said "What were the places like?"

"What would you two say?"

"Maybe you had to be her," Roy said, "to see what she saw."

"Or you can let them speak to you," Bella said.

An uneasy memory of Halfway Halt prompted me to ask "What did you hear?"

"They speak like her paintings, Patrick. Speak to your soul."

"I'm afraid they don't speak to mine," Julia said.

Roy's look might have been implying she had none. Not least for fear that he would voice the thought, I said "Magister Stellarum."

Everybody turned to me, and Bella's eyes were widest. As though he'd expected someone else to speak, Roy said "What was that supposed to be?"

"Didn't you hear it at Halfway Halt?"

"Just heard the trees, and it was cold even though there wasn't any wind."

"If there wasn't a wind, how did you hear the trees?"

"There must have been one up where they were. How about you, Bell?"

"Don't mind me," Julia said, "but I'm afraid I'm feeling uninformed again."

Roy and Bella gazed at me as if I was responsible for deciding how much to reveal. "All the places Thelma wrote down have to do with magic," I said. "Maybe there are people buried there who did."

"What makes you think that?" Bella said.

"I found a map of them."

I was tired of withholding the truth from Julia – in fact, I'd begun to feel I might welcome her support. I brought up the atlas on my phone, and Roy peered at it while Bella gave it just a lingering blink. "May I see as well?" Julia said.

Roy passed the phone across the table occupied by soft drinks and wine depleted by respectful sips. Julia used a finger and thumb to expand details on the map, a process that enlarged her frown as well. Eventually she said to nobody specific "Well, I hope you won't be doing this much longer."

"There aren't too many, are there, Patrick? Just the ones Thelma had to visit."

"Did you notice Third Mile Wood is on that map?"

"Maybe that's why she bought her house there," Roy said.

"She wasn't online then."

"Maybe she didn't need the map to feel the magic."

I thought Julia might object, but she appeared to think she'd made her point. "It's where Diana Arborum is meant to be buried," I told her. "Don't ask me where."

"I wasn't about to. I shouldn't think anyone cares."

"Supposedly a witch. Real name Mary Hodge. The most recent of them on the map." Since this brought no response, I turned to Roy and Bella. "Whoever's planted somewhere around Halfway Halt liked to call himself Magister Stellarum," I said. "Master of the stars, which he must have thought was more impressive than Harold Lambkin."

I was hoping this would amuse my listeners — better still, strike them as pathetically absurd — but not even Julia smiled. "Names help to make us," Bella said. "You'd have changed yours when you married, Julia."

"And now I've changed it back." Perhaps Julia felt this was unnecessarily insensitive at the wake. "What about yours, Bella?" she said as if to leave her remark well behind. "I don't know the rest of your name."

Roy laughed at Bella's answer. "Bella Knowall?"

"That isn't what I said, Roy. I wouldn't take that name."

"It sounds a bit like you sometimes."

"Bella Noel," Julia said to forestall any quarrel. "I'd call it musical."

"Thank you, Julia. I'm glad it has some charm."

"Does it mean you were born at Christmas?" Roy said.

"Something like that if you like."

"Roy, you're confusing us," his mother said. "Her surname wasn't changed, was it, Bella?"

"It's the only one I've ever had."

"I was sure it must be," Julia said and handed me my phone, which had blotted out the atlas and was demanding identification. Apparently she thought her blank look was eloquent enough about the map. She didn't speak again until she'd taken a sip of wine followed by a resolutely final one. "I really should be going, Patrick," she said, and told Bella "I hope I'll see you again soon."

"We ought to be making tracks as well if Patrick doesn't mind."

I couldn't very well expect my son to linger by himself. "Thanks for coming," I said.

"I wouldn't have felt right otherwise," Bella said. "Could I ride part of the way with you, Julia?"

"Of course you can. We can start to get to know one another better."

Outside the pub Julia gave me a terse loose hug, and Roy came up with an embrace that consisted mostly of slapping my back. Bella delivered an enveloping squeeze that lasted long enough for Julia to raise her eyebrows. "See you soon, dad," Roy said, and Bella left a look that seemed to convey the same, while Julia's touched upon the possibility. I watched them drive away, engrossed in a conversation I couldn't hear. I had a sense of having missed an opportunity, and perhaps that distracted me from grasping how much else I'd missed.

CHAPTER SIXTEEN

Someone on the Roof

"What can I do for you now, Patrick?"

"We didn't really have a chance to talk much yesterday."

"I'm sorry if we left before you wanted."

"I mean I wish we could have been alone."

"Patrick, I know you must be upset about your parents, but—"

"So we could talk properly, I mean. Can you now?"

I thought her pause might hide a silent sigh. "What do you need to talk about?"

"Roy and his lady. Did you learn much about her?"

"We just chatted. They mostly did. She wasn't with us long before I dropped her off."

"Where?"

"The nearest station."

"You don't know where she was headed for."

"I didn't ask. Why do you want to know?"

"You said yourself we don't know much about her."

"I'm not so sure I ever said that, and I don't doubt we will if they stay together."

"Are you hoping they will? I thought you'd be bothered by the things she's making Roy do."

"I'm busy right now." I thought Julia was dismissing my observation and quite possibly me as well until the sound of a door let me know that someone had looked into her office. More sharply still she said "What things, Patrick?"

"Not just visiting the places Thelma went but taking samples of them."

"Samples," Julia said as if it mightn't even be a word.

"Souvenirs if you like. Some of the earth."

"I don't know if I like or not. Whatever gave her that idea?"

"My aunt used to do it. She kept them in jars in her studio."

"That's what you made such a fuss about at her funeral. You accused your parents of throwing them out." With too little of a pause to let me speak Julia said "So Bella must have picked up the idea from you. She never met your aunt."

"I suppose it may have come from me indirectly, but—"

"A good deal more than indirectly. Weren't you there with her and Roy?"

I did my best to be prepared for the response I would provoke by saying "No."

"You certainly led me to think you were. May I ask why you'd do that?"

"As I say, I wanted to discuss it when we were by ourselves."

"I don't know what sense that makes." As I willed her to find it justified, her voice slowed down as though burdened by her thoughts. "Now I understand what Bella meant. She must have wanted me to realise."

More uneasily than I could quite conceal I said "What did she tell you?"

"She said it to you and they left you to explain to me, but you didn't."

I recalled this style of accusation from our marriage. "Explain what?" I knew I wouldn't learn unless I said.

"She said you'd been following them. What have you been up to, Patrick?"

"Not following in the way you mean. Just going to some of the places they've visited."

"I wonder how you think I meant it. What's this really all about?"

"I told you, I'd have expected you to be more concerned about their behaviour."

"If you mean going places your aunt went, I'm hoping it lets them work her out of their system. Or have you something else on your mind? It's not at all like you to object to anybody showing interest in your aunt."

"Their kind is different. Even I think it may be too much."

"Then you should take it up with Roy yourself. How do you

know they've been collecting what you call souvenirs? Is he keeping them at your flat?"

"No, but—"

"And they certainly aren't at my house. Have you even seen them?"

"Bella must have them wherever she lives."

"In other words you haven't. I wonder if there's more to this than you're admitting."

"Tell me what there would be."

"Do you suppose you might be a little jealous?"

"Jealous?" When this failed to convey all my disbelief I said "Of what?"

"Of our son and the relationship he seems to be developing. You do seem rather anxious to undermine it."

"I'm nothing of the sort if it's good for him."

"If it is." Once she'd made it plain that the doubts were wholly mine Julia said "You might want to be a bit more careful round her, Patrick."

"Careful of what?"

"You were getting rather affectionate yesterday. You gave her quite a hug."

"That was her, if you noticed. She gave it to me."

"You shouldn't blame a girl of her age. At the very least it's irresponsible."

"Whatever age you think that is."

"That's the kind of excuse worse men than you make. At least, I hope you aren't like them." As I tried to gather words to use in not too furious a retort, Julia said "I hope we've said all we need to say about her now. Speak to me if you need to talk about your loss."

I couldn't judge whether she was inviting this immediately or later, nor did I care. "I don't," I said.

"Just look after yourself," Julia said, which I could have taken for a warning not to interfere, and ended the call.

For a moment I thought a dormant voice was making itself heard on my phone, but a train in the station was counselling vigilance. On the horizon a solitary windmill in the middle of the rank stirred as though regaining life and then reverted to emulating its neighbours. I went back to poring over Colin Wilson, determined to read him more attentively than he appeared to have treated some of the texts he'd read. I wished I could approach the book more carelessly, because the theme of the need for magic had grown less than welcome. I'd just learned that both Crowley and Strindberg believed they could render themselves invisible when my phone announced an unknown caller.

Bella's was the name I immediately thought of, and yet I had an odd conviction that she couldn't be the caller. I hadn't time to ponder why as I said "Hello?"

"Is that Mr Semple?"

Though the voice wasn't Bella's, it sounded familiar. "It is," I said.

"Which Mr Semple?"

"Patrick of that line."

"The father or the son?"

I wondered if I should feel flattered or less positively commented upon. "Which do I sound like?"

"You could be either. Phones do that to people."

"Well, I'm the older generation."

"People don't always seem the age they are." Apparently she needed to explain her doubts before saying "This is Hattie Dennison."

"Miss Dennison."

"I heard about your parents."

I found even less of an answer. "Yes."

"I was sorry when I heard." Having reduced me to wordlessness, the old lady from the Stonefield cottage said "I hope you're getting over it."

"I may be."

"It can take time. It did when my hubby passed. Please say if I'm intruding." When I held back from doing so she said "I just wondered if they told you what I told them."

I could only think her memory was failing. "You told me yourself."

"No, the second time."

My bewilderment felt too close to unease. "Which second time?"

"I'm afraid it was the day they had their accident."

How apologetic did she need to be? "You don't mean they were driving when you called."

"No, they were just looking in at their office when I caught them."

A silence meant I had to ask "So what did you tell them?"

"About whoever has been lurking near my house. I didn't see it at first, but it's the eyes that give them away."

"My mother said something like that." It disturbed me to realise "Almost the last thing she ever said."

"She would have." As if to leave this less ominous Hattie Dennison added "Would have wanted you to know."

"I still don't, so could you tell me?"

"The people who were here..." I assumed her pause denoted thought rather than reluctance. "I'm sure they were related," she said.

"Me and my son?" I wondered if she'd lost her sense of my identity. "We said that's who we were."

"Not then." Less directly to the phone she remarked "There now."

"If you're thinking of my aunt, of course she was related to us."

"Not her. Don't make this so hard for me." After a silence that might have been designed to measure the difficulty I'd caused, Hattie Dennison said "The one that was here when she was."

I had to think her mind was misbehaving. "Forgive me, but you told me she was by herself."

"That's because she was. I've still got some brains left." Her latest silence could have signified resentment or reproof, and I was about to end it when she said "They were loitering near her after she fell. They were the first there, and they stayed in the crowd."

"Why didn't you mention them earlier?"

"I thought they must have been in there for drugs. I didn't care to be singled out as an informer. Call me a coward who wouldn't take responsibility if you like."

"No," I said to some of that, "why didn't you mention them to me?"

"Because I didn't realise they were so significant."

"And now you think they are because..."

"Someone like them has been skulking around here. I've no idea what they think they are, but I saw them with—"

At first I thought she'd been cut off, and then I heard a protracted shaky breath. "Yes, with?" I urged.

"They're out there now, watching me. Come and see for yourself."

This sounded like a challenge, unless she was accusing me of disbelief. "Can't you just say?" I protested.

"I want someone else to see them."

Presumably this was a refusal. "I'll be with you as soon as I can," I said.

The blank white tube that led beneath the river seemed to hollow out my mind, and by the time I drove out of the far end I was losing any sense of purpose. All the way through Liverpool traffic lights greeted me by turning red, and roadworks contributed to hindering me as well. Cones like headgear for my ignorance narrowed the motorway, slowing most of the traffic down, not least my car. Once I left the motorway the flat land felt like the absence of a destination. I ought to see what Hattie Dennison had seen, if it related to my aunt, but I'd begun to wonder whether she'd imagined it. Perhaps her vagueness on the phone should have alerted me to her state of mind.

The tower blocks of Stonefield rose grudgingly to meet me as the road wandered closer. Lower containers for tenants surrounded them to make up the town. As the row of old cottages came in sight I saw the church, which looked mass-produced, hiding most of its length behind Block Five. I was nearly at the cottages before I noticed a small crowd outside the tower block.

Would Hattie Dennison want her neighbours to see me? Suppose they thought she'd informed on some of them? There was no point in parking further away when they would see me at the cottage. Surely she would have phoned if she wanted to put me off. I was drawing up outside her cottage when my feet faltered on the pedals, and the car jerked to a halt. The crowd had gathered around a woman who lay face up on the concrete.

As I climbed out of the car I had to grab the edge of its roof for support, having seen more of her state. The back of her head looked flattened, as if it had been deflated by emptying out a considerable crimson stain. I felt as if I'd returned not just to the scene of my aunt's death but to that time as well. This wasn't why the dead woman looked familiar, but I had to venture closer to be sure that she was indeed Hattie Dennison.

Her swollen eyes stared at the height of the tower until a man who'd just joined the gathering went down on one knee to finger them shut. Her jaw stayed fallen in a silent scream. As I approached I looked away, fixing my attention on faces in the crowd. When several people stared at me I demanded "What happened to her?"

More of the crowd turned to eye me, but everybody appeared to be delegating someone else to respond. Eventually a longhaired scrawny teenager in torn jeans and a singlet did. "Fell," he said and raised a fist to point a thumb up the tower block.

Surely the gesture couldn't signify approval, and I was about to enquire further when his companion – an equally undernourished girl whose jeans came to a ragged end an inch above her knees – said "Are you her son or something?"

"No, I'm just," I said and felt driven to think swiftly, "just a friend."

"We saw you round at hers before."

More than one listener stared hard at me, and I thought it wise to say "When?"

"The other week."

Hoping this had absolved me of suspicion, I said "Did anybody see what happened here?"

"We did," the girl said. "We were coming home."

"What did you see?"

"She doesn't live in our block," the boy said or complained, "but she went up on our roof."

"Someone chased her in," the girl said.

"Don't know who they were. Didn't really see them."

This sounded blunt enough to be designed to end the conversation, until the girl said "She didn't let them in the lift but they were waiting for her on the roof."

"No way they were. The other lift's still fucked."

"You never believe anything I tell you. I saw them. I said."

"You were stoned, that's all. Still are."

"No more than you are, so you should of seen them too."

I had to interrupt for fear the argument would deny me any further information. "You keep saying they," I said. "How many are we talking about?"

They gave me identical unfavourable looks. "One," the girl said as though it was too obvious for words.

"Don't know if it was a her or a him."

"And what do you say happened on the roof?"

"She went up and they were there." When the girl aimed her defiance at the corpse, I kept my eyes on her face. "They didn't chase her any more," she said. "She ran away from them and fell off."

"They must of been some runner if they went up all them stairs when she was in the lift."

While the girl looked stubborn, this led to silence. "Do you know where they went after she fell?" I said.

"I saw them going to the church." With the first hint of doubt the girl said "Going round there, anyhow. They couldn't of got in, it's nearly always locked. And then they weren't there at all."

"Never was at all," the boy said, "that's why."

This time her silence was plainly final, and I could think of nothing else to ask. I was retreating when the man who had closed Hattie Dennison's eyes said "Aren't you staying? You're meant to be her friend."

"I wasn't much of one," I said, so truthfully it was dismaying. I made for my car, not looking back until I was safe inside. Spectators were raising their heads at the sound of an oncoming siren. I drove off as fast as I dared, because I wasn't anxious to be interviewed by the police. Could I have prevented the tragedy if I'd arrived sooner? My sense of guilt was putting off the need to think what had happened on the roof.

I felt anxious to speak to somebody I knew. Not just anyone – my son. As the distant siren dwindled into silence I parked on the verge of the deserted road. Roy's phone had hardly started ringing when he said "Hello."

It sounded closer to a protest than a greeting. "Yes, hello," I said.

"What, dad?"

This was even less welcoming. "Can't I talk to my son?"

"I'm just waiting for the bus."

I didn't want to take this for a refusal. "Where are you?"

"Why do you have to keep asking that? The bus station."

"Which one, Roy?"

"You're talking to me like I'm little." A pause suggested this might be his only answer until he admitted "Leeds."

I heard a voice several times the size of his announcing a coach to Hull. Leeds was at least an hour away from me, and I felt still more remote. "Are you on your own?"

"Bell's here now. It's my dad. You were a long time, Bell."

"Where was she?"

"Oh my god, do you want to know everything? Where girls go and we can't."

"I'm sorry," I said, feeling unexpectedly close to hysterical mirth. "I think I'm a bit shaken up."

"Why, dad? What's wrong?"

"I've just been to see Miss Dennison."

"Who?"

"The woman who saw Thelma fall," Bella said.

"Her, right." With no lessening of puzzlement Roy said "Why were you seeing her?"

"She wanted me to see someone she said was watching her."

"Did you see her?" Bella said. "Miss Dennison, I mean."

"Saw her, but I was too late." To stop the phone trembling I laid it on the dashboard. "It's as if history's repeating itself," I said in the hope of rendering the memory less immediate. "She'd fallen from the tower block just as my aunt did."

"Is she dead as well?" Roy said.

If this seemed callous, he'd known her no better than I had. "Very," I said as if this might fend off the recollection.

"Did you speak to her, Patrick?"

"She'd gone by the time I got there. I did talk to her on the phone, but she didn't really say much. As I said, she wanted me to see for myself."

"Why did she go up the block?" Roy said. "I thought she didn't want anything to do with it or anybody in there."

"I think she may have been running away from whoever she called me to see."

"Maybe she was just pretending to be down on drugs. Maybe she was after some and that's why she went in."

This struck me as wildly unlikely, and I was about to say so when the enlarged voice announced a bus for Mountfoot. "There's ours now," Roy said, and dutifully "Will you be okay, dad?"

"I'll do my best to be," I said, which felt like a sly rebuke for leaving me on my own. Before I could reassure him or myself, he'd gone. So he and Bella were on their way to yet another site from Thelma's journal. I gripped the wheel and then rested my hands on it, all of which gradually helped them to stop shaking. After a while I started the car, though I felt as if I was distracting myself from some recent observation I'd failed to make. If there was something I ought to have noticed, I couldn't help dreading what it might be.

CHAPTER SEVENTEEN

Beneath the Trees

"What's wrong, dad?"

"Nothing, I hope. Why does anything have to be wrong?"

"Just you never call me this early."

"Apologies if I woke you up."

"You didn't. I'm making coffee. You might have woken someone else, though."

"Apologies to your mother if I did."

"Anyway, I'm here now if you need to talk."

"I just wanted to be sure of catching you before you head off wherever you're going today."

"Okay," Roy said after a pause like a withheld answer, "you did."

"Where might that be?"

"Dad, why do you keep wanting to know?"

"Is there any reason why I shouldn't?" My resentment wasn't entirely feigned. "You wouldn't be making all these visits," I said, "if I hadn't let you copy Thelma's journal."

"Doesn't mean you have to keep asking where we are. It's embarrassing."

"It shouldn't be." In an attempt to sound less unreasonably insensitive I said "I'd like to know what her places were like too."

"You didn't get much out of the one you went to."

"Perhaps I need to be with someone who finds more in them. That's one reason I'm calling you now. I was thinking you and Bella shouldn't have to go to so much trouble for your tour."

His pause suggested reluctance, and so did his answer. "How's that going to work?"

"As long as I'd like to see the places too, I can drive you both."

"I'd better speak to Bell."

"Why don't you phone her now and—"

"Hey, Bell." He sounded almost as surprised as I felt, if rather more delighted. "Did we wake you?"

"I just heard my name."

"It's my dad again, asking if we want a lift to Thelma's places."

"You don't look too keen."

"I am if you are."

"You'd expect him to be as interested as us, wouldn't you? And he knew her before—"

"Before what, Bell?"

"That's what I said. He knew her before."

I would have spoken if Roy hadn't said "So where are we going today?"

"I was thinking Brightspring."

"That's not too far, is it? No need to make dad drive all the way here as well."

I wondered if I should have established "Are you at your mother's, Roy?"

"She was kind," Bella said, "and she found me a bed."

"It's no trouble to pick you and Roy up there. It's on the way to Brightspring, isn't it?"

"Might be," Roy admitted.

"Let your father come, Roy. Maybe with more people we'll see more. How long will you be, Patrick?"

"I'm leaving now. Less than an hour."

I'd already showered and breakfasted. As I climbed into my car a train in the station declared it was a train. Driving through the tunnel and then through Liverpool onto the motorway, I felt more purposeful than last time, though uneasy too. At the edge of Manchester I left the motorway for streets where shops were opening with a celebratory rattle of shutters. Pensioners determined to make the most of their day were at large in the suburb, speeding on motorised scooters or leaning on wheeled frames. Quite a few pedestrians looked no less preserved than the buildings, which dated from before at least one world war if not both. Julia lived in the midst of a grid of increasingly new and narrow streets, in a tall terraced house topped with the window of an extra room beneath the roof.

I'd just parked opposite the compact regimented garden, where each variety of flowers was named on its own miniature notice, when Julia stepped out of the house, closing the stout ambitiously panelled door all but an inch. "What's this about, Patrick?" she said.

"The youngsters want me to give them a lift."

"You're saying they asked you."

"I believe I can say that."

"You didn't suggest it."

"I'm saying I think it's appreciated."

Julia glanced at the house and took a pace forward, lowering her voice. "What do you actually think you're doing?"

"It won't do any harm to keep an eye on what's happening with them."

Another pace took her voice lower. "What do you imagine is?"

"I won't know until I see." Her weary stare provoked me to retort "Has anything been going on at your house?"

"Nothing whatsoever. What on earth would have been?"

"The usual, I should think. Bella told me you gave her a bed."

"I have, yes. Her parents aren't around just now, so that's two problems solved."

"Do we know where they've got to, these parents of hers?"

"Away for the summer is my impression. She doesn't like to talk about them much."

Somewhere I heard the sharp flat pats of a game of tennis, which our conversation resembled rather too much. "So what problems do you say you've solved?" I said.

"Not leaving her and Roy alone at her house and not having to sort her stay out with her parents."

"What are the sleeping arrangements, then?"

"Patrick." In case this was insufficiently reproving Julia said "They're under age."

"I just wondered where you've put her."

"She's at the top and Roy has his room. She likes the high view. Satisfied now?"

I glanced at the roof, where I thought I'd glimpsed someone gazing down at me through the vertical window. "I just wonder if we ought to be a little more concerned."

"About what, Patrick?"

I wasn't sure enough to put the feeling into words, and in any case I had no chance. The front door had opened, letting out Roy and Bella. "We're ready," Bella said.

Their arrival threw me so much that I demanded "Is there anyone else in the house?"

"No."

All three said it, pretty well in chorus, which made them laugh. I did my best to feel they weren't laughing at me. Perhaps I'd seen a bird reflected in the window, or a cloud. "My mistake," I said.

"Try not to make any more, Patrick," Julia said and followed us to the gate. As I unlocked the car and let my passengers into the back she said almost too low to be heard even by me "Just be certain you want this and why."

I couldn't answer when I was uncertain of both. As the car moved off she sent Roy and Bella a smile she hadn't found for me. While they weren't sitting particularly close together, they were loosely holding hands. Their clasp rested on Bella's shoulder-bag between them, a gesture I thought reminiscent of a séance. Perhaps I owed the notion to the chant I heard somewhere ahead: "Appear... appear... appear..." The voices fell silent, and then a soloist began to sing: "Sprites of earth and air..." I wasn't expecting much of an answer when I said "What am I hearing?"

"It's *The Sorcerer*," Bella said. "Gilbert and Sullivan's firstborn."

"Sounds like somebody's rehearsing," Roy said. "Do you like old music, Bell?"

"Older than that."

"Put some on for her, dad."

I switched on the radio, which was already tuned to the BBC's classical station, and notes streamed out of the speakers. Within seconds Bella said "That's when he was starting to become himself."

"Who, Bell?" Roy said with admiration.

"George Frideric." As if she thought she should sound more teenage Bella added "Handel doing old Julius Caesar."

The overture was ending. The opera accompanied us onto the motorway and through Stockport towards the Peaks. The road narrowed through a succession of small towns before rising towards a sky so blue that it suggested its depth was infinite. On both sides of the road slopes blazed variously green along with purple shades of heather or shone grey with bare limestone. As we reached the heights the spiky drystone walls gave out, leaving the road bordered just by ditches. We'd started to descend when a pine forest closed around us, shoring up the intense burden of the sky. Bella looked engrossed in the music — her wide eyes might have been full of reminiscence — but she turned to look at a signpost for a town called Moonwell. "What's that about, Bell?" Roy said.

As the gloomy side road through the trees fell behind she said "There's something down there."

"Do you want to go and look?"

"It's not for us."

The opera saw us out of the forest, and the green lowlands extended ahead. Despite the expansive view, I wasn't sure of the route. "I may have to switch this off," I said, "so I can hear the navigator."

"I'll direct you," Bella said and took out her phone. Miles of downhill road brought us to a junction where none of the names on the sign told me the way to Brightspring. "Turn left, Patrick," Bella said.

Hulking hedges cut the view off, and by the time the road meandered to another junction I'd began to wonder whether we'd taken a wrong turn. If the crossroads had ever been provided with a sign, it wasn't there now. "Right this time," Bella said.

"Are you sure, Bell? You haven't been using your phone."

"We don't need it. I can feel the land."

"Forgive me," I said without wanting it much, "but how does that work?"

"Trust me, Patrick."

"You can, dad. I do."

As I turned along the unmarked road I wondered whether I was just indulging his confidence in his girlfriend. Wildly high hedges bordered the road as though bent on forcing it to change direction every few hundred yards or even less. I had no idea how far I'd followed it before a side road almost hidden by beech trees came in sight. A sign scaly with rust was partly obscured by a hedge and its tangled shadows, which made the pointer say **RIGHT IN** until I turned along the lane, transforming the words into **RIG I** and **I PIN** and **I SPIN** and **I SPRING**. "You could turn off the radio now, Patrick," Bella said.

The trees and their shadows that netted the tarmac seemed to have trapped a silence. Apart from the rubbery mumble of tyres, I heard my breath and more faintly Roy's, and felt as if Bella was urging us to hush. The lane curved without haste, and a strip of it reared up to greet us. No, it was a watery illusion created by haze, even if it persisted longer than such effects usually did. The car had almost reached it when it disappeared, absorbed by a glistening mass of shadow. I might have commented if fingers hadn't tapped on the roof above my head.

They sounded thin but eager to be recognised. Of course, they were drops of water falling from a tree. All the foliage over the road looked wetter than the arid August day ought to have allowed. I supposed it had rained here recently, though I'd seen no previous evidence. This would explain the glint of water on the road ahead, unless that was another summer mirage. When it refused to disappear I saw it was an actual trickle, the tip of a stream that meandered along the middle of the tarmac, following every turn of the lane. Condensation started to obscure the view, and as I set the wipers working I said mostly to myself "That's real."

"It all is, Patrick."

Water hissed beneath the wheels on my side of the car, and more drops struck the roof, sounding impatient with my speed. I wasn't about to increase it while the wipers were hauling condensation aside on the windscreen. A large drop like an omen of a storm shattered on the glass, making me glance at the strip of cloudless sky between the treetops. As the road hissed louder I saw our destination, a bright gleam between the trees to the right of the lane – a nearly vertical gleam. Water was streaming down a rift in a slope of mossy rock, and the edges of the cleft looked illuminated by the stream, which was borrowing its light from shafts between the branches overhead. "Is that it?" Roy said.

Given the signpost at the far end of the lane, I would have expected the spring to be marked for visitors, but there wasn't even a parking area. I might have concluded that someone thought the place was best forgotten. Nevertheless I said "It must be."

"It is," Bella said. "I remember."

"From the map, she means," Roy said.

I parked on a bank at the opposite side of the road. The wheels slithered over wet dead leaves until I dragged the handbrake on. As I climbed out I felt moisture settle on my skin. The stream that had followed all the convolutions of the lane led through the trees to the mossy ridge. Trees grew close together around the ridge, and I was looking for a route to use when Bella said "Let me go first, Patrick."

She hadn't found a direct path. As she dodged between the trees I kept losing sight of her, and following her gave me only intermittent views of our goal. I couldn't walk too fast on the sodden leaves that made up the squelchy track, especially when I kept needing to confirm Roy was behind me. Though I'd thought the spring was no more than a couple of hundred yards from the road, it took minutes to reach. Bella had her left hand in the downpour, which made her fingers glitter like a crystalline explosion of power. "It's here," she said.

Her words seemed redundant unless they were ominous. The ridge was perhaps fifty feet high, and surmounted by a line of trees that entangled branches with their neighbours in the small dense wood, creating shade that very little direct sunlight penetrated. The spring emerged about halfway up the slope and collected in a hollow in the rock, from which the overflow streamed between trees to the road. The rift the spring followed was as good as straight, and the bowl at its foot was virtually circular. Once again I had a sense that the place had been abandoned, quite possibly on purpose. No doubt the shade was why I felt a chill as Bella raised her cupped hand to her mouth. "Isn't everybody thirsty?" she said.

"Are you sure it's safe to drink?" I said.

She tipped the water into her mouth like somebody older dashing back liquor. "It always has been."

"Bell looked it up," Roy said, and drank. I found I was holding my breath, because he'd grown as still as the ridge. I was about to ask why when he said "I'm seeing, Bell. I'm hearing too."

I was seized by a suspicion I would very much have liked to disbelieve. "Roy, have you taken something?"

"Dad." Just as reproachfully he said "Never since I met Bell."

"You shouldn't need drugs either, Patrick. Just be open to what's here."

While I found this less than tempting, it was surely my responsibility to learn what my son had experienced. "Is anybody going to tell me what to expect?"

"Nobody should," Bella said. "Let it come to you."

As I leaned forward to reach into the spring, a shaft of light caught my hand and my bare forearm. I was disconcerted by how cold they immediately felt, as if something had drained all the heat from the sunshine. My shadow fell across the hollow in the rock, and I could have thought that darkness was taking shape in the water and rising to welcome me – that the pool itself had grown deeper. I could even have fancied that a face had peered up from the depths. Of course one had – my reflection – and only the irrepressible ripples had made it look unstable, desperate to cling to its identity. Just the same, I wasn't anxious to linger, and I thrust my hand into the cleft in the rock.

The spring was so cold it sent a shiver through my arm into the rest of me. My gasp made Roy and Bella laugh. Perhaps they were simply acknowledging a similar experience, but their united response displeased me so much that I held my hand in the stream for several seconds, determined not to flinch. When the face below me started mouthing – my reflection, distorted by ripples jittering with brilliance – I felt I could easily begin to hear a voice in the breathless rush of water, the incessant chatter of the pool. I took a handful from the spring and brought it to my mouth.

Some of it went in. Some trickled down my arm, and the remainder splashed my chest. At once I felt as if all the heat had been snatched from my body, departing with a convulsive shiver. The violent chill seemed to fasten on my brain, gathering around it like ice. As I blinked my eyes clear of the moisture that had filled them, Roy said "Are you getting it, dad?"

Either the chill was lessening or I'd become acclimatised. It appeared to have lent my perceptions a clarity that wasn't far from painful. The insistently glittering water and the misty shafts of light had grown so intense I had to look away, only to notice mist hovering beneath the treetops, like a cloud that had descended almost to the earth. I realised I could hear no birds, just the endless monologue of the spring. It grew louder, at least in my ears, and set about forming words — a crass ram meant he. "Aqua Sacramenti," I said more or less aloud.

"You're hearing him, Patrick."

"I'm hearing what I may have expected to hear. The name was on the atlas." Just as defensively I said "Why would anyone want to call themselves that?"

"They get their names from their powers. That one means mystery of water."

I would rather Bella had said so, not my son, but no doubt she had previously told him, unless he'd read it in some book his mother ought to disapprove of. Now that I'd heard the name I couldn't stop doing so. It sounded hungry for acknowledgment, and I told myself it was nothing but a sound. "Are we staying here much longer?" I said.

"Is it affecting you too much, Patrick? Trust me, you'll get used."

I waited for Bella to complete the phrase, but had to assume she thought this was unnecessary. "I want to be sure I'm fit to drive," I said.

"Let's just remember Thelma and we'll go."

She took a glass jar out of her bag and handed Roy the lid. "You call that remembering," I said.

"It's what she did."

I was waiting for Bella to produce some digging implement when she scooped up a handful of mud from the stream at the base of the ridge and let it slither into the jar. For a moment I thought the illusion of a voice was repeating its syllables inside the jar, and then Roy screwed the lid on. As Bella rinsed her hand in the spring I said "Don't you use a spade?"

"That way brings me closer."

I had to look elsewhere as she shook her hand dry in a shaft of light, because it looked as though the outlines of her fingers were shattering like crystal. She retrieved the jar from Roy, who was cradling it as though he'd been entrusted with a sacred relic, and dropped it in her bag. "We've finished," she said. "I've got him."

Her turn of phrase made me anxious to learn "What do you think you're actually doing?"

"What you see, Patrick."

"You didn't mind when your aunt did it," Roy said. "You wanted to get them all after she died. I remember you asking your parents."

I found I didn't want to continue the discussion while we were in the woods. It was hard to separate their voices from the unrelenting repetitions of the water, the syllables that threatened to grow clearer still. I was turning towards the road when Bella said "Best let me again, Patrick."

I tried to feel relieved that she was offering, since I couldn't see the car. I hadn't realised the wood was so dense. We must be taking a different route back, because even after dodging around several trees I was no closer to locating the car, and Bella kept slipping out of sight. At least whenever I looked behind me I saw my son, but I was acutely aware that the watery syllables had yet to grow fainter. Perhaps the stream that led through the trees was transmitting the sounds from the spring, but I couldn't help associating them with the mist that loomed high overhead. I glanced up, only to wish I hadn't, because the shifting pallid mass beneath the treetops appeared to have ambitions to assume a shape, and I could have thought it was emitting the persistent syllables. Another glance might show me the approximation of a face, hunching grub-like across the underside of the foliage while it mouthed the words with dangling lips. Surely I could fend off the impression so long as I refrained from looking up, but as the leaf mould sucked at my shoes I heard a plop of moisture on the woodland floor. Was it a fragment of the dripping face? What might happen if a drop of it fell on me or, worse still, on my son? The idea brought me so close to panic that I didn't immediately grasp what I was seeing ahead – a glimpse of my car. There was Bella too, heading as nearly straight for it as the trees permitted, and I did my best to catch up with her while making sure I wasn't leaving Roy behind. "Go on, dad," he said with impatience shading into resentment, and as I was rewarded by a clear sight of the road he tapped me on the shoulder to alert me to its closeness. No, that wasn't Roy, and it wasn't a finger, unless the finger consisted of a substance that was seeping through my shirt. I lurched forward, almost colliding with a tree that glistened with trickles of water that followed every crack in the bark. All the trunks around me were frantically active with water, so that I could have fancied a presence overhead was using the wood to reach with a multitude of tendrils for us, the intruders. I floundered between them, as desperate to avoid touching them as I was not to be caught by another drop of water. When I stumbled onto the road at last, Bella was standing guard beside the car, and slipped in as soon as I unlocked it with the fob. Drops of water plopped around me on the tarmac, and I thought the road felt far too much like sodden earth. I waited by the car, having almost lost my footing on the saturated leaves, to make sure Roy was safe, even when he protested "You can get in, dad." I clambered in as soon as he joined Bella, and locked the doors at once.

I had to sweep the befogged windscreen clear once I'd started the car, and then I wondered whether I was safe to drive, if my senses stayed as chronically heightened as they'd grown by the spring. I was grasping the wheel and staring through the passes of the wipers when Bella said "Would you like me to drive, Patrick?"

"It's kind of you to offer, but you can't any more than Roy can. You won't have a licence at your age."

"If you need help there's nobody about to see."

"I'll be all right," I vowed, and eased the car forward despite yearning to accelerate out of reach of a sound like liquid fumbling at the roof. The trees receded behind us, letting sunlight into the car, and I wasn't even slightly blinded. I was celebrating how fast we could speed away from Brightspring when the road straightened out, revealing that it came to a dead end.

My mouth grew parched at the thought that we'd have to go back, but I tried not to betray to my passengers how I felt. As I swung the car back and forth and twice again across the constricted road, the movement seemed to rouse the jar in Bella's bag. I was certain I heard a whisper of mud, although surely it wasn't articulate. It ceased as I sent the car back along the lane, but soon it was replaced by a spongy hiss beneath the wheels, the whisper of the stream that traced the windings of the road. I didn't want to hear this separating into syllables, but I couldn't ignore the peremptory tapping of drops on the roof, which sounded as if they were determined to penetrate the metal. However much the wipers squealed while they strove to keep the windscreen clear of moisture, the glass persevered in growing as mistily grey as the underside of the treetops. When I glanced at the efforts of the rear wipers in the mirror, I saw Roy had closed his eyes, surely not from fear. Bella's were as wide as ever, looking eager for experience. She met mine and gave me a smile that might have been sharing a secret, except that I had no idea what it might be – perhaps no wish to know.

The trees and the impatient tapping fell behind at last, and the sun shone into the car again. It seemed to waken Roy, though with a shiver. "Are you all right, Roy?" I said.

"I'm fine, dad."

Despite having provoked all his teenage resentment, I had to carry on. I felt somewhere between prudent and irrational for checking Brightspring and its environs were out of sight before I said "Are you sure all this is good for you both?"

"If it is for Bell it is for me."

"We're helping each other grow, Patrick," Bella said, and I didn't immediately realise why my hands clenched on the wheel as my foot jerked on the accelerator.

CHAPTER EIGHTEEN

Home

Throughout the drive to Julia's I was aware of Bella's bag on the back seat. Her hand and Roy's were clasped in front of it like a protection or a pledge. Its contents were silent, and as far as I could judge they were still. Whenever Bella looked at me in the mirror, her eyes were so wide that they might have been eager to fit in more innocence. I found this and the presence of her souvenir increasingly hard to bear, and on the final stretch of motorway they made me break my silence. "Will you be taking your trophy to Roy's mother's?"

Roy shivered, perhaps at the prospect. "Mum doesn't have to know, does she?"

"I think she does if anything like that is being brought into her house."

As he looked betrayed Bella said "No need for any trouble. I'll keep it at mine."

"Where might that be?" I said and met her innocence with a version of the same.

"Not far from Julia's. I'll tell you when we're close."

We'd hardly left the motorway when she directed me along the outskirts of the town towards the river. In less than ten minutes most of the houses were left behind, and the remainder were split into flats, unless the families whose bicycles – toy and teenage and motorcycles too, not to mention scramblers – occupied some of the front gardens were extravagantly large. Although more than one house sounded like an outsize stereo system mainly devoted to drums, nobody was to be seen. The buildings on the right side of the road gave way to a high brick wall that was losing a struggle to restrain trees. "I'm here, Patrick," Bella said.

Before I could suggest it Roy said "Shall we come with you?"

"I'll only be a minute."

She grabbed her bag as she unbent with a ballerina's litheness from the car. I expected her to head for one of the houses, but she crossed the road and vanished through a gap in the wall. "Where's that supposed to be?" I said.

"Don't know." Roy made it plain that he resented both his ignorance and having it exposed. After a minute or so he said "Maybe we should look."

I wished he'd proposed it sooner. I was reaching to open my door when Bella reappeared in the gloom beneath the trees beyond the wall, brushing at herself with both hands. As she slipped into the car Roy said "Where did you go?"

"Where I live. What did you think?" With a laugh at his bemused expression, she recaptured his hand. "That's a short cut to it," she said.

He obviously wanted to be satisfied with this, and I refrained from commenting. As I turned along a side street, the dark beyond the gap in the wall appeared to close around the trees. Not many minutes brought me to Julia's house, and I was first to the front door. When she answered the politely mellifluous chimes I loitered long enough to prompt her to say "Would you like a coffee before you drive home?"

"I wouldn't mind at all." As Roy and Bella followed me into the hall, where framed Edwardian photographs of Manchester overshadowed the discreetly silver pattern of the wallpaper, I said "And a talk."

Julia led the way into the clinically metallic kitchen, where just the chairs and table and cupboards were composed of wood. While she made coffee for the two of us, Roy found chilled juice in the refrigerator. I wondered if the drink would revive his shivers, but perhaps they'd finished with him, unless he was bracing himself. Nobody seemed eager to prompt conversation until Julia set a steaming mug in front of me with a rap like a judge's gavel. "So what did you find today?" she said.

"Let them say."

"I wasn't preventing them, Patrick, but you were the one who wanted to talk."

"I hope we all do. No reason not to, is there?" When Roy looked wary of speaking and Bella's eyes stayed guileless, I said "We went to a spring. There used to be a sign for it, but I think it's been abandoned because it's a bad place."

"There's still a sign," Roy objected.

"It looked to me as if people wished there weren't."

"Bad how?" Julia said. "Poisoned, do you mean?"

"Not in that sense. Bad for anyone to visit."

"Is that what you both thought?"

"I didn't, mum. It was just somewhere that gave dad's aunt an idea."

"You saw something," I reminded him. "Heard as well."

"What did you think was there, Patrick?" Bella said.

"Some kind of trace of someone. Like their voice, and I almost saw them."

"Was there anything like that, Roy?" his mother said.

"Don't know."

"I should think you don't," she said and turned on me. "Let your fancies wander if you must, but don't impose them on these two."

"I've imposed nothing. I've just followed what's already going on."

"I think you want to be involved too much, and I wouldn't be surprised if you're making it worse."

The unfairness almost rendered me inarticulate. "How?"

"Turning it into something it wasn't in the first place."

"We didn't mind you coming with us, Patrick," Bella said. "We appreciated your help."

This failed to let me feel supported. "Which help?"

"Giving us a lift," Roy said.

With a hint of disappointment Bella told me "I thought you might see what Thelma saw."

"I'm afraid I think I did."

"May we hope that's the end of it, then?" Julia said.

"It won't be while you have the souvenirs you took, will it, Bella? The ones you didn't think you should bring here."

"Thank you for showing consideration, Bella," Julia said.

"Why did you think you shouldn't bring them?"

"Because you told her not to, dad."

"I don't think that's quite the case, and—"

"If it's even slightly true," Julia said, "that's just as bad."

"I'm asking Bella what she doesn't want you to know."

"Dad, why are you doing this? What's making you behave this way?"

As I saw Julia find an answer, Bella said "About what you call my souvenirs, do you mean, Patrick?"

"What would you call them?"

"By their names."

"Hear that, Julia. That's the kind—"

"I'm with Roy," Bella said. "I don't understand why you're having to act like this now. Is it for Julia's benefit?"

"I assure you I'm not putting on an act," I said mostly to Julia, "and—"

"You weren't like this at Brightspring, dad. You were into it then."

"And Patrick," Bella said, "you didn't have this attitude when Thelma was collecting from the sites. You were interested then and you were later."

I wanted to believe she'd trapped herself, not me. "How would you know that?"

"Roy told me."

"And how would he know? He wasn't even old enough for school when Thelma died."

"Because you told me, dad."

All of them were gazing at me. Julia looked concerned, but only about me. "It's true, Patrick," she said. "You were definitely fascinated. I'd like to know what's changed."

"I'm sorry, Bella, but you have. That's to say you've changed my feelings."

Julia opened her lips in an unhappy shape as Roy demanded "What's Bell done to you, dad?"

"Not just to me in particular." Bella's innocently puzzled look was making me determined if not desperate to penetrate beyond it. "I believe you're keeping secrets from us all, Bella."

Julia closed her mouth, apparently to prepare another contribution, and Bella said "Tell them then, Patrick."

"I believe I've met your father."

Julia parted her lips without speaking, while Roy grimaced with surprise if not denial. Bella's eyes widened, which I took for confirmation, and Roy demanded "When?"

"Before you were born."

"Why are you only saying now? Have you been trying to trick Bell?"

"I'm not the one—" I cut the accusation short by saying "Because I only saw the truth today. Maybe the spring woke my mind up, Bella."

I wasn't sure I thought this – it was more a sly gibe – but she said "What truth was that?"

"Things you have in common with your father. I expect you can think of a few."

"Just like you and Roy have, but I don't know which you mean."

"Nor do we, Patrick," Julia said without much patience. "It's past time you said."

"Turns of phrase, for one thing. Bella, you told me you and Roy help each other grow."

"I could have said that," Roy protested. "It's the truth."

"It's true of quite a lot of people," Julia told me. "It isn't as unusual as you seem to think."

I hadn't time to grasp how many criticisms this might contain. "That wasn't all. When we were at the spring you said you're what we see, Bella."

"Don't you think I am?"

"I'll say she is as well, dad."

"Have you any reason to suppose she isn't?" Julia said.

"That's not my point. It's what her father said as well."

"I shouldn't think that's too uncommon either. So are you going to tell us who you've made up your mind he is? You're the one who's creating a mystery here, not Bella."

"I should think she can say who her own father is."

"I'm sure she can, but why don't you? What on earth are you trying to achieve?"

"I just wanted to be certain, and I am. It's your eyes, Bella."

"What about them?" Roy demanded, and Julia said "Yes, what, Patrick?"

"She doesn't look much like her father otherwise, which is why it's taken me this long to realise. They have the same eyes, though. I still remember them."

I was willing Bella to admit her parentage when Julia said "Stop harassing the poor girl and just say who you mean, for heaven's sake."

"The man my aunt took up with at the end."

"Good God with a capital, does everything have to come back to her?"

"I'm afraid it mostly seems to just now. It does in this case, doesn't it, Bella?"

She turned her eyes to Roy, and I thought she was about to appeal to him until she said "I'm sorry, Roy, but yes."

He reached for her hand on the table but stopped short of touching. "Sorry for what, Bell?"

"Patrick's right about my father."

"Why are you going to be sorry about that?"

"For not telling you who I was. I was afraid you'd think I'd been lying in wait for you that first time at the gallery. At first I didn't realise, and when I did I thought it was too late."

His hand had found hers now. "Why do you think it'd have mattered?"

"It's as Patrick started to say before. You could have thought I was playing some kind of trick."

"For what?"

"Yes, Patrick," Julia said. "For what purpose?"

I couldn't say. I felt robbed of insight, not least by how the revelation seemed to have relieved the girl. "I thought Roy was supposed to do the thinking, Bella."

Everybody gazed at me as if I were the trickster, and Julia looked weary and sad. "I shouldn't think anyone even knows what that means."

"I'm saying it was Roy who was supposed to be suspicious."

"Well, I'm not," Roy said.

"I meant to say—" I had a sense that trying to explain would simply aggravate the confusion, however deliberate it might be. "Let's leave it," I said. "I apologise if I went for you, Bella."

"Nothing I can't handle, Patrick."

"I'm glad to hear you say so." Just as deviously I said "What's the plan for tomorrow?"

"We thought we'd visit Monks Cross."

I was hoping Julia would object, but it was Roy who said "By ourselves."

"Forgive me, when was that decided?"

"For heaven's sake, Patrick," Julia said. "When do you think?"

"Roy, I've apologised. I will again if you think I should. I'll happily save you the trouble of getting there."

"No need," he said without glancing at me. "We'll be together."

I hoped Bella might coax him to relent, but her eyes were blank all the way to their depths. "I'll see you out, Patrick," Julia said.

She didn't speak again until she'd shut the front door behind us, and then she said low but fiercely "How else are you going to try and spoil their relationship?"

"Do you honestly accept what she said about her father? Do you think that's any kind of explanation?"

"I think you showed her she was right to be afraid people would be suspicious for no reason. Just one person, Patrick."

"No reason." I was struggling to keep my voice as low as hers. "You really believe what she said was reasonable."

"A lot more so than you're being. Just tell me if you can what other explanation she would have."

"She hasn't got one. That's my point. We don't know what she wants, and we need to know."

"She's fascinated by your aunt. She got that from her father, the same as Roy picked it up from you."

"Which we both know you wish hadn't been the case. Are you going to let them make another of their trips tomorrow?"

"You've made the situation worse and now you're leaving me to deal with it, are you? All you've done since you got here is make them more determined to go." Before I could argue Julia said "I don't think we'll be wanting to see you again until you've got rid of whatever this fixation of yours is. I don't want to know any more about it either."

If I hadn't felt unbearably provoked I might have managed not to say "Are you sure you aren't under her spell?"

"That's your kind of thing, not mine." She gave me a look that didn't quite own up to the accusation it contained, and turned her back to ring the doorbell. Before I could find a response it might have been worth giving or advisable to give, Bella opened the door. "It's only me," Julia said, which was plainly meant as reassurance that I wasn't following her in. I saw Roy frown at me along the hall, possibly expressing regret, and thought I glimpsed triumph in Bella's eyes as she smiled at me or at the sight of me. I was taking an angry step forward when she shut me out of the house.

CHAPTER NINETEEN

Finding Words

I was minutes away from the motorway junction when the Beethoven symphony on the car radio was invaded by a local station, and the choral contention that all men were brothers gave way to a phone-in. The subject was the homeless, quite a few of whom had gathered at a site one contributor called the uptown cross. They were in there, so let them stay, another caller urged. They left their muck in there, so they should clean it up, a woman declared — it wasn't up to no one else. They were stuck in there, though, another female caller countered, and they deserved some compassion. I was distracted by the phrases that felt close to a repetition of a single bunch of syllables, and concentrating on the traffic helped less than I would have liked. I was boxed in by caravans bound for the Lakes or further north to Scotland, and a bid to overtake trapped me in the outer lane. I needed to return to the inner lane well ahead of the exit for Monks Cross, and as I veered into it between a pair of speeding motor homes, a caller complained that some people were talking about the homeless at the site as though they weren't human. It was up to Ned Cross to put them right, she told him, or was his name Ted Ross? Perhaps I'd misheard the entire sentence while I tried to focus on driving and ignore the face that was spying on me from the rear window of the motor home ahead. It kept ducking out of sight and inching up the glass — no doubt a child who'd found a game to fend off boredom — and my impression that the face was growing larger every time it reappeared must mean it was coming closer to the window. I held back from looking as long as I could, and when I glanced up it dropped out of sight like an unstringed puppet before I had a chance to make it out. Now here was the motorway exit, and I hadn't even thought to indicate. I signalled my departure and swung down the ramp, and as the motor home raced onwards overhead I could have fancied I glimpsed the face falling from the window to slither down the dusty metal. It was light from a headlamp, I told myself.

The slope led down to a skein of six roads, some of which passed beneath the motorway. The ramp and the motorway, along with the opposite incline, were supported by so many hulking concrete columns that the area underneath resembled a cage. The nearest road was shut in by warehouses as windowless as walls of rock. Although I couldn't see beyond them, I suspected I'd reached what locals called the uptown cross, since Monks Cross was the junction itself.

As I parked on a deserted stretch of cobblestones by the nearest warehouse, the radio presenter told me I was listening to the Fred Russell show. I eased the car backwards to make sure it wasn't visible from Monks Cross, and was switching off the radio when I heard a caller describe the site as somewhere uptowners doss. I tramped to the junction, hoping to be met just by the sounds of the motorway – by no kind of presence.

The roar of traffic grew in my ears as I ventured under the ramp. Beyond the first of the wide square pillars I saw signs of the homeless, sleeping bags and huddled blankets, hidden from the road. All the makeshift beds were deserted, and nothing like a face had started to creep out of a bag in the shadow of a column before it was snatched back like a creature surprised in its lair. Regardless of the August sultriness, someone appeared to have set about building a fire beneath the motorway, and I couldn't avoid noticing how much the wooden structure resembled an inverted cross.

I'd pieced together the history of the site from the occult atlas and a page for the town the junction served. It had originally been named for a stone cross, a monument erected at a crossroads to commemorate a monastery blessed by a mediaeval saint. According to legend, if only to that, the cross had repeatedly been found turned upside down despite its massiveness, on nights that bore a magical significance. Eventually it had been destroyed, perhaps by people who blamed the cross itself for its antics. Even the fragments were disposed of, and nobody had tried to reconstruct it or erect a substitute. By the time the motorway was built, the source of the name of the site was virtually forgotten. I'd found the mundane information on the local page, and the rest embedded in the occult map, which tagged the place with the name of a practitioner – Crux Inverso, which it translated as Upturned Cross.

I might have liked not to recollect all this. I could easily have fancied that the rush of traffic overhead had begun to shape the Latin syllables, especially once the swish and echo of wheels seemed to grow louder with each pass. As I made to retreat from the onslaught of sound, I saw I was surrounded by graffiti. They were confined to the inner sides of the pillars, and the distorted faces peering out of tangles of unrecognisable symbols might all have been bids to depict the same swollen contemptuous face. I didn't want to find it reminiscent of any I'd recently seen, and was even less eager to see anything similar begin to protrude from a sleeping bag or a heap of blankets. I was still under the motorway when it fell abruptly silent. There must be a gap in the traffic, but the pause felt like a held breath, and it let me hear a voice I knew. "There it is, Bell."

Roy was somewhere near my car. I was afraid he'd noticed it until Bella said "Look for cracks. They're how we'll get to the earth."

More than one column hid me from her and my son, but I didn't know how much longer they would. I retreated under the far ramp to lurk behind a pillar. The noise from the motorway was no less overwhelming here, and sounded increasingly repetitive – a prolonged utterance of "Crux" followed by "Inverso" shaped by the wheels of the next vehicle. Surely it was common enough to imagine that wordless noises contained words, and they were distracting me from listening for Roy and Bella. I had so little sense of where my son and his companion might be that I risked a glance around the column. They were approaching beneath the other ramp, examining the concrete floor, and I hid before I could be seen. I heard no more from them until Roy spoke, sounding close to awe, which I didn't like at all. "Are those his face?"

"They will be," Bella said.

"And there's his name."

"You'll hear that. Him and his kind, they try to cling to life however they can."

Her comment revived the syllables up above, which I'd been

managing to ignore. As I strove to concentrate on her and Roy he said "Look, there's a crack by that thing like a cross."

"That's what it's meant to be, a cross. Here, hold my bag."

Unseen vehicles raced past, trailing syllables, and then Roy protested "Be careful, Bell. Do you want me to try?"

"Don't underrate me, Roy. I'm getting my strength back."

I heard a crunching thud – the fall of a chunk of concrete. "Open the jar," Bella said, and moments later "Wipe my hands for me." I strained to hear more, but when neither of them had spoken for at least a minute I inched around the column. They had their backs to me and were already on the road.

As I followed, using pillars for concealment, I saw a jagged lump of concrete lying beside the rickety cruciform construction. It was at least two feet across at its widest point, and dauntingly thick. I would have needed both hands and a considerable effort to lift it, and how would I have dislodged it with my bare hands in the first place? I was staring at the patch of earth it had exposed, a handful of which had been scooped up – I was imagining how many insects it might have roused to scramble back into the soil, a thought that produced the unwelcome illusion that the faces on the columns all around me had begun in some way to swarm as though they were about to hatch – when I heard Roy say "That's never..."

I felt robbed of breath until he spoke again. "It fucking is. It's my dad's fucking car."

Julia and I had seldom heard him use such language, and I had a sense of encountering an aspect of him I was unaware of. What others should we know about? "Where are you, dad?" he was shouting like somebody more savage than I recognised. "We know you're here."

There was no point in hiding further, and I was glad to leave the blurred voice of the motorway behind along with the graffiti, even if a glance reassured me that the reiterations of a face didn't appear to have stirred. As I emerged under the ramp Roy folded his arms, not by any means unlike a parent preparing to deliver a reproof, while Bella crossed her hands on her breasts, a gesture that looked placatory and yet oddly secretive. Roy didn't speak until I was almost within arm's length, alongside the car. "What do you think you're doing, dad?"

He might have inherited Julia's weariness with my behaviour. "Something like you are," I said.

"I don't see where you've got a specimen."

"Not that. Just exploring, the way we did before, forgive me, before you met Bella."

"So why are you still doing it?"

I aimed my question at them both. "Is there any reason you wouldn't want me to?"

"We said we didn't need a lift."

"I don't believe I gave you one."

As Roy looked tricked rather than defeated Bella said "Patrick learned where the places were before you did. He had Thelma's journal."

"He didn't have to come to this one now. He only knew we were because you told him."

With a portion of the truth I said "I wanted to find out what you might be subjecting yourself to."

"Me and Bell, you mean." When I mutely allowed that she could be included Roy said "So did you?"

"I think it's a thoroughly unpleasant place, and I wouldn't want any part of it."

"But your aunt did, Patrick."

"It didn't do her any good, did it? I can't recall a painting of anywhere like it."

"I know which one it must have been, dad. Where all the sleeping bags are dancing in the street at night."

"They weren't here then, Roy," Bella said. "How about her painting where the cars on the motorway are escaping the traffic jam by driving into the sky?"

"I don't see much of a connection," I said.

"Perhaps that's because you're not an artist, Patrick."

"You're saying you are."

"No, I'm—" She closed her eyes while she shook her head. "You've already heard me say what I am."

Some of Roy's resentment might have been provoked by how I'd apparently inhibited her. "Are you giving us a lift, dad?"

"I thought you didn't want one."

"You can as long as you're around." With no increase of enthusiasm he said "Unless you want to leave us here."

"Let's get away by all means," I said.

I started the car as soon as the doors were locked, while my passengers were fastening their seat belts. I was driving under the motorway when the radio let out a mutter. Had I left it on or switched it on without realising? "Cross," it mumbled, unless this was a distorted fragment of the presenter's name, and I could have fancied that it added "Inadvertent," not a welcome comment just now. As I made sure the radio was turned off, a face whose outline swarmed with symbols peered at me from beneath the motorway, and then it did so from a second pillar. I felt not just watched but threatened with some hindrance all the way to the homeward ramp. I sped onto the motorway, wishing the traffic would let me go faster. We'd travelled less than a mile when Roy said "Can we have some music on for Bell?"

I felt uneasy as I poked the button. I'd had enough of several words, and wasn't anxious to revive them. The strains of an opera came as a considerable relief. "It's Orpheus," Bella said at once. "Even older than Handel."

"How old's that?" Roy said, which I thought was a bid to contribute.

"Nearly as old as anyone here," Bella said with a laugh and a nudge. "Listen and you'll hear her brought back from the dead."

We did while Monks Cross fell behind, despite a sluggish tailback that made me wish we could take off like the vehicles in Thelma's painting. By the time we picked up speed Orfeo had looked back, inadvertently returning Euridice to the underworld. I would have been happier with the distance I was putting between us and Monks Cross if the mirror hadn't kept reminding me of Bella's relic, even though it was hidden in her bag. Shades from Hades brought the act to an end with a chorus, declaring that virtue was immune from the passage of time, and Bella caught me glancing at the bag. "Would you like to have it by you, Patrick?"

"I'd rather not have it anywhere."

She'd provoked a response I should have known Roy wouldn't like. Orfeo reappeared to perform a lament answered by an echo – a bid to borrow aspects of the human – before Apollo raised him to the stars to be rewarded for his sufferings, though only with an image of his lost love in the sky. "We never really go away," Bella told Roy. "There's always a trace if you search."

Since he didn't answer I said "You're talking about the likes of Monks Cross."

"What else could I be, Patrick?"

I heard a question, not the confirmation Roy plainly took it for. I was overtaking a parade of elongated lorries while outdistancing an impatient truck three times the height of the car, and couldn't risk meeting her eyes in the mirror. Some Mickey Mouse music by Dukas struck up as I managed to return to the inner lane. Bella was looking somnolently innocent, even more so when I held her gaze. "Did you want to ask me something?" she said.

A shiver seemed to waken Roy from dozing. "Like what, Bell?"

"I know you don't. I was asking Patrick."

"I heard you telling Roy about Monks Cross," I said.

"You mean you were spying on us," Roy objected.

"Was there anything to spy on?" When nobody answered I said "You seemed to know a lot about it, Bella."

"She read about it in the library."

"Didn't you as well, Roy? Why would you need to be told?"

"Because Bell read more than me. She went back."

I remembered hearing her return when I'd phoned him at the library the day my parents died. I felt as if my attempt to trip her up had sent me sprawling instead, but there was more I ought to question. "Bella, you said I knew about places like Monks Cross before Roy did."

"It's true, isn't it? You had Thelma's journal."

"No, I mean you didn't say I'd known before you did."

"She meant us both, dad."

"That's how I think of us. I didn't think I had to specify myself."

They were staring at me in the mirror as if I'd been at the very least unreasonable, and Roy took a firmer grip on her hand. I had one last dogged point to raise. "You said there were no homeless at Monks Cross when Thelma was there. How could you know that?"

"Do you really think they were there back then, Patrick?"

"Not those in particular. I'm saying—"

"Any, dad," Roy said, using Bella's hand to point at me. "They didn't live under motorways then."

I had no idea whether this was true, but if he believed it, mightn't Bella? I'd run out of questions and of conversation, or rather any that felt advisable to risk. Seeing my doubts had antagonised Roy, I let a concert on the radio take the place of dialogue. We were leaving the motorway when Bella said "Could you drop me by the house, Patrick?"

"I'll drive you to your front door by all means."

"Honestly, no need. Just take me where you did last time."

I stopped opposite the gap in the wall undermined by trees, and Bella squeezed Roy's hand before retrieving her bag. "Are we waiting again," I said, "or are you inviting us in?"

"Neither, Patrick. I'll come to yours tomorrow, Roy. Now I'll leave you in case you need to talk."

We palpably did, but when I made to begin Roy gave me a shake of the head, so violent it resembled a shiver. I was parking outside Julia's when he spoke. "I don't know what you're trying to do to Bell and me," he said, "but you can stay away from her till you've given up." He let himself into the house without looking back, and I remembered Bella's triumphant expression last time the door had shut. I had the idea, surely close to deranged, that she'd planted doubts in my mind today so that I'd sound irrational when I voiced them. That would mean she'd known I was eavesdropping, which left me feeling as foolish as my son must believe I was. As I drove away I was struggling to think what else to do – how much further I might have to go to learn the truth.

CHAPTER TWENTY

The Contents of the Bed

"Archives."

I was sure Julia would have gone home by now, and this wasn't her voice. "I'm hoping you can help me," I said.

"If we can we will."

"I had a book out from you the other day. I read it there, I mean."

"I see."

I was glad she couldn't, not least my grimace at the difficulties I might be destined to encounter. "I'm afraid I've forgotten the title," I said.

"What can you tell me about it?"

"I believe it's in your witchcraft archive."

"The Sutton Collection. Is the book rare, do you happen to know?"

"I wouldn't be surprised if it's the only copy."

"Then that's certainly where we would keep it."

"And it's supposed to be somebody's diary."

"I see." This time I hoped it might be so, but she said "I should think we can find it for you. May I have your name?"

Posing as my son didn't mean I had to lie. "Semple," I said.

"That's a coincidence."

Although I knew, I had to say "What is?"

"There's someone here who used to have that name."

"There," I said so cautiously I was afraid it might sound suspicious.

"Yes, working in the archive."

Even more warily I said "They're with you now."

"No, she's finished for the day. Why do you ask?"

"I didn't." In haste, and hoping this would distract the woman from my unnecessarily nervous denial, I said "As you say, it's a coincidence. Will my name help?"

"Let me ask." Her voice had started to recede when it came back. "Well, here's another coincidence. She's here now."

I suppressed a gasp and wished I'd been able to do that to my name. "I've got someone on the phone, Julia," the woman said.

"Is it for me?" Julia said altogether too close.

"No, it's just—"

"Is it anything I need to deal with immediately?"

"It's nothing you need to deal with at all. I only—"

"Then will you excuse me if I scoot, Hannah? Otherwise I'll be stuck in even more of a jam."

"You shoot off." All the same, Hannah added "It was just this reader had a name you'd know."

I was afraid this might bring Julia back, and Hannah's next remark fell short of reassurance. "Sorry about that, Mr Semple. I'll ask for you now."

I heard her murmur away from the phone, which sounded partly covered by a hand, and an answering voice. I had to strain my ear until that side of my head began to ache before I was convinced her colleague was a man. Her hand left the mouthpiece as she said "We're looking for you, Mr Semple."

Surely Julia had left by now, but held breaths had my lungs competing with my ear for aches by the time Hannah spoke again. "We've located your request. It was for Lumen Scientiae."

"That sounds like him." In a bid to appear more informed I said "It means light of science, doesn't it?"

"More like light of knowledge, of all knowledge. That's what he imagined he had or was going to get." A hint of disapproval lingered while she said "*Lumen Scientiae, His Life and Explorations.* That was your book."

"Thank you very much for tracking it down. Can I come in for another look?"

"By all means, but you'll need to send us a new application."

"Where—" I needed to seem to have known that, and I said almost too fast to separate the syllables "I mean, when can I see it? Tomorrow?"

"The earliest would be the day after tomorrow. Apply online as you did last time."

At least that would be Julia's day off. In my nervous eagerness I'd nearly booked a visit when she would have been at the archive. On my phone the application form was microscopic, and I brought up the archive on my computer. The Sutton Witchcraft Collection contained twenty-six items, and the one I wanted was the last, a number I refused to find ominous. *26: Lumen Scientiae, His Life and Explorations. Handwritten journal of "Lumen Scientiae" (identity unknown), n. d., poss. C 17th.* I ticked its box and saved the selection, and a button let me reserve the book. I was feeling in charge of the situation until the form asked for my borrower number.

It would be on my Manchester library card, except I didn't have one. On the horizon twitching windmills mimed the antics of my nerves while I tried to think. Eventually, though not entirely confidently, I retrieved my phone and called the library again. This time it was a male voice that said "Archive."

"I was speaking to a lady there before. I wonder—"

"The archive's actually closed now. Can you call back tomorrow after nine?"

"I just need help with reserving a book. Can you put me through to someone who'll advise me?"

A silence let me think he had, unless he was unprepared to comply, until he said "What seems to be the problem?"

"The form wants the number from my card, and I haven't got one."

"Are you the gentleman who was asking about the Lumen Scientiae item?"

"That was me," I said despite a sudden sense that I ought to have been warier.

"But you had your number when you viewed the book."

I tried and failed to find a response other than "That wasn't me."

"I think you'll need to explain that, Mr—" Just as suspiciously he added "You said your name was Semple."

"It is, and his was too. He's my son."

By no means signifying comprehension, the man said "Yes?"

"He's quite a young chap if you've seen him. Young enough that we need to keep an eye on what he reads."

"I'm afraid that's not part of our job, Mr Semple. If you're asking us to ban him from the library—"

"I'm just saying we may need to look at the kind of thing he reads, me and his—" Before I could stray into perilous territory I said "I'd like to take a look at it, that's all."

"We can't prevent you from doing that."

"Your system is. How do I get round it?"

"Just email us asking for the item to be made available."

"I will right now." My eagerness had already brought me trouble, and I was anxious that it shouldn't twice. "I'll email you personally, shall I?"

"If you wish. Address it to Derek Lister."

"And I'd appreciate it if you wouldn't mention all this to anybody else."

I had Julia more in mind than Roy, but couldn't say. "Not necessary," Lister said.

Did he mean informing anyone, or had my request offended him? Asking might antagonise him, and I ended the call so hastily that I almost neglected to obtain his email address. It took me some time to compose a wary message. Further to our phone discussion, this is to confirm my request to consult *Lumen Scientiae* in your archive on Thursday. Sincerely, and I had to tell myself there was no reason why Julia should see the email. Pa, I typed, which expanded into my stored name at once. I stared at the message in case there was a less explicit way of conveying the information, and then I sent the email.

Waiting a night and a day and its night as well before I could discover what Bella had wanted to learn felt like frustration rendered ponderously solid. By dawn I knew I couldn't spend the day without involving myself somehow. Since I had no idea which site she and Roy planned to explore, I couldn't risk visiting anywhere on Thelma's list in case I encountered them. I thought of inspecting somewhere they'd already been – hadn't Roy named a place? – and then I saw they were giving me the chance to carry out a different investigation. After a shower and an equally swift breakfast I made for my car.

In less than an hour I was leaving the motorway, and in a few minutes I was at the short cut Bella used. I parked outside a capacious Victorian house whose doorframe was buttoned with bellpushes next

to handwritten tags. The deserted street was quiet except for the
barking of a dog in an upstairs room. Fragments of brick clinked
together as I stepped through the gap in the tottering wall.

The sharp shrill sound might have been displacing birdsong from
the trees. A thin path elaborately patterned with dead leaves wound
between them from the opening in the wall. Otherwise the trees
grew so close together that it was impossible to see more than a few
yards ahead. A solitary beer can lay just inside the wall, a token of an
adventurer. I'd advanced several hundred yards through the greenish
gloom when I caught sight of a house.

At least, it was a red-brick building. By the time I reached the
end of the path, which led onto an overgrown expanse of gravel, I'd
seen it was a derelict hotel. Every window was boarded up. From
the remnants of the sign above the awning, a wrought-iron structure
barbed with shards of glass, I gathered that the small hotel had been
the Little Imperial, though at first I misread some of the remaining
letters as **IMP REAL**. On the far side of the gravel the path continued
through another mass of trees, and I made for Bella's house.

I hadn't struggled far through the tangle of trees when I was
rewarded by the glint of a window ahead – indeed, several. The
effort of advancing further prevented me at first from seeing my
mistake. The light was reflecting not from glass but from water, and
the choked path led to a viewing platform above the river. The
handrails had mostly rotted away, and sections were strewn down a
slope twice the height of the three-storey hotel. I could see both ways
along the riverbank without venturing onto the decayed platform. I
took some time to peer in each direction, shading my eyes and then
straining them until they stung, but it made no difference. The only
building on this side of the road was the abandoned hotel.

While I made my way back through the trees I stared about as
though a house might be persuaded to appear among them or take
shape from them or otherwise prove to have been overlooked, but
nothing like a fairy tale took place. I emerged from the silent gloom
onto the gravel, to be confronted by the uselessly unhelpful hotel,
which was as long as several of the nearby houses stuck together.
Beneath a steep slate roof sprouting four enormous chimneys, the
boarded windows left the frontage so anonymous that the remnants

of the sign suggested at best a failed attempt to lend it an identity. The door under the awning was covered up as well, and I was making for the road without a coherent idea in my head when I saw those boards weren't entirely secured. The door was furtively ajar.

Only frustration and aimlessness made me go closer. Glass crunched underfoot as I stepped on the concrete threshold, and one of the slates that had smashed the panes of the awning splintered as I trod on it. Though the boards had been prised away from the doorframe, where the nails had left rusty stains, the door wasn't open wide enough for even a child to slip through. I made a token bid to shove it wider, but it didn't budge. I was about to turn away when I noticed a faint trail leading into the darkness inside the hotel.

Switching on my flashlight, I poked the phone through the gap. The marks were footprints, leading across a carpet that looked imbued with soot, and ending at a staircase. They were significantly larger than a child's. Though I hardly knew what the sight meant to me – perhaps I wasn't anxious to know – I pocketed the phone so as to grab the edge of the door with both hands and exert all my strength. It juddered inwards, hindered by an obstruction that felt soft but resolute. As soon as I'd made enough of a gap I retrieved the flashlight and edged in.

Darkness swooped at me as I turned the beam on the obstruction. The door had rucked the carpet up, tearing it loose from the boards. Massive shadows dodged into rooms as I shone the light around the lobby. Beyond a doorway on my left, long rectangular shapes were draped with pallid cloths – tables in a dining-room – while to my right a faint roundish glow rose out of the dimness to greet if not entice me like a will-o'-the-wisp from a marsh, the reflection of the flashlight in a grubby mirror behind a bar, where inverted bottles glimmered without visible support. The ceiling loomed over me, untouched by the light, and the carpet underfoot yielded like moist earth. I was heading for the stairs beside the reception counter when I noticed the visitors' book.

It lay open on the counter, displaying several entries. At first I was sure I'd misread the dates. I leaned closer to look without touching the counter, which was encrusted with grime. Although all the entries were in the same old-fashioned script, every one was dated this month, and the names were dismayingly familiar, though they weren't the kind anyone would expect to see in a hotel register. *Crux Inverso, Aqua Sacramenti, Magister Stellarum*...

I came close to grabbing the blackened scabby counter as I tried to understand what I was seeing. The entries suggested some kind of secret joke nobody was meant to appreciate, unless logging them was a gesture of defiance or triumph. My mind felt unable to struggle beyond knowing who must have written them, and the names clamoured in my head as if they were importuning me to pronounce them aloud. I had a fearful sense that speaking any of them might summon its owner. Perhaps a face would sprout from one of the pigeonholes at the back of the reception recess, if not from all of them. Or might a piecemeal figure make itself apparent in the chair behind the counter, an occupant in the process of putting on some kind of flesh? Unwelcome as these notions were, they were trying to distract me from an unenviable task. I had to see where the tracks on the carpet led.

As I swung the flashlight beam towards the stairs a shape leapt up from the chair – an enlivened shadow. I didn't know how much longer I could bear to stay in the building, and to prevent myself from fleeing I climbed the stairs at once. Many of them gave way, some with a creak like a tree in a gale, some with a squelch of the carpet. I felt as if the narrow passage had extinguished the summer day, draining all the heat. Shadows mimed the instability of the handrails, which I refrained from touching once I'd nearly dragged the left-hand rail free of the wall with a crunch of sodden plaster. The passage turned back on itself at a boxed-in landing, and a second flight of stairs brought me to the middle floor. Corridors gaped on both sides of me, but the flashlight beam didn't reach even halfway down either. There was no point in wondering what the darkness further down might hide. The footprints led to the top floor of the hotel.

I was at the enclosed bend at the foot of the last flight of stairs when I realised what I'd somehow failed to appreciate – that there was just one set of prints. Had their maker trodden in them more than once? More grotesquely still, had she walked backwards in them? The idea of someone moving in reverse put me in mind of witchcraft, a similarity I would rather not reflect upon just now. Or did the prints mean she was still upstairs? I held my breath, which had begun to taste of grime, but all I could hear was emptiness or its pretence. "Bella, are you here?" I shouted, and my voice came back flattened, reminding me how shut in I was. Only silence responded, and though it made me feel awaited I followed the tracks and my nervously unsteady light to the top of the hotel.

The footprints led beyond the light into the left-hand corridor. All the doors were open, revealing rooms where objects more shapeless than they ought to be crouched in the dark – beds with disarranged drooping quilts, unless the beds themselves were sagging. Beyond them a face peered out of the lightless depths at me, the same blurred face in every room. When the beam caught the first of them it flinched back before the light erased it. My reflection had recoiled because I had. I shone the beam into each room, where it roused shadows to dance a greeting. Perhaps I was searching for a reason why the corridor was growing so much colder as I advanced. A framed print hung between each pair of rooms, but the images were so obscured by stains that I saw just my own faint image, as though they were parodying Thelma's portraits of me. The glimpses paced me to the end of the corridor, where the footprints disappeared into the furthest left-hand room.

They ended at a double bed. For a moment I thought it was occupied, but so far as I could see from the corridor the quilt was emptily humped up. When I ventured into the room a face swelled at me like a worm out of the darkness. It was mine once more, faintly illuminated by the beam. Something pale reared up much closer to me – my breath. A shiver travelled through me to the flashlight, and as shadows swarmed up the walls to nest beneath the ceiling, I made for the bed.

The footprints ended near the headboard, where the pillows looked as if they'd been kicked out of shape. From beside them I could see under the quilt, which was raised like the entrance to a burrow. When I shone the beam under the grubby stained material, the hollow it revealed put me more than ever in mind of a lair. It was empty apart from a collection of objects at the far end. I leaned reluctantly closer while shadows leaned closer to me. The glinting items were jars that housed samples of earth.

The sight brought me near to a kind of uncomprehending panic. From the position the quilt retained, I could tell that the jars had been stored there by someone crawling head first into the burrow, and I couldn't help fancying that she slept there in that fashion. Discovering the jars had revived the clamour of names in my skull. I pressed my lips together so hard that they ached, but perhaps I didn't need to utter any syllables, because I glimpsed movements at the cornices around me – a suggestion of several scattered objects fluttering like masks in a wind. When I peered up without raising the beam, I had the impression that they resembled tethered balloons, imperfectly inflated and nodding as though windblown, unless they were repeatedly attempting inflation only to deflate afresh, not least their eyes. I was about to shine the beam at them in the hope that it might banish them when I wondered if it could attract them instead, drawing them to cluster around me if not on me. The prospect almost made me drop the phone as I fled.

Grime caught in my throat, and my breaths grew unhealthily harsh while they kept appearing in front of my face. Darkness lurched at me from every room I passed. I would have taken several stairs at a time if I hadn't been afraid of falling. Even running down them one by one meant I had to keep thumping the unstable wall with my free hand. I dashed across the lobby, to find that the door wasn't open nearly as wide as I'd left it. I had to drag at it, bunching up the carpet that must have settled into place, before I could struggle past. Once I was outside I didn't immediately think to switch the flashlight off, because the sunshine felt like a pretence that I'd escaped the dark. I stumbled across the gravel into the trees and dodged doggedly along the path to the gap in the wall. There was my car outside the houses, and surely this ought to reassure me that some of my life remained normal, but even having reached the driver's seat and locked myself in, I couldn't drive by any means at once. I was desperate to think how I could use what I'd learned at the hotel – desperate to understand what I'd seen.

CHAPTER TWENTY-ONE

A Disappearance

"Semple."

"Mr Semple."

The librarian said my name a good deal louder than I had. He might almost have been announcing my arrival. Remembering when you were expected to be quiet in libraries, I glanced about the long white room. None of the readers at the tables appeared to have been disturbed, but I was looking for Julia too, although it was her day off. As I turned back to the desk beside the glass door in a wall of the same material, the librarian said "You were worried about your son."

I took this for a means of identification, but perhaps his long tanned extravagantly hirsute face was offering sympathy as well. "You'll be Mr Lister," I said.

"Mister Lister, that's my cross." Having acknowledged with a pout how the name sounded like a joke, he said "If you could put yourself in the book."

He meant the ledger lying on the nearest table. I added my name and date and place of residence and the reason for my visit – research. The process reminded me of the visitors' book at the derelict yet inhabited hotel, and I turned the pages until I found Roy's entry and Bella's. I didn't realise how much I'd been hoping to be proved wrong until I saw her handwriting, the same old-fashioned script I'd found in the hotel register. She and Roy had given research as the excuse for their visit too. I was nowhere near dealing with my thoughts as I asked Lister "Were you here when my son came?"

"Mr Semple, as I told you on the phone, we had no authority to deny him access to the item."

"I was only wondering what your impressions might have been."

"I'd say he was a fine young specimen."

"And the person with him?"

Lister rubbed his chin as if to conjure up the memory, producing a noise like a mouse scrabbling in litter. "I can't really recall."

"Anything you can bring to mind." Unease beyond defining made me urge "Anything at all."

"I think they did most of the reading." Lister raised a forefinger, signifying inspiration. "So perhaps you needn't be too worried for your son," he said.

"What difference does that make? He's still with someone who's mixed up with that stuff."

I'd embarrassed the librarian, who said "Let me fetch your book."

"Hold on." When he turned without bothering to display enthusiasm I said "Were you here all the time they were?"

"I was, yes."

"How long would you say that was?"

"About an hour," he said, having mimed deliberation.

"And after they left she came back."

"Did they?" Apparently this needed pondering as well, and so did adding "No."

I felt more disquieted than I understood. "What do you mean, no?"

"They, that's to say your son's friend, they didn't come back. Not while I was in here, at any rate."

"Ah," I said with the hope of relief. "How long was that?"

"The rest of the afternoon. At least a couple of hours, and I never went out the door." Lister gave me a decidedly doubtful blink before saying "Anyway, your book."

My appearance might well have been a source of concern, given that I'd barely slept since visiting the abandoned hotel. I'd managed few coherent thoughts, none of them reassuring. Presumably the jars of earth had been left unguarded because anyone who touched them would be given good cause to regret it. At least Bella was keeping the items away from Roy, but no doubt she was with him at this moment, and exerting what influence? What did she actually want from him? I was desperate to confront her, though perhaps not until I could find her on her own, and surely learning what she'd discovered in the archive might help. I did my best to focus on the moment as Lister returned with the book.

I'd expected an imposing tome, but this wouldn't have covered much more than the palm of my hand. The exterior was utterly black, not just the binding but the edges of the pages. I saw the library had bound the book, but if the title and classification number on the spine had been gilded or otherwise emphasised, they were all but engulfed by blackness now. The volume looked as monolithically solid as a lump of coal, but when Lister passed it to me I felt it shift in my hand, betraying that it was less stable than it looked. I could have fancied that I'd wakened it somehow, especially when Lister said "If you could rest it on a pillow."

There were cushions on the tables, so that readers could prop up books they were consulting. When I dumped the item on the nearest unused cushion the journal sprawled open, revealing that the front board was loose, while the pages were losing their hold on the spine. Someone hadn't shown the book much respect, and I couldn't help suspecting it had been the previous reader, though why would Bella treat such a rarity that way? The endpapers were as black as the binding, which gave me the unsettling notion that their darkness was designed to contain more of the same. I had to glance about for mundane reassurance — the sockets embedded in the tables for powering laptops, the cables lurking in recesses by the sockets, the high windows displaying office workers at their lunch on benches in the street — before I opened the first page.

Lumen Scientiae, His Life and Explorations. Although these were the solitary words on the page, the elaborate script was minute. It seemed introverted, addressed only to its author, as if the intricacies of the penmanship were designed to obscure any secrets it contained. I felt inexplicably reassured to see it didn't look much like Bella's writing, and I needn't think hers suggested an attempt at imitation. How could it when her writing dated from before she'd seen the book? I tried to leave my confusion behind as I turned the page.

The true mage is conceived by the cosmos, and is its fleshly incarnation. He belongs not to the human, for the instant of his conception epitomises the ancient will to reach beyond the stars and to exhume the secrets of the earth. In the womb he is privy to arcane lore, and bears occult truths into the world upon his birth. Such an one am I, and who else shall say it? Did the Christ raise the dead to stand guard at his manger? Did Mahomet split the moon in twain while he yet crawled on all fours, or was the Buddha seen to tramp the sky while still an infant? Once grown they were compelled to strut their powers to confound their followers, but I have no disciples or apprentices, nor any need of such. Nonetheless, I summoned presences whom men would name angels to watch over my crib, and my dissatisfaction with my clumsy infantile limbs sent me to emulate the flight of birds while my body played at teeter-totter to amuse my parents. My first words were in no language they had the wit to recognise, and my first steps enacted a forgotten ritual dance which those doting dullards applauded ape-like. Turned five years old, I grew alert to the whispers graves conceal, and at less than twice the age I was adept at locating those from which I could profitably learn...

Deciphering all this had cost me the best part of ten minutes — disentangling the cramped words from the inky efflorescences that surrounded and frequently obscured them. I could have thought the extravagant curlicues contained a separate message meant for initiates. No wonder Roy had given up trying to read the journal, but had Bella carried on out of perseverance or from some affinity with the material? I closed my eyes to rest them for a few moments, only to hear a surreptitious noise like a wakeful head shifting on a pillow. The pages had sagged shut, confronting me with the front endpaper as though the book had tired of my attention or found it intrusive. I had to hold it open with my fingertips on the margin of the scrawny verso and the recto that felt fat with secrets.

He who draws his powers from the stars or from beyond that luminous multitude may, upon relinquishing his flesh, be raised into the empyrean, while he who depends upon the earth and its aspects hidden from the herd of men, may rest beneath the land from which he gained his powers. Yet the mind of the mage is not restful, nor shall it sleep. He may be heard to insist upon his name like an infant hot to establish its identity, and be observed making shift to piece together his lost form out of the environs of his grave. His thoughts and his discoveries remain available to the initiated, for the earth itself shall grow eloquent when questioned. The merest handful contains the essence of its occupant, and shall yield all its knowledge to the searcher...

I lifted my eyes from the page, not just to give them a respite but in a bid to put my thoughts in order. Had my aunt gained any esoteric knowledge from the samples she'd taken from the sites — the burial sites? Or had that been the purpose of the man who'd ingratiated himself with her? Was Bella attempting it, and far more importantly, was Roy? I was distracted by a face mouthing so fiercely at me that it seemed to be opening too much of a mouth. I could have thought the book had summoned it until I realised it was beyond the window, which muted the shouts of a man calling to a friend across the road. I returned to the book, only to be daunted by the task, and started leafing through it in the hope that anything I ought to learn would catch my eye. I was somewhere near the middle when a word or phrase snagged my attention, and I used my blackened fingertips to pin the pages down.

...such rites and expeditions as require a helper or companion. No true mage imperils his secrets by educating an apprentice; nor should he hire the ignorant to aid in ritual, no matter how imperfectly it may be comprehended, for this is to invite a thief into his life. Let him rather conjure forth a servant which must conform to his desires and remain bounded by them. It shall be his wisest friend, for its nature is founded on the most ancient secrets; yet he must guard against permitting it to develop beyond his needs. It is his creation; it is but a parasite on him; yet all life contains the seeds of aspiration. If not adequately trammelled, the parasite may acquire powers in the very act of aiding its master in such rites as call for its participation. Perhaps the servant seeks to counterfeit humanity or even yearns to attain that state. However pitifully incomplete it grows in the absence of its master, this may spur it to importune others of his kind. Its flawed nature may compel it to pursue the companionship of those within whom it detects any hint of arcane vision or of sympathy therewith. Its victims will be blinded to their plight while it battens upon them in its hunger to regain power. How perfect are the

"Patrick."

The whisper was so close that my ear felt invaded. I managed to confine my immediate reaction to a gasp as I twisted to face Bella. But the newcomer was Julia, meeting me with a look of weary disbelief. "What do you think you're doing now?" she said.

"I might ask you the same question."

"You'd sound foolish if you did. I work here, if you remember."

"Not today you don't."

"Is that why you're here?" Julia said and stared at the book, which had shut its pages on the finger that was marking my place. "Because you thought I wouldn't see?"

"I'll ask you one of those too," I said, raising not just my eyes to Lister but my voice. "Did your colleague tell you I was coming?"

"Patrick—"

"Is that why he made such a noise about my name, to let you know I'd arrived?"

"You're the only one who's making a noise, and please make less." Without lowering her own voice Julia said "Believe it or not, your behaviour isn't as important to so many other people as you seem to think."

"Is that why you were spying on it?"

"Nobody was spying. I really think you need to take a long hard look at the way your mind's working these days, and if you can't or won't, find somebody who will. I don't believe it's been right since Bella came into Roy's life. Do you resent her having such an interest in your aunt that you can't share it with him any more? Is that why you're jealous?"

"I've already told you I'm nothing of the kind. I'm glad you brought her up, because—"

"And for the record, I'm here today because I swapped days off so Hannah could go to a wedding."

"Good luck to the happy couple." At once I wished I hadn't said that, at least not so cynically. "Look, we oughtn't to be arguing," I said and opened the book on the cushion, which shifted like a bag of worms. "We should be talking about this."

Julia kept her displeased gaze on me. "You always wanted to control our disagreements, didn't you? Calling a halt as soon as you'd had enough, especially if it was going against you."

"I'm just suggesting you might be more concerned if you saw what Roy's been reading."

"I'm perfectly familiar with the contents of our archive." As I opened my mouth to doubt she'd read every book Julia said "And if anyone's responsible for Roy getting involved in that sort of thing I'm very much afraid it's you, Patrick."

"I didn't bring him here to see this. Bella did."

Julia looked sad, though hardly sympathetic. "Is that what it's all about? Finding somebody to blame for what you wish you hadn't done?"

"I didn't even know the book existed." When Julia gave this a stare that scarcely bothered to express weariness, I said "Just read some of this and perhaps you won't be so—Just read."

She leaned over my shoulder, taking care we didn't touch. Far sooner than I would have hoped, she straightened up. "I'm not wasting any more time on that. If there's something in it you want me to see, show me."

"Nothing specific that I've found yet, but if you read just one page—"

"I've told you I haven't the time. And I'm surprised you're so anxious now for me to read it when you obviously didn't want me to know you'd been here."

"I would have told you if I'd found anything we ought to be worried about. That's to say I've been trying to tell you now."

"Only because I caught you out, and I really don't think I need to know." Julia stepped back while her discontented gaze remained on me. "Carry on, then," she said. "Read to the end if it makes you happy. Just don't go harassing Roy and Bella about it, or anything else for that matter."

If I'd sent a retort after her it would have involved speaking up, which might even have provided an excuse to eject me from the room. As I peered at the book I heard Julia murmuring to Lister at the desk. I needn't imagine they were discussing me, let alone act on the notion. By the time I managed to locate in the midst of the inky labyrinth the point where my reading had been interrupted, I was virtually unaware of them.

How perfect are the curbs which I have set about my servant? In my absence it is powerless; yet perhaps I should reinforce its dependence upon myself and no other. Though it be an avatar of the demonic, its essence is my creation and my triumph. It lives but to serve me, and should give thanks to me for its existence. Ought it to be permitted to retain the name it brought out of the dark, or might renaming it confirm my mastery? For the nonce it responds when called Bal or yet Bel...

I had no idea what sound I made, or how loudly. The sight of the variations on a name paralysed not just my body but my mind until I heard a noise like the tolling of a glassy bell. It was the door, and Julia had left the archive room. I lurched to my feet with my finger in the book, and was making to chase her when Lister said "Excuse me, can you leave that here?"

"I need to show Julia."

"You mustn't take it out of the search room."

"All right, then will you stop my wife?"

He glanced after her as I dumped the book on the cushion, which uttered a sound like a muffled breath. "Your wife."

"She used to be," I said and stalked fast to the door. "Forget it. I'll catch her myself."

I felt brittle with the information I had to impart, as though it had reduced me to a sketch of my nerves. The shrill note of the door could have been expressing my state. "Julia," I called, and louder "Julia."

At least a dozen people seated at computer terminals in the expansive outer room turned to stare at me. They were more responsive than Julia, and I was on the edge of shouting when she halted with her back to me. She didn't speak until I'd overtaken her. "What is it now, Patrick?"

"I've found something in the book you need to see."

"No, I need to be upstairs. I'm already behind on some work."

"It won't take a moment," I urged, only to regret neglecting to mark the place in the book. How long might it take me to find it again? "It's more than important," I said, trying to restrain my voice. "You'll see."

Very little like an invitation Julia said "Just tell me, Patrick."

"You have to see for yourself. You won't believe otherwise."

Julia gave a shrug that appeared to pump out an equally fierce sigh of resignation. "For heaven's sake show me, then."

She marched back to the search room and held the door open barely long enough for me to follow her in, and then she swung to confront me. "Where is it?"

"I told you, in the book," I said and dodged around her, only to falter. On the table in front of the chair I'd shoved away at an angle, the cushion lay indented as though it had supported a sleeper's head, but now it held nothing at all. "Where's the book?" I demanded.

"That's what I asked you, Patrick."

"I left it there, right there. Mr Lister knows I did. He made me. He saw me do it."

Lister stared at the table and rose halfway to his feet to confirm what he was seeing. "I'm afraid that's not the case."

"How can it not be? What are you trying to suggest?"

"I'm saying you asked me to go after your wife and so I wasn't looking."

In a dangerously neutral tone Julia said "Did you really call me that, Patrick?"

"I was in a hurry to catch you, and if you recall, Mr Lister, I immediately said she only used to be." I felt reduced to nerves again. "I'd think you would be more concerned about finding the book," I said.

Julia gazed at me as Lister did. "We are," she said.

"If that look's supposed to mean you think I've got it somewhere, come and search." Not far from hysteria I said "After all, this is the search room."

"I won't be going near you, but perhaps Derek should."

"Examine me by all means, Derek. Really, pat me to your heart's content. Feel wherever you like."

Too late I realised this might sound like a clutch of homophobic comments. Perhaps that was why Lister rendered his face blank before approaching me. I emptied my pockets – phone, wallet stuffed with plastic cards, comb, handkerchief as crumpled as a schoolboy's – onto the cushion, and Lister responded to my invitation by patting me pretty well from head to foot with a fastidiousness that might have conveyed disdain or distaste. The process worked on my nerves so much that I had to restrain more than one twitch. At last the librarian said "Mr Semple appears not to have the book."

"Just appears? Is there somewhere you haven't poked around you'd like to? Up my—" This wouldn't help the situation, and rather than say it I said "So someone else took it. Did they go out?"

"Nobody has left this room since you did."

"Then they've got it somewhere in here."

"Nobody else has been to your table."

"How can you know that if you didn't even see me leave the book?"

"Because it's my job to be aware what people do in this room."

"It's in here somewhere," I insisted and began to search, peering at every book and less directly at their readers, not to mention under all the tables and at the librarian's desk. Before I'd finished I heard Julia and Lister murmuring together. "I'm afraid we've called security, Mr Semple," Lister said.

"A joint effort, was it? You can tell them not to stir themselves. I'm gone."

Just the same, I stared around the room. Nobody was looking at me, and I could have imagined everyone was determined to render me unseen and unheard. I had an absurd impulse to slam the door on my way out, but it wasn't playing. As it gave its faint chime behind me I heard Julia say "I'm sorry about all that. We were together years ago." She was apologising to everybody in the room, but that wasn't why I stared hard through the glass. I half expected the book to have reappeared on the cushion, but there was no sign. As I tramped through a maze of computer terminals and emerged into St Peter's Square, across which a segmented tram was worming with a metallic moan, I was close to storming back into the search room. I had a nagging sense that the book was hidden in plain sight, having been made invisible – that magic had invaded the sunlit room.

CHAPTER TWENTY-TWO

The Second Call

When my phone rang I wondered dully who it would announce, and the only name that came to mind was Bella's. I couldn't imagine why Roy would be calling after our last confrontation, and that would equally apply to Julia. Then I realised my phone didn't know Bella's name or number, and as I fumbled it out of my pocket it said "Roy" with a hint of electronic enthusiasm.

"Roy."

"Dad."

We might have been competing to sound less expressive than the voice of the phone. I was confused by feeling that a thought I'd just had was mistaken — that I needed to realise what I'd overlooked. I stared out at the bay as if the bony twirling of the windmills could enliven my brain, and Roy said "What were you doing?"

"I've just about finished getting ready for next term."

The prospect felt not merely remote but irrelevant to the life I was living just now. "No," Roy said as if he doubted I'd misunderstood, "what were you doing at the library?"

"The same as you and Bella did."

"All we did was read. Mum says she doesn't know what you did with the book, and—"

"I did nothing with it. I left it on the table while I went after your mother, and when we came back it was gone. What has she been saying I did?"

"Like I said, she doesn't know."

"She knows she had her colleague grope me to find out if I had it. And I'm sure it would have set off an alarm if I'd tried to take it out of the building, so she knows perfectly well I wasn't responsible."

"If you got groped you ought to put in a complaint."

"I won't be bothering. I take it the book hasn't reappeared."

"Mum says not." A dry cough might have been why Roy paused before adding "She says you were annoying everyone, acting like they'd pinched the book."

"Would you rather think I did?"

Another cough did duty as an answer before Roy said "They had to call security, she says."

"And did she tell you I left without being escorted? The lazy bastards never showed up."

If this was my bid to make Roy feel we were having a laddish conversation, it expired in transit. "Dad, we're worried about you," he said.

"And I am about you, Roy, more than you know." This hindered my demanding "Who's we?"

"Mum and me and Bell."

"Bel." Of course he couldn't hear the difference, but I saw it as though it had appeared on the computer screen like writing on a wall. "Why should she be worried?" I said as unemphatically as I could.

"Because she's part of the family now. Mum says she is."

I choked down my initial response and said "I mean what might be worrying her."

"Your behaviour, dad." Less as if he were addressing someone half his age Roy said "She's fond of you. She often says she feels like she's known you for years."

I nearly let the truth out, but what would have been the point? Roy would never have considered it without the evidence of Lumen Scientiae's journal, if even then. "What exactly about my behaviour, I wonder," I said.

"Christ, dad, don't you really know?"

"I'm interested what she would say." With equal restraint I said "Is she there?"

"She's coming from her house."

I felt shamefully devious for asking "Have you been there yet?"

"Haven't tried."

More sharply than was helpful I said "Why not?"

"I think she's embarrassed by it. Maybe it's a bit of a tip if she's there with just her dad, if he's not as tidy as you are."

"If you're planning to stay together—" Just in time I refrained from suggesting he insist that Bella should show him where she lived, because I had no idea what this might provoke. "Perhaps you're right," I made myself say. "No need to harass her."

"I expect she'll let me see when she's ready."

I hoped whatever this might entail would never come to pass. As a preamble to risking more conversation I said "Your mother will be at work."

"She said you tried to check she wouldn't be there. What didn't you want her to know?"

"Roy, I'm not the one you should be asking that."

His cough might have been a bid to fend off the remark, but he said "Not getting you."

"Whose idea was it to visit the archive while your mother wasn't there?"

So bluntly that it might have been the final syllable he had for me Roy said "Mine."

"Bella didn't choose the day."

"Maybe she sort of did, but she didn't know mum wouldn't be around."

I couldn't argue with this, however little I believed it. "So you want to know why I did the same as you."

"You keep doing it. It's like you want to copy Bell."

Withholding my immediate response took more of an effort than ever. "How much of that book did you read?"

"Some."

"Did you read how he created a familiar?"

"Missed that bit." In a tone that might have denoted condescension Roy said "I don't believe any of it. It just helps Bell get hold of what your aunt did."

"So what did you read?"

"Not much." Defensively enough to sound resentful Roy said "The writing hurt my eyes."

"Mine too, but I carried on. You'd have thought Bella would have wanted you to."

I thought nothing of the kind, and Roy retorted "Why would she want anything to mess me up?"

I suspected she wouldn't care, but confined myself to saying "Suppose there was something in that book you wouldn't want to know?"

"That's pretty much everything I read."

"No," I said while my nerves endured my reticence. "I mean suppose someone wouldn't want you knowing?"

"Maybe that's why he wrote it like that, so nobody else could read it."

"Bella seems to have succeeded."

"That's because she didn't find the writing hard. She's more into the past than me. Anyway," Roy said as I took a breath to answer, "you succeeded too."

"I wish I had."

"I don't know what you mean, dad, but I hope it's over now."

"What do you think is going to be?"

"Upsetting mum. She still cares about you even though you've split up, and it's hard on me as well. She says you're being like this because of Bell, but I don't know why you would be."

I struggled to say only "That's how your mother thinks sometimes."

"I'm glad Bell doesn't, then. Are you going to accept her?"

For a moment my mouth felt unlikely to work, and then I said "I'll do whatever you need."

"Then I expect we'll see you soon. I'll talk to Bell." Doubt lingered in his voice as he added "And don't upset yourself either, dad."

I'd found no more to say by the time he rang off. The call had left me feeling ineffectual as well as devious. I would do anything necessary to protect my son, but how should I proceed when I didn't even really know what I was shielding him from? Surely I had to confront Bella by herself, perhaps by loitering near the derelict hotel. If only I had her phone number – and then the thought that had been taking form when Roy rang made itself plain at last, and my mouth fell open as though it was yearning to speak.

Was my memory correct? There was only one way to learn, and I brought up the contact list on my phone. I'd never deleted any entries, and it took just a few seconds to revive the one I had in mind. As I touched the call icon I felt as ridiculous as I was sure several people thought I was. No doubt the number would prove to be unobtainable – dead – but it rang and was answered almost at once. "Patrick, you've found me."

"Bella." I found it unexpectedly difficult to articulate "Or should I call you Bel?"

"Roy does."

"Not the way I've seen it spelled and you have."

She released a low sound that might have implied mirth. "How much do you think you know, Patrick?"

"I'd rather tell you face to face."

"I'm nearly at Roy's. We wouldn't want him to think you've been going for me again, would we? Shall we make a date instead?"

I found the discussion unnervingly banal in the circumstances, and almost intolerably grotesque. "I'll find you at the Little Imperial, shall I?"

"Yes, you left your mark there. I wondered if you were intending to own up." Before I could retort she said "I'll find you, Patrick. That's a promise on my soul, and soon."

"You mean you've got one," I said, a riposte that was useless at best, since she'd ended the call. As I stared at the phone I grew aware of the windmills sporadically twitching on the horizon, and it felt as if they were picking at my brain. So my mother had indeed recognised something when Roy had phoned Bella from the restaurant. The number Bella had was my aunt's old number.

CHAPTER TWENTY-THREE

Conversations in the Dark

As the windmills on the horizon began to glow like branding irons prepared for an interrogation I grew tired of waiting for Bella. Sunset bruised the sky with elongated welts of cloud while waves flocked towards the dimming bay as if they were recoiling from the prospect. I felt trapped in my apartment, nervous with undefined anticipation but unwilling to indulge Bella any longer. Was she reluctant to confront me? Perhaps the showdown would take place at the derelict hotel after all, despite what she'd said. I wasn't about to drive there tonight – I hoped to sleep eventually instead – and I refused to be made to feel I was at her disposal. Rather than speak to her I sent a message. Please let me know when I can expect you, it said.

The formality felt like an attempt to bring the situation down to the banal – to exert control, at any rate. I disliked the notion of receiving a reply that would appear to come from my dead aunt, and so I substituted Bella's name in the contacts list, only to feel I should have saved the evidence. What could it prove to anyone who didn't know as much as I did? No doubt Bella would simply claim she'd acquired the phone from her supposed father, even if this failed to explain how he'd come by it. I knew Julia and our son would find some way of exonerating her. Perhaps I should have phrased my message differently, since it brought no answer. Even if she didn't mean to let me know until she was imminent, I was going out for a walk.

A few families with toddlers howling to be carried were toiling up the hill towards the station. Sand from the beach glinted where they trod, and I did my best to recall seaside days with Roy and Julia – a crab attempting a clumsy escape from Roy's plastic bucket until he took pity on it and returned it to the sea, ice creams piled so high and solid that they toppled from their cones at the initial lick, a turreted fort built of sand by all of us, which borrowed grandeur from the evening shadows as we made for home – but the footprints put me in mind of the tracks I'd found in the abandoned hotel. I felt as if Bella could be following me unnoticed if not less naturally than that as I headed for the promenade. Whenever anyone I met looked past me, I had to glance uselessly back.

A lane to the seafront led between chain restaurants, as crowded outside as within. At my approach a crouching shape leapt up from behind an outside table, baring discoloured teeth – a dog roused by the offer of the remains of a burger. Opposite the restaurant was a multiplex, the Light. "Go towards the light," Roy used to intone as a joke. Through the window I caught sight of a title on the list behind the counter, *A Midsummer Night's Dream*. Whichever version it was, the film might provide distraction and ideas for next term as well.

Half a dozen old folk were scattered about the small auditorium, which was spasmodically illuminated by a trailer for a remake of *Snow White* where it was the prince who needed wakening or, as the trailer put it, to be woke. As I sat on the back row I silenced my phone. The screen counselled the audience to hush, and then the overture began. More than one person turned to peer if not to frown at me for laughing, which was simply owning up to my mistake. The film was an opera by Britten.

The overture resembled a magical lullaby, an invitation to dream, and it wasn't long before I started nodding in a species of agreement. Between inadvertent naps I glimpsed the fairy horde and the enchanted couples in the forest and the comic rustics at rehearsal. Bottom entered wearing a donkey's head, to a cry of "thou art changed," at which point my awareness lapsed again, to be recaptured by a chorus of "bless thee, thou art translated." Not just the voices brought me back. I'd sensed a breath like a waft of fog on my cheek.

A shiver overcame me as I twisted in the seat to confront my neighbour. Her large eyes widened as though to let their darkness out, and a smile that might have signified a greeting or secret amusement shaped her small mouth. Her face moved so much with the unstable light from the screen that I could have imagined it was seeking a form, but I was sure it had filled out since the last time I'd seen her – perhaps almost imperceptibly each time I had. "You wanted me, Patrick," she said, "and here I am."

"You were supposed to let me know when you were coming."

This felt like a pathetic bid to retain some hold on the banal, and so did consulting my phone, which showed no message. "How would that have helped?" Bella said. "How would you have been prepared for me?"

I had a sense that now we were alone she'd abandoned trying to sound Roy's age. "I am now," I retorted with all the conviction I could feign.

"Then tell me why I'm here."

"Because you want to find out how much I know."

"No, Patrick." A smile or the flickering illumination twitched her lips. "I'm asking why you called me, if you know."

I felt as though I'd fallen short of wakefulness and might be dreaming my unnatural companion. "I know everything," I said. "Everything you'd rather nobody knew."

As the smile parted, a man leaned over the back of his seat to growl "Take it outside."

Even this failed to restore reality around me – the angry silhouette beneath the screen on which Bottom was asking each fairy its name. "I'm taking it," I said with an attempt at grim humour. "It's leaving now."

I didn't look back until I reached the exit from the auditorium. As I shoved the door open I glanced around, but Bella was nowhere to be seen. When I stepped into the corridor I found she'd somehow slipped past me unnoticed. "You'll have to be nimbler than that," she said, "if you're planning to catch me, Patrick."

I kept quiet as we crossed the lobby, where the girl who had sold me the ticket said "Didn't you care for the film?"

"We just need to talk."

This earned a puzzled look. The automatic doors gave an uncertain jerk as Bella made for them, and then glided apart as I approached. The dog outside the restaurant began to snarl before barking so fiercely it sounded like canine hysteria. Though its owner tugged the lead hard enough for me to hear, the outburst didn't subside until my companion and I reached the promenade. "Animals can tell, can they?" I said.

"Unless you were the problem, Patrick. You were about to add to my store of knowledge."

"I can't imagine I know anything you don't."

I turned along the promenade, where scattered cyclists were following a track marked out for them, swerving around pedestrians who apparently found the symbols on the concrete too arcane. At the distant limit of the dark sea the windmills resembled thorny sticks charred black. "Regale me with a little of it," Bella said.

"I believe you're some kind of parasite."

"Do you believe everything you read?"

"If you're telling me that book isn't true, why were you so keen on reading it?" As headlights from a seafront car park caught her teeth bared in a smile, I said "And so anxious to hide it, which I'm sure you did?"

"You credit me with a good deal, Patrick."

"I notice you aren't denying it." When her teeth continued glinting in the dark the headlights left behind, I said "If you aren't a parasite, what do you want with my son?"

"For shame, Patrick. Just because you made an unsuccessful marriage needn't mean that others can't form meaningful relationships."

With more anger than I cared to feel I demanded "So what does your relationship with Roy mean?"

"Mutual nourishment. Developing together."

"Helping each other grow." My cynicism might have been mistaken for bitterness. "I've heard you say that already," I said, "and now I've heard it more than twice."

"I doubt Roy or his mother would agree."

"Of course they wouldn't." With an increasing sense of speaking in or to a dream if not a nightmare I said "They weren't there the first time. Roy wasn't even born."

"What are you suggesting? Do put it into words."

"It was you Thelma brought out of Third Mile Wood. It's been you all the time."

A dog approaching with its owner began to bark, though I couldn't judge whether it was protesting at my fierceness. "You sound close to persuading yourself," Bella said.

"And maybe other people," I said, more a desperate hope.

"Do you sincerely believe that? Do you even really believe what you said about me?"

"I know you do, and that's good enough."

"You read minds, do you, Patrick? That's a power I haven't gained yet."

"Which are you claiming you have?"

"You've had a hint of some. Perhaps you'll invite more of a demonstration."

This made me glance over my shoulder. Although I hadn't thought we were far from the lights of the car park, the deserted stretch of unlit promenade seemed unnecessarily elongated. My companion's outline appeared to squirm as if experimenting with its shape. Surely the illusion was produced by the dim relentless advance and retreat of the sea, and I said "You won't deny where you got your phone or how."

"I might or I might not, depending what you have in mind."

"You took it from my aunt. You were with her on the roof."

"Patrick, you shouldn't stain my memories of Thelma."

I felt as if the night had lurched at me, flooding my mind with darkness. Up to that moment I hadn't fully accepted my suspicions – deep down I must have hoped they would be disproved – but now they were embodied in the creature at my side. "You admit it," I said with not much of a voice.

"Your aunt died of herself. She couldn't encompass the knowledge she'd gained. She wanted to send it back where it came from, but you can't unlearn what you've learned."

"You're admitting you were there." I peered at Bella's face, but it might as well have been the gathering dark that gazed back at me. "What exactly happened?" I made myself ask.

"She was frantic to silence the relics. I tried to show her their voices were alive within her too, but the knowledge cast her down. I may also tell you that I didn't steal her phone."

"How did you end up with it, then?"

"She was in such haste to destroy the relics that she left it at home. I found it when I made a last visit to her house."

Could this be a bid for understanding, even for sympathy? I

thought it as nightmarishly grotesque as the rest of the conversation, and it inflamed my anger. "And now you're using my son the way you used her."

"You seem determined to mistake the situation. I come only when I'm summoned."

I stared hard at her face, an inexpressive oval set against the restive dimness stretching to the horizon. "Don't lie to me. Roy never brought you."

"No, Patrick, you did."

I wanted to believe this was false as well. "How could I have?"

"You wakened me by delving into Thelma's journal."

"Then why are you with Roy?"

"Because you shrank from following her journey. You weren't as open to experience as you liked to think. If you hadn't changed so much since you lost her example I would have stayed with you. When I met you at the gallery I was expecting the old Patrick. Sadly not all the past survives."

I felt acutely guilty, though only for having invoked her. I was discomforted to think my question could have sounded jealous. Bella turned to lean on the railing above the black waves as though she was calling down the night to settle on the world. I grabbed the rail with one hand, though its chill failed to make my situation seem entirely real, and kept my gaze on her. "And what are you doing with him?"

"According him the vision you once wished you had."

"The one you say my aunt died of."

"No more than he's able to contain. Why are you so afraid of it, Patrick? You've shared some of it. You insisted on experiencing it for yourself."

"If you mean when I drove you to Brightspring—"

"And when you lay in wait for us at Monks Cross. You saw everything we did and raised no objection."

"That's just where you collect your dirt. It's what you do afterwards, with my aunt and now my son."

"You know quite well that's not the case."

Her surge of righteousness took me aback. "What are you claiming I know?"

"Thelma kept the relics in her studio and communed with them, but you've good cause to know they're nowhere near him."

The thought of the unlit hotel drained this of much of the reassurance it might have conveyed. "So why do you need him at all?"

"It's how I was made. My summoner couldn't perform all his rites without calling upon one of us, and I need a companion to live as I should. I trust you appreciate how wrong he was to write of parasites and fancy he was my maker. He couldn't bear to depend so much on me."

I felt as if the swarm of words might be a spell – a means to confuse me, at any rate – but a phrase nagged at my mind. "One of us, you said. One of what?"

"Some fell from the stars, and some rose like fire from the earth."

With a revival of the sense that I hadn't managed to wake up I said wildly "Which are you?"

"We are all one in the state we attain in your world."

"You're talking like the book you hid. Are they even your own words? You sound as though you're quoting someone else."

"Don't you believe I exist in myself? Do you want to inhibit me as well?"

"How am I inhibiting you?" As I spoke the word it took on an ominous significance. "Tell me the truth," I said and stared into her eyes, though I might as well have been gazing into the depths of the night. "Are you having sex with my son?"

"What a small mind you do have, Patrick. There's so much more to life."

"That's not an answer."

"Why, he isn't even of the age. You surely wouldn't think I'd risk being separated from him."

I wasn't sure this was the reply I needed either. "What about my aunt?" I said, though I scarcely grasped how much I was implying. "I'm sure my uncle thought you were mixed up together."

"Another small mind, Patrick. Do try to understand I bring Roy wisdom."

"His mother and I can do that perfectly well. That's what we're for."

"Not my kind." Bella turned towards the waves, which appeared to be helping the night to advance. "Don't be too concerned," she said. "I'm not here to replace you. He'll still have a use for you both."

Before I could control my helpless rage enough to speak she said "Are we done for the moment?"

"I want you to be done with Roy for good."

"I'm for his good as he is for mine." A chill breeze emerged from the dark, infecting me with a shiver, and seemed to mingle with her voice. "There won't be much more need," she said.

I might have been making a threat or a plea as I said "When are you going to leave him alone?"

"You may count the days. Meanwhile I advise you not to trouble us." She turned her face to me, and I could have thought darkness had spread from her eyes to erase every feature. The whole of her looked like a shadow rendered solid. "I can come to you at any time," she said.

"Is that meant to be—" My retort trailed off, because I was addressing the night alone. A gust of cold air that could have been a loitering breath found my face, and then the dark was still. I stared about at the deserted promenade and headed for the nearest streetlamps, almost running before I broke into a run. The lights felt so distant that I could have fancied someone was withholding them from me, and the dark seemed altogether more real.

CHAPTER TWENTY-FOUR

A Search for Evidence

Bel was Bal, and both had been Abel, and now all of them were Bella. The names clamoured all night in my head, blocking every bid to think beyond them. They might have been a spell somebody had laid on me, unless I'd brought it on myself. I could have imagined the obsessive repetition was designed to prevent me from reaching a thought it was crucial to have. Knowing the names all belonged to one creature was a cognitive peak I had repeatedly to scale, only to slip back into defensive disbelief and begin again. Whenever I awoke from a doze almost too shallow and fleeting to count as one, I felt as though the knowledge had been just a dream I could dismiss. The recurrent parody of reassurance was a mockery of hope, and yet I persisted in feeling as if I must have dreamed the encounter on the promenade and everything it confirmed. If only I could talk to someone about all this, but who would believe me without evidence? I felt as though I'd been drawn deeper into my aunt's world than I would ever have wished – the world of her paintings, where the mundane offered no defence against the unknown, and everyday sights collaborated with the unnatural. I felt like a child isolated by a secret nobody but the culprit would accept. Bella had said she could come to me at any time, and often when I lurched out of another loss of consciousness I expected to find her watching me in the dark.

Eventually the room grew brighter, but I could just as well have been lying in gloom. I might have concluded that my encounter with Bella had depleted my energy besides reducing my ability to think. Though my eyelids had an additional excuse to droop – to fend off the increasing glare – I told myself I must get up soon, in case this helped me conceive some kind of plan. Let me have some real sleep first for just a few minutes, but I'd experienced none of that when a large insect landed on the bedside table, buzzing as it crawled towards my face. Once it began to trill I recognised my phone, only to wonder if it was about to announce my dead aunt. Of course I'd substituted Bella's name, but the one the phone spoke was my son's. "Good to hear you, Roy," I said.

A pause gave me time to fear it wouldn't be his voice I heard, and then he said "I'm in Liverpool."

"Just you on your own?"

"It's the last day of the exhibition. Bell said she didn't need it any more."

"As long as you're so close we ought to get together."

"I've only just got here. I'll be here for a while."

I was already struggling out of bed, squeezing my eyes shut as they met sunlight through the window. "Will you stay there till I find you?"

"I'll be here at least an hour."

While nothing he'd said was a direct invitation, I wanted to think it all was. After a rapid visit to the bathroom, I grabbed an apple from the kitchen as I hurried to my car. I left the gnawed remains in the cup-holder beside the gear lever, and in seconds the exposed flesh grew discoloured. For some reason the display of ageing reminded me of Bella. Since she wasn't with my son, where might she be? I couldn't help glancing at the back seat in the mirror all the way to the tunnel and for the miles beneath the river. Once I reached the waterfront I found I wasn't anxious to use the underground car park. Having located a space in the open, I made for the Tate.

I was sending the lift up to the third floor when the doors reopened, admitting nobody that I could see. I was glad to leave the pallid metal box, and didn't look back as I heard the doors falter while closing. The title of the exhibition – *Reaching Further* – no longer inspired me. I could have taken it as a warning, especially for Roy. As I hurried through the first room, which was full of influences on Thelma's work, I reflected that a crucial influence was nowhere to be seen, though need this mean Bella wasn't there? I could only hope so as I caught sight of my son.

He was in front of Thelma's final painting. My footsteps made him turn, a shivery movement that he seemed to hope would go unnoticed. He took a moment to raise a smile, by which time I'd seen how thin and pale he was, his eyes underlined by dark skin that looked bruised. I could easily have thought his smile involved some bravery, however resolutely hidden. "Good God," I said, "what's happened to you, son?"

My outburst made a gallery assistant give us rather more than a glance while Roy caught a desiccated cough in his fist. "That's all, dad."

For a moment I thought he was dismissing my concern and me as well. "What is?" I protested.

"Just a summer cold, mum says."

"That can't be all. How much weight have you lost?"

"No more than I can afford, mum says. It's all the walking we've been doing, Bell and me." Defensively if not resentfully Roy added "Bell says I look good."

I was dismayed to think he was depleted to the same extent that she'd grown plumper. "Does it matter what I say?"

"Course."

I found the word too terse for conviction. "Have you been to the doctor at least?"

"For just a cold? You never would. I'm not going to waste their time."

I had to restrain my anxiety so as not to alienate him. "So why did you want to meet up?"

Even this appeared to provoke him. "Have I got to have a reason?"

"Not at all. If we're friends again I'm glad."

A cough was his immediate answer, followed by "I figured we could get together while I wasn't with Bell."

I managed not to betray how I wished this were wholly so. "We could when you are if you like."

"Maybe soon. I'll talk to her." Before saying any of this he turned back to the canvas. "I'm through here if you are," he said. "Just wanted another look."

I gave Thelma's final work a last glance, and then I peered closer. While the tree displaying traits of every season was as diversified as I remembered, the distant figure was entirely faceless. On my previous visit I'd made out the hint of a face. It looked as if the features had been erased, leaving an oval smudge of paint like the mark of a thumb without a thumbprint. "Excuse me," I called to the attendant, "what's happened here?"

She approached at speed, only to slow down. "That's her last piece," she said. "She left it unfinished."

"Not that unfinished. This figure here, she'd begun the face."

"No, she wouldn't have. That's a recurring motif in her late work, the faceless figure in the distance. You can't even tell the gender."

"I can." Rather than say far too much I said "I'm her nephew."

"In that case I should think you'd recognise that element."

"Recognise it, yes." I was close to saying too much again. "Is the painting in the catalogue?" I hoped aloud.

"I'm afraid not."

"And it isn't in any of the books about her, dad."

"Can you confirm what I told your father?"

The attendant was just a few years older than Roy, as far as I could judge, and I felt as though they were turning their youth on me. "I think she's right," Roy said. "I think Bell would too."

As words struggled to escape me I managed to say just "You're both wrong about this painting."

"Honestly, dad, your aunt never put the face in. I know Bell would have pointed it out if she had."

Yet again I had to suppress a response, saying only "Why do you think she never painted it?"

"It's consistent with her style," the attendant said. "Another enigma she's left us."

"Unless the subject didn't want to be recognised." When Roy and the attendant kept their reactions to themselves I said "That's how this painting looks to me."

"You aren't suggesting anybody touched it." In case my silence wasn't a denial the attendant said "Nobody could have without being seen."

"Are we finished now, dad?"

I'd said all I could risk saying, and it hadn't been enough. It had achieved nothing except to embarrass my son. As I gave up, the attendant said "I promise you we look after your aunt's work, and I'm sure that's true of every gallery that shows it."

Though none of this had been the point I felt bound to say "Thanks for the thought."

As Roy hurried downstairs, possibly to demonstrate vigour, he said "You weren't very nice to her, dad."

"I didn't realise you cared." When he left this unanswered I said "Where shall we have lunch? You've not gone vegetarian, have you?"

"Why would I? Bell doesn't need me to be."

I stifled my response as I led the way along the colonnade to a dockside fish and chip emporium. Each fish overhung both ends of the cardboard container it was served in, and Roy attacked his with an enthusiasm I found heartening. It nerved me to ask "Are you beginning to think about moving on?"

"Can't we sit and finish it?"

"Not lunch. Moving on from Bella."

His laden fork hovered halfway to his mouth. "Why should I?" he retorted more than asked.

"You seemed quite taken with the young woman at the Tate."

He saw off the mouthful before speaking. "Dad, maybe you just don't get how relationships work."

Once again I was on the brink of saying far more than would be wise or useful, but he'd provoked me to enquire "You said Bella doesn't need you to be vegetarian. What does she need?"

"That's exactly what I mean, dad."

He looked saddened by my lack of understanding, a reaction that frustrated me almost beyond control. "All right then, what does she give you?"

"That is too."

Before I could be driven into useless recklessness I said "Are you still being taken to those sites?"

"I'm taking Bell, or we're taking each other."

"And what is all that giving anyone?"

"Rash." Despite its force, this was pronounced so distinctly that it sounded like a warning not to pursue the subject, but its repetition owned up to being a sneeze. Once he'd dealt with his nose, having grabbed a wad of paper napkins, Roy said rather less intelligibly "Brings us closer to your aunt as well."

"As well as each other, you mean."

"You've been there with us, dad." This sounded not unlike an accusation, and so did "You know what happens to us."

I became aware that several of the diners who'd laughed at or otherwise reacted to Roy's sneezes were listening. However I might have replied to him, I couldn't now, and we settled into an uneasy silence until Roy said "Thanks, dad, I've had enough."

Though he'd left almost half his meal, entirely untypically, I knew even the gentlest nagging would only annoy him. I'd already finished my lunch. "I'll give you a lift," I said.

"Just going to the wee room."

I hadn't heard him use Julia's term for it since he was a toddler, and it left him seeming oddly vulnerable. "Find me outside," I said.

I retreated along the colonnade while I searched my recent phone calls for a number. "Archive," a woman said, not Julia.

"I was reading a book in there and then it got lost somehow."

"Is this Julia's son?"

In case identifying myself would lose me information I said "I was just wondering if it showed up."

"It hasn't, no. I'm afraid we think your father may have been involved."

I tried to let out no more anger than my son might have. "How?"

"He had it when it disappeared. We still haven't established what happened."

I had some idea of that, which left me more frustrated than ever. "No need to say I called," I said as Roy wandered out of the restaurant, peering around in search of me. The phone was in my pocket by the time he reached me, and I was deciding on a plan as we made for the car.

I drove as directly through the city centre as the convoluted traffic system allowed, but turned away from the main railway station. "Drop me anywhere here, dad," Roy said.

"No, I'll take you home." Having neglected to lock the doors, I remedied this at once. "Back to your mother's, I mean," I said.

"You don't need to. I've got a return on the train."

"Save it for another visit." We were speeding up a slope as cars on either side did, and I wasn't sure if I felt more like a racer or a kidnapper. "There's something I have to do over there," I said.

I was hoping he wouldn't ask what, and he didn't speak. I might have switched the radio on if it hadn't brought Bella to mind. I was anxious not to think of her in case this acted as a summons. Roy stayed quiet as far as the motorway and along it too, except for the occasional dramatic sniff, which I eventually quelled by directing him to the tissues in the glove compartment. When we left the motorway I turned towards the river. I thought Roy might ask where we were going, but perhaps he knew and didn't want to say. Even when I parked opposite the gap in the overgrown swollen wall he stared at me before protesting "Dad, what are you trying to do?"

"As long as we're here we may as well visit" – I tried not to pause long enough to betray my search for a phrase – "your lady friend."

"I don't even know if she's here."

"Then we can see her house at least."

"Maybe she wouldn't like us sneaking around."

"Why should she think anyone is doing that? I would have thought she'd be glad to see you."

He grimaced as though he'd strayed into a trap. "I'm calling her," he said.

I thought of offering to call, but I couldn't show him Bella's name. I watched while his phone roused a bell – just a bell. At last he said "She's busy or she's blocked where she is."

This sounded like the start of a refusal to explore, and I hastened to leave the car. "I'm going to see what's to be seen," I said.

Roy climbed out at once despite making his lack of enthusiasm plain. "Better not without me."

I was first through the jagged gap and along the twisted path between the trees. Had they grown closer together? Certainly it was darker still beneath them, and the gloom seemed more extensive than it ought to be. When I glanced back I could barely make out Roy's unhappy look, and the wall was nowhere visible. I was starting to feel we were on the wrong path, unless the hotel had somehow been rendered unseeable, when I glimpsed a hint of gravel through the trees ahead. I struggled through the undergrowth, which had unquestionably grown since my previous visit, and saw the hotel. As I experienced a version of relief Roy tramped off the path with a clatter of gravel, demanding "Where's Bell's house?"

I oughtn't to display too much prior knowledge. "Let's see along there," I said.

The path to the viewing platform on the riverbank was less overgrown, as though it had no need to hinder intruders, none of whom could have reached it from the river. Roy halted by the platform, glowering around him. "So where is it?" he said as if I were to blame.

"I'm seeing what you're seeing," I said, only to wonder how often this was still the case. "You tell me."

"We must have come through the wrong bit of wall."

"I guarantee we didn't. I recognised the house we parked outside."

"Then where's she been going?" Roy said not entirely unlike a plea.

"There's only one place it could be, isn't there?" When he simply stared I said "The hotel we just passed."

Roy stalked along the path to kick up gravel on his way to the building. He confronted it without a word until I joined him, and hardly needed to say "Nobody's going to be living in there."

"It looks as if someone got in."

"That's not the same as living." Quite like an adult indulging a child's fancy, Roy made his way onto the threshold strewn with glass and slate, where he sent his flashlight beam through the gap between the door and its frame. "You're right," he said. "Somebody's been in."

"Then let's explore as long as we're here. It's been a while since we had an adventure together."

Might this sound like a complaint about his escapades with Bella? Perhaps the look he gave me simply meant he thought I was being childish or treating him as less than his years. All the same, he took hold of the edge of the door to exert a tentative shove before pocketing the phone so as to heave two-handed at the door. Soon he desisted, swabbing his forehead with the back of a hand. "You try if you want, dad."

I did my best not to feel too dismayed by his lack of strength. Surely it was just a symptom of a summer cold. As I made for the door a shard of glass cracked underfoot with a shrill sound that seemed to pierce my nerves. Seizing the door with both hands, I threw all my weight against it, and it stuttered reluctantly inwards, forcing a soft but determined hindrance to retreat – the carpet, of course. "No reason not to go in now," I said.

Was I urging Roy or trying to reassure myself? I switched on my flashlight as I sidled through the gap, beyond which the carpet felt not much less soft than loose earth. Roy's light followed me before he did, and confirmed a sight that had made me falter. Bella's long thin footprints were nowhere to be seen. All the prints in the derelict lobby, leading to the reception counter and the stairs and returning to the exit, were my own. "Looks like there's only ever been one person," Roy said.

"I can see how it looks." I shouldn't have let the trick provoke me so much. "Let's see what they found," I said.

Roy swung his light back and forth as we crossed the lobby, and I trained mine on the counter. Long shrouded shapes lurched out of the darkness, roused by his flashlight – tables in the dining-room – and on our other side the beam summoned a solitary vagrant star. However unnaturally displaced a star would be, the depth of the darkness it inhabited seemed equally abnormal, even if it owed half its distance to the mirror behind the bar. "Nobody there," Roy muttered.

I might have replied if I hadn't been distracted by another absence. Louder than I would have planned I said "Where's the book?"

"Christ, dad, you can't think it's in here."

"Not that one," I said, though I wondered if it could be. "The visitors' book. It ought to be here."

Roy stared at the rectangular trace it had left in the grime on the counter, an impression that put me in mind of a grotesquely shallow grave, and then at the footprints on the carpet. "Looks like whoever came in took it," he said.

I felt sure this was true, but not as he imagined. "Let's find out where they went," I said.

I moved fast to the stairs, following my own trail. The beam from Roy's phone set my pallid shadow prancing on the wall, which our lights rendered even more unstable than the torn wallpaper sagging with dislodged plaster. When we reached the middle floor he swung his light from side to side, and doors opened wide along both corridors. No occupants emerged – just shadows that the light had brought to life – and Roy repeated his formula. "Nobody there."

I hoped it was unnecessary, although surely accurate. As I climbed to the top floor the carpet yielded underfoot so much I could have thought the boards were rotting too. I waited at the bend in the stairs for Roy to catch up while my shadow mimed restlessness, but he said "Go on" with all the breath he could spare, and I thought he might feel trapped. Halting at the top, I shone my beam along the left-hand corridor. My footprints and the returning set overlapped as they vanished into the dark. "Go on then, dad," Roy said more edgily than ever.

Far too belatedly I wondered whether his experiences with Bella had left him more sensitive than me, more alert to anything that might be at large in the abandoned hotel. I made my way along the corridor as fast as he seemed capable of keeping up. Doors crept wide to greet us, or their shadows did, and blotches crawled across the framed prints between the rooms, stains that were the shadows of the frames. Every time we passed a room, faces glided alongside us to peer out of the dark. I thought the repeated sight of our reflections would prompt Roy to utter his formula again – his spell, as I very much preferred not to think of it – but he stayed silent apart from his dogged breaths all the way along the corridor. I made space for him in the doorway of the final left-hand room and shone the flashlight in.

The quilt on the double bed was still raised like a burrow. As the beam found it, the elongated hump stirred as though its denizen was about to rear up or squirm forth. Surely this was just a trick of light and shadow. Dim faces wormed out of the dark as we ventured into the room, but they were our own. We hadn't reached the bed when Roy halted, jerking up his free hand as if to fend off something he'd seen or otherwise sensed. I wasn't sure he'd simply wanted to detain me until he said "Must be someone homeless, dad."

"Shall we make certain?"

"We shouldn't wake them." As I took a step forward, since he refused to move, he muttered "You wouldn't like it."

When I kept on he aimed his flashlight at the bed to add to mine, revealing how the burrow had begun to quiver with apparent eagerness, or its shadow had. He stayed between the doorway and the bed as I reached the open end of the burrow. I sent the flashlight beam in, and a dark shape slithered to huddle in the depths. It was yet another shadow, and I leaned closer to thrust the phone into the mouth of the burrow, which smelled of musty fabric. It showed me no more than I'd already seen. "They aren't there," I complained.

"They must have found somewhere better. Wouldn't be hard."

I meant the jars of earth. I gave the empty tunnel in the quilt a last frustrated look and straightened up, imitated by a figure like a dimly illuminated specimen in a glass case. "Unless they're somewhere else in the building," I said.

"They can't be. You can see from their footprints they went out."

How could I have suggested that the absence of a trail was no proof? Roy still had homelessness in mind, which wasn't relevant in any sense I would be able to explain. "Can we go now?" he said.

Once again I felt afraid that he might be more sensitive than I was to presences in the dark. If I made him confront them, how might that harm him? My duty was to protect him, and I mustn't risk failing out of confusion. "If you think we should," I said.

He swung his flashlight towards the corridor at once, and a mass of blackness dodged aside beyond the doorway. He was making me more nervous than I already was, and I hurried after him, trying not to glance into the rooms we passed, where I glimpsed faintly luminous heads bobbing in the depths. As we approached the stairs the flashlight beams strayed into the opposite corridor, and I was afraid that they might rouse something in the dark – that the ill-defined activity at the limit of the light would resolve itself into a crowd of faces that swelled to fill the passage before swarming out of it to overwhelm us. Was I sharing Roy's perceptions or at least a hint of them? If this was in any way akin to his experience, I felt more desperate than ever to rescue him.

Nothing but jittery light had appeared in the corridor by the time we reached the stairs. As I stumbled down after Roy, resisting an urge to take more than one stair at a time, the walls staggered around us as if they were enacting their dilapidation. The middle floor yawned on both sides of us, and I didn't risk sending any light into the blackness. The last flights of stairs felt as insecure as the reeling light made the walls look, and the lobby floor didn't feel much solider. I was about to follow Roy out of the hotel when he peered at the footmarks leading to the reception counter and then raised his flashlight along with his gaze. "Is that what you were looking for, dad?"

I saw a blackened slab propped on the chair behind the counter, and then I recognised the visitors' book. "That wasn't there when we came in," I said.

"Must have been. We missed it, that's all."

Arguing was less important than showing him the truth. I had to hold my light close to the encrusted counter before I could locate a flap to lift. When I threw it back, fallen plaster rumbled across the rotting wood, and more of it thumped the carpet. As I grabbed the ledger the rickety chair gave a wakeful squeak. I retreated fast through the gap and opened the book on the counter. I was hoping I'd turned too many pages one-handed when I came to the last one that wasn't blank. It bore just a single entry, not the list of occult names I'd seen. Turning back, I saw exactly what I feared. The preceding page had been torn out. "She—" I blurted.

"Who what, dad?"

"Never mind. You'll see." I'd already noticed that the final entry was in Bella's handwriting, and this would have to be enough – whichever name she'd left, having forgotten she'd written it down. "Look here," I said, planting my hand on the blank section. Then a shaky breath escaped me, and I wished I'd shut the book or never opened it. The entry consisted of the date I'd previously visited the hotel, and my name.

Roy stared at it before pointing his flashlight at the only set of footprints that led out of the hotel. "I thought I was tripping, but it's true. You've been here already. You wrote that in the book. What the fuck are you trying to do?"

"That's not my writing, Roy. You know it's not."

He gave it a disgusted grimace and made for the exit. "So what's it supposed to be?"

"Don't you recognise it? Surely you must have seen it somewhere. Try and think."

He shoved the phone into his pocket, having extinguished the light, and hauled at the door to shift the carpet that had forced it almost shut. "Can't even fucking—" he snarled and twisted to face me. "Can you let me out, please?"

As I strode across the yielding floor I felt as if I were trying to erase my own tracks. I'd hardly opened the door wide enough for Roy when he shouldered his way out of the hotel. "You were trying to make it look like the writing in that book in the library, weren't you?" he said while I struggled out onto the littered threshold. "Why would you ever want to do that? Did you bring me just to see?"

"Roy, you have to know that makes no sense." When his face admitted nothing I said "Have you honestly never seen Bella's writing?"

"Why would I? We've got phones." His eyes widened and his mouth sagged open, a mask of disbelief. "You're still getting at her when you said you wouldn't. That's enough and more than. I'm going home."

"Roy," I tried pleading, but he was already striding across the gravel. As I followed him I had a sense that we were being watched triumphantly from the hotel — that the darkness inside was victorious. By the time I reached the street, having dodged along the path that felt too much like the lightless interior of the hotel, Roy was tramping past the houses. "Let me give you a lift at least," I called in desperation.

"Don't bother. I'm walking." As he put on speed without looking back I could have thought he shouted "Rush" and then "Whoosh." He wasn't directing himself or referring to his pace. Once I might have laughed at the pronunciation of his sneezes, but not now. I only hoped they were merely symptoms of a cold he ought to be more than able to recover from at his age. If his energy and strength were being drained as much as I feared, it was all the more urgent to think how to save him.

CHAPTER TWENTY-FIVE

A Return Visit

"You know who this is and why," I said. "Let me have an answer."

A simulated voice, if no more artificial than I suspected hers might be, had answered on Bella's behalf. I'd begun to wonder if anything about her wasn't false. I was too enraged by how she'd managed to estrange me even further from my son to leave her any more of a message. Suppose she let Roy hear what I'd said and perhaps played it to Julia too, demonstrating yet again how deluded and obsessed I was, bordering on dangerous? So long as my call made her respond, I couldn't afford to care. "Do your worst," I said, having ended the call, and laid the phone on my desk.

I'd withheld that challenge until it couldn't be recorded, but might it reach her by some means? There was no point in antagonising her more than necessary, but I was determined to ensure she left my son alone. My final words had started to disturb me in a way I couldn't grasp, as if they ought to convey more to me than they did. The impression lay like a shapeless weight on my mind while I waited for the phone to ring, if that was how Bella would respond. Half an hour crawled by, followed by another half, each marked by the emergence of a few commuters from the station and the voice of a train listing the stops on its route. I peered at every distant face, none of which resembled Bella's. Perhaps she wouldn't arrive that way, but I thought it best to watch the street as it grew secretive with twilight, and in any case I felt confined to my desk by my inability to think. I watched the sunset on the faraway windmills drain into the sea. The spindly vanes continued to work, plucking without result at an upright oval of pale cloud, so apparently insubstantial it was barely visible. I did my best to hope that Bella might end up as ineffectual as the windmills looked. After all, she'd caused me no physical harm, and how much longer was she going to need Roy? They must be close to finishing the expeditions they were basing on my aunt's journal. Surely she couldn't do much worse to Roy than she already had – and then, far too tardily, I wondered whether anybody else could have been another kind of victim.

Had I already learned the worst she was capable of, or at any rate seen examples of it? As my thoughts took a dismaying shape I was distracted by the spectacle at the horizon, the unnaturally regular oval cloud hovering over several windmills. Of course they couldn't shift it, but it hadn't moved of itself or altered any of its outline, though it had been loitering for minutes since I'd noticed it. It was the sort of phenomenon that gave rise to tales of alien visitors, and I imagined people phoning the authorities, but these thoughts were simply hindering the ones I was afraid to have. Had someone besides me recognised or at any rate suspected Bella? At once I was certain who had, and as though my realisation had wakened it along with my brain, the phone rang. "Bella," it said, and another voice followed it as the ringtone fell silent. "I'm here, Patrick."

It appeared to come from the hovering cloud, which had opened its mouth. The cloud had eyes as well. If it hadn't just produced the features, presumably the darkness gathering at the horizon had let them grow clear. The cloud was a reflection of the intruder behind me, the source of the voice. I twisted around in my chair, grazing my arm on the edge of the desk, to see Bella in the middle of the dim room. In an attempt to fend off panic I demanded "How long have you been there?"

"Since you called me. I was waiting to be noticed."

With all the force of the realisation that had come to me I said "I thought you didn't like to be."

"Every girl does, Patrick," my visitor said, accompanying it with a simper. "Whatever can you mean?"

"There are people who learned to their cost that you didn't." It appalled me to have to add "There were."

"You can speak freely. We're all alone."

"Yes, you wouldn't want Roy or his mother to hear."

"I was thinking of you, Patrick. I shouldn't think you'd want to estrange them even further."

"If that's what it takes to get rid of you it's worth the risk."

"You don't think you could be risking them."

"Don't you dare harm them. Leave them alone."

"I'm afraid I shan't be doing that quite yet. What would you propose to tell them? You haven't even made it clear to me."

"About the woman who saw my aunt killed, for a start."

"Miss Dennison."

"That was her name, and I ought to have seen how it gave you away."

Bella widened her eyes, which appeared to darken faster than the room was darkening. "How was that, Patrick?"

"When I spoke to Roy after she'd seen both of you he didn't know her name, but you did."

"Unless he'd forgotten it and I reminded him."

"Why would you know it at all?"

"Why shouldn't I? You did."

I felt as though Bella aimed to let the darkness overwhelm my mind, and I clung to the knowledge I'd gained. "I should have realised what she meant to tell me when she rang."

"What might that have been, Patrick?"

"That it was you she'd recognised, not Roy."

"How would she have managed that?"

"Because she saw you when you were using my aunt the way you're using him."

"Do try to remember what I told you and your family. That was my father."

"I don't believe you ever had one."

"Good gracious," Bella said, and it was as if the darkness tittered. "I'll look forward to watching you attempt to convince your family of that."

"If nobody's going to believe it, why did you do away with Miss Dennison?"

"Precisely, Patrick. I'm sure that's an objection they would raise."

"I'll tell you why," I said furiously enough to overcome the dread that was massing around me like the dark. "Because you didn't want to risk being found out then, but now you've got such a hold over Roy and his mother you feel safe."

"And will you be explaining to them why I'm supposed to have killed your aunt as well?"

"I didn't say you had, but now I know you did."

I wished I could distinguish her expression, but the light switch was beside the door beyond her, and I'd grown nervous of venturing closer to her in the dark. "You haven't told me why," she said with grotesque coyness.

"Because you couldn't stop her destroying the relics you'd made her collect. I think you lost the control you're so determined to keep and went for her."

"She oughtn't to have done it. She knew full well I was just a step short of achieving what I'd set out to achieve."

I felt as eager as afraid to learn "Which was..."

"My powers that waned when my summoners died. Each time I return to the earth."

I had a sense that the foundations of reality, or at any rate my notions of it, were under threat. "You don't mean the people who are buried at those sites."

"Those, yes. When they're all gathered I shall be free."

"To do what?"

"To be myself, as the likes of you are."

For an instant I felt seduced into sympathising, and then I retorted "Not to kill even more people."

"Patrick, you're becoming dull. I wouldn't have expected Thelma's nephew to grow up such a monomaniac."

"Better than the kind of maniac you are." I was furiously aware that my response might well be taken to exemplify dullness. "You killed my parents, didn't you," I said as my lips grew stiff.

"Now, Patrick." She might have been addressing a dotard. "What evidence do you think you have of that?"

"I don't need to give you any. We both know the truth. It wasn't just your mobile number my mother recognised."

"Do remind me."

"When you wouldn't meet us at the restaurant because you were afraid she'd know you or my father would. She saw your picture on Roy's phone when he rang you."

"She remarked on it, did she?"

"She began to, and I think you know it. I'm guessing you were there and not letting us see you. That's one of your powers, isn't it? The power to sneak about and spy on people."

"Do try to think clearly. If nobody knew I was there, how could that have stopped her speaking up?"

"Because she couldn't have been sure what she was seeing." I was answering so as to clarify the truth in my own mind. "She was when she'd spoken to Miss Dennison again," I said. "She knew you and my aunt's man were related somehow."

"Her ideas weren't as imaginative as yours, then."

"They were close enough for you to want to silence them." My mouth was growing unwieldy with rage again. "She recognised your eyes," I managed to pronounce. "And my God, the last thing my father said, he was starting to tell me you were there in the car."

"You really think you heard enough to say that was what he meant."

"How would you know how much he said if you weren't there?"

A silence admitted it had no answer. By now the room was so dark that I could scarcely make out Bella's shape. Another surge of fury left me struggling to say "That's why you were so ready to get together the second time, because you knew they wouldn't be meeting us. Christ, you even said you'd been feeling you should meet them when you already had."

"Tell me this, Patrick. If I've silenced all these people, why haven't I silenced you?"

"Because you've made certain nobody will believe me."

"Then perhaps you should trouble yourself less and leave me to finish my mission."

"I'll leave you alone if you leave my family alone. I will if you finish it by yourself."

"I regret that isn't feasible. Besides, I've grown rather attached to your son."

When I dug my nails into the arms of my desk chair I didn't know whether I was trying to contain my rage or preparing to launch myself at my visitor. "Parasitic, you mean."

"Can you truly not appreciate how much I've given him? He does, you know. You should ask him."

"I've seen how much you've taken. He's so weak I had to open a door for him." At once I realised "You were there in the dark, weren't you? You saw."

"You do seem bent on blaming me, Patrick. It's those beneath the earth that feed on your energy. You felt cold where they were, didn't you? That's how they draw on you to help them to return."

"And you're using Roy to make them."

"They have to be vital when the relic is collected for my purposes. We won't be making many more excursions, so do try to content yourself."

"Content." The word came out of my mouth like spitting. "I won't be that until Roy's rid of you," I said.

"You shouldn't force me to protect myself again, Patrick."

"What are you threatening me with now?" I demanded, staring fiercely at the dark. I had no idea how long it took me to grasp that I was confronting only darkness. I shoved myself to my feet and strode to the door, which was shut – unopened for at least two hours. The light confirmed that I was wholly alone in the room, and I went through the rest of the apartment to confirm that it was deserted as well.

Surely the threat had been merely a warning; what else could she do to me? I was as ineffectual and unconvincing as she could wish. I had no evidence of any kind against her – and then I thought of the item she'd given me the first time we met, the rarest of the books that used a painting by my aunt. At once I was sure whose name had been blotted out inside the cover, and it must still be under the erasure. I hurried to the shelves where I kept all the books to do with Thelma, but that book wasn't where I'd filed it. It was nowhere to be found.

I couldn't help wondering if Bella was spying on my useless search. When I gave up at last, I felt compelled to listen for any hint of trespassing as I made myself get ready for bed. Once I started pacing through the rooms to persuade myself that the intruder hadn't returned, I was reduced to muttering "Go to bed. Go to bed." Even there I found it hard to close my eyes, and harder still to shut my thoughts down. I did my best not to think of Bella, in case this functioned as an involuntary summons. I tried to recall memories that wouldn't bring her to mind, but thinking of my parents only revived my father's loss of control when they'd found her with them in the car, and any attempt to remember my years with Julia simply reminded me how thoroughly Bella had ingratiated herself. Any thoughts of Roy led straight to her and my fears for him, and a bid to reminisce about my aunt and uncle found me walking in Third Mile Wood, but now I knew I wasn't alone with Thelma. Our companion was dodging behind the trees, constantly changing from one side of the path to the other, even though I never saw the presence cross the track. This was the nearest I came to dreaming, which wakened me enough to prompt me to struggle not to think of Bella. Suppose striving to keep her out of my mind simply invited her? As I tried to fend off the possibility I heard a sound outside the bedroom.

Somebody had dropped an object, or at any rate something had fallen. I wanted to think one of Thelma's sketches of me had dropped off its hook, but I felt less than eager to check. Enraged by my reluctance, I flung off the quilt and strode to throw the door wide. The dim corridor was strewn with rectangular items – the portraits that had hung on the wall. I switched on the light and uttered several words I seldom used. All the pictures were still on their hooks. The objects scattered the whole length of the corridor were pages torn out of a book, and the empty binding lay on the carpet outside my bedroom.

Not just the sight of all the litter had provoked my outburst. I'd recognised the archaic handwriting of Lumen Scientiae's journal. I grabbed the binding and retrieved the pages, only to discover one was missing – the page that gave the names of the writer's familiar. Its absence might have been an especially sly gibe at my helplessness, since if I showed anyone the book I was bound to be accused of theft and vandalism, unless the culprit had simply taken extra care not to be identified. "Still here, are you?" I said rather more than conversationally as I headed for my desk. "Aren't you going to make yourself known?"

Only silence replied while I laid the remains of the book in the drawer, having shoved pens and printer cartridges aside, and locked it in. I wanted to believe that Bella had made a mistake at last – that I'd been given evidence I could use if I could only think how.

Perhaps sleep would clear my mind, if I was able to sleep, unless I had to think first. I turned off the light in the corridor and hurried to take refuge in the bed from a sudden chill that made me shiver. I slipped under the quilt, and as my head found the pillow a face rose out of the dark to loom over mine. "You came to my bed and so I've come to yours, Patrick."

A convulsive shudder hindered me from recoiling. "Get away," I protested in a voice that my throat choked almost beyond hearing.

"Don't you know what you want? I'm here because you called again for me."

Her body had reared over mine, and her face was descending towards me. I could have thought it was starting to extend itself from the head. My hands jerked up to stave her off, but they hadn't made contact when I felt I was about to be fooled into touching her more intimately than I would be able to explain, not least to myself. I seized her by the shoulders while I scrambled out of bed, and my fingers sank deep into a pair of hollows in the flesh. As I gave a cry of dismay she writhed out of my grasp, and I thought she grew thinner and supple as muscle untrammelled by bones in order to make her escape. Before I could take a breath I was alone in the room, but I floundered to the door and switched on the light, feeling as though I might never dare venture back to the bed. When at last I did I left the light on, but I still didn't sleep until well after dawn.

CHAPTER TWENTY-SIX

Separations

I awoke knowing what I had to do and immediately dismayed by what it would entail. It mustn't matter how Julia and our son would think of me; only keeping Roy safe did. I was eager to phone at once, but I shouldn't risk letting Bella anticipate my plan. I oughtn't to alert her in any way, which meant avoiding any thoughts of her. I did my best to concentrate on work, rereading all my preparations for next term, and managed to come up with additional ideas, though the preoccupation with the magical threatened to bring Bella to mind. At the edge of my vision the restless windmills might have been trying to snag my attention, to undermine my focus. Every train that waited at the station warned the public about safety in the same unalterable female voice, reminding me of other elements that apparently couldn't change — the eyes my mother had recognised. I stared at the computer screen and stuck my thumbs in my ears, shading my eyes with my fingers to shut myself in with my work. I imagined I could still hear the insistent voice, so faint it sounded as if it were speaking from beneath the earth. Every repetition meant another quarter of an hour had passed. At long — unbearably protracted — last it was late afternoon, and I made the call.

"It's Roy. Don't know who you are or what you want, so."

I waited for his recorded voice to finish its brusque invitation, but that was all. The truncated message sounded like a dismissal, which I was about to ignore when Roy spoke in a voice that was thinner and harsher. "What?"

"It's your father, Roy. It's dad."

"I saw that. What do you want?"

I'd begun to wonder how much Bella might have told him — certainly not all. "Just to find out how you are," I said.

"Okay." With a cough that suggested otherwise he said "I'm good."

"Better than you were last time I saw you?"

Another cough left him sounding reluctant to say "Bout the same."

"I trust your mother's looking after you."

"Bell is." With additional resentment he said "I can look after myself."

Though the reference to Bella left me nervous of being overheard, I had to ask "Where have you been today?"

"Here at home reading about your aunt. Looking at everything she did."

Once I would have welcomed this more than I did now. "Did it help you much?"

"Just trying to get ready for our next trip so I'll get more out of it."

I was dismayed by how routinely he assumed I'd know that this didn't include me. "How many of those are there going to be?"

"Not many now, Bell says. We're nearly finished."

I wished I could find this reassuring. "And what does she say will happen then?"

Perhaps the pause conveyed his disbelief that I should ask. "We'll stay together," he said.

I couldn't risk enquiring whether she'd said so, a question likely to antagonise him further. Before I could think of a safer response he said "How are you doing, dad?"

"Just working on my latest task."

"I mean have you sorted out your shit."

"I believe I will have soon."

As I hoped this might satisfy or at any rate silence him, I heard a doorbell ring beyond him. "She's here now," he said.

I could have thought our conversation had summoned her to put an end to it. "We'll talk more soon," I said.

This was far from the promise it resembled. It felt more like an omen of the unavoidable. Pocketing my phone, I grabbed my car keys from the desk. I'd learned what I needed to know – that Bella would be at Julia's – and could only hope she wouldn't sense my purpose.

The suburbs, the underwater tunnel where the rush hour had already begun, the city centre on the far side full of queues of traffic, the relative release the motorway eventually provided, adding my car to the race home – I was much less aware of any of this than of the glances I kept having to give the mirror. There was never any sign of an intruder, but had there been until just before she'd sent my parents to their deaths? Perhaps my thoughts weren't quite enough to bring her, unless she couldn't find an excuse to absent herself from where she was. Only my own nervousness had undermined my driving by the time I reached Julia's house.

The shadow of the tall building dulled the colours of the tagged flowers in the front garden. When I opened the gate the latch gave a clank loud enough for a doorbell. It could easily have alerted someone, but the house was so quiet that except for seeing Julia's car on the road I might have imagined the place was deserted. More likely someone was lying in wait, since I felt observed. I had barely rung the bell when the door was snatched open. I thought Bella might have sprung the trap, but Julia confronted me. "We're about to have dinner, Patrick."

It was plainly not an invitation, although I could have taken the aroma of Asian spices for one. No doubt she'd made a vegan feast on Bella's behalf. I saw her have a second thought, which didn't lead to hospitality. "Who are you going to pretend to be now?" she said.

"Me." This was both a statement and a protest at the question. "I'm not the one who—"

Before I could finish she turned her back on me to call "It's your father, Roy."

The announcement sounded no more welcoming than her initial greeting had. The kitchen door opened at the end of the hall, and Bella was first to appear, carrying two glasses. Roy was behind her with another glass and a creaking plastic bottle of red juice. He looked no happier to see me than Julia and his companion did, though Bella's face outdid theirs for blankness. "What do you want, dad?" he said.

"I don't know why people keep asking me that sort of thing. The answer has to be the same until it's done."

"I'll ask you as well," Julia said.

"I need to speak to everybody while I have you all together."

Julia's face withdrew even more expression, and then she stepped back. "I need to do that too," she said. "Come in but don't expect to stay long."

Roy looked not far from dismayed as I crossed the threshold, while Bella betrayed a smile too faint to admit defiance. "Just put those on the table," Julia told them. "We'll go in the front room."

Cacti were arranged in the order of their dwarfish stature along an ornamental mantelpiece as roughly stony as a desert. Cushions importing patterns from Mexico squatted on a pair of chairs and on the couch, where they framed a stack of gallery catalogues and studies of Thelma's work. When Roy and Bella took the couch I wondered if they meant to join hands on top of the books. I sat on the chair Julia had left unoccupied, opposite an extravagant television screen like a blackboard waiting for a lesson to be chalked on it. "Just say what you told me before, Roy," his mother said.

His grimace almost shut his answer in. "Which?"

"Did you ring the archive to ask if a book had been found?"

"I didn't. I said."

"That's absolutely true," I said. "I did."

"And you claimed to be Roy."

Now that I understood her accusation of pretending, I liked it even less. "I did nothing of the kind."

"Hannah says you led her to believe you were."

"No, she assumed it and I hadn't time to put her right. I needed to find out about the book."

"You mean you were afraid she wouldn't tell you if you owned up. I hope you're satisfied with the result of your performance. We still have no idea where the book is."

"I can tell you someone does, and you shouldn't be accusing me."

Was I hoping Bella would own up to some reaction? Her expression – faintly puzzled and concerned, as the ignorant might expect her to look – didn't change. I was appalled by how unnatural her pose appeared to me, not to mention her very presence, and how natural to Roy and his mother. They saw a girl sitting next to her boyfriend, but I could still feel how my fingers had sunk into her flesh. I was so busy trying not to shudder that I failed to realise how fiercely I was staring at her until Roy said "Dad, stop doing that."

"What do you think I'm doing?"

"Harassing Bell. You said you wouldn't any more. You did yesterday as well."

Julia turned to face me, simultaneously leaning back as though recoiling from the sight. "What did your father do?"

"Took me looking for Bell's house and didn't even ask her first. That's all right because we never found it, because he got the place wrong."

"I didn't, Roy. If you think back—"

"Then you went there to make me think Bell's been playing tricks on me. That's the truth and I was trying not to say," he said as though I'd forced him to accuse me in front of Bella and his mother. "You tried to make it look like she'd been in that old hotel and all you did was show me you had."

"Why don't we all go and see where she lives right now? Or you can tell us why you wouldn't like it, Bella."

"We'll do no such thing," Julia declared. "When are you going to give this up, Patrick? I've told you to stop and now Roy has. Carry on if you want to lose him."

"If that's what it has to take. However much it has to." I was struggling not to let my dismay at the prospect hinder me. "How about you, Bella?" I said. "Are you feeling harassed?"

"I feel the same as Roy."

"Don't say you have no feelings of your own, or is that part of how you're made? I'm sure you've convinced Roy you have some."

"Patrick, I think it's time for you to leave." Before I could reply Julia added "And I think you'd better stay away."

"Mum's right, dad."

"Surely you won't let everyone do your talking for you, Bella. You had plenty to say to me."

Roy kept his unhappy stare on me as he said "What does he mean, Bell?"

For the first time she seemed disconcerted, and I experienced a surge of vicious satisfaction. "Patrick," Julia said, "for the second and last time—"

I held Bella's resolutely innocent gaze with mine. "Give her a chance to speak. You can see she wants to be heard."

Perhaps this provoked her, unless it simply left her no option except to respond. "All right, I feel harassed. I didn't want to say."

"There's your answer, Patrick, and now will you please—"

"What don't they know about, Bella?"

Julia had let her recover herself. "You'll have to explain that, Patrick."

"You haven't told them what I meant before."

"I should think you ought to know that best of anyone."

"Come on, Bell," Roy said and looked at her at last. "If you know, you tell us."

With a wistfulness that turned my mouth sour Bella said "Has he made you suspicious of me?"

"If he says you know what he's on about I expect you do, unless he's mad."

I saw her consider suggesting some version of this, but then she reached for her bag. "Since you're insisting, you can hear for yourself."

I couldn't believe I'd guessed her intention until she produced the phone – my aunt's phone. Before I could identify it aloud I was silenced by my own voice. "You know who this is and why. Let me have an answer."

"That's harassment if ever I heard some," Julia said. "An answer to what, may we ask?"

"To a lot of things that need one. What do you say, Bella?"

"I assumed you just meant I should call you back. And to save Patrick the trouble of pointing it out, this phone used to belong to his aunt. I had it from my father."

Though she was forgetting to sound Roy's age, nobody else appeared to have noticed. "Father," I said with no tone at all.

"Yes, Patrick," Julia said, "her father. What are you trying to imply?"

"I was wondering if we're ever going to meet him."

"I'd say there's increasingly less reason why you should."

"Are you making other people speak for you again, Bella?"

She met this with a sad look that I was dismayed to think might be enough for Roy and his mother. I was about to provoke more of a response when Roy said "Bell..."

His hesitation suggested doubt, and I found I was holding my breath. "What do you want to say, Roy?" she said.

"How could your dad have got that phone? Dad's aunt wouldn't have given it to him, would she?"

"I wasn't suggesting she did. He acquired it after, you'll forgive me, Patrick, after she'd no more use for it."

How much longer would it take her listeners to notice that Bella's speech had stopped pretending to be youthful? I hoped Roy was about to comment along those lines, but he said "Still doesn't make sense."

As I nearly shut my eyes to contain a surge of hope Julia said "Roy, you shouldn't let your father come between you."

"I'm not. I'm only thinking." The hand he extended towards Bella resembled a plea. "How come it wasn't broken when she fell?" he said.

"Because she was so preoccupied she left it at home."

When he failed to question this I said "How would you know that?"

"I don't believe I did. I should think we can guess that's what may have happened."

"Or her father could have told her, Patrick."

I saw Roy accept at least one explanation. I had to carry out my plan, however devastating the result would be. I was taking quite a breath when Julia said "Dinnertime now or it'll be ruined."

As we competed to be first at standing up I said "I suppose I'm not included."

"I'm afraid that's very much the case."

"Then I hope you're better soon, Roy. I'm worried, and I expect your mother must be."

"It's just a cold," Julia said as Roy hid the evidence of a cough behind a hand. "How these men do suffer, Bella. I've seen you survive worse, Patrick."

I was dismayed by her insistence on the commonplace, but hadn't I previously tried that myself? Caution left me as I said "And let's hope your condition improves, Bella."

She and Roy and his mother stared at me, and Bella looked no less uncomprehending than they did. "What one's that?" Roy said.

"The problem with her back."

"She hasn't got a problem." With a little less conviction Roy said "Have you, Bell?"

"I wouldn't say so. I hope you won't give me any, Patrick."

The disguised threat only provoked me to tell Roy "You don't know her as well as you should. She mustn't have needed to let you that close."

"I believe you were leaving, Patrick," Julia said in a voice that had stiffened with control.

"Give us a minute, mum," Roy said and confronted me. "What aren't I supposed to know?"

"Why don't you show them, Bella?"

Her look was maintaining its innocence. "I've nothing to show."

"Then show them that."

As I willed her to betray understanding, she turned up her empty hands. "How can I show nothing?"

"You can hide how you are the same way you've hidden other things, can't you? Only you forgot to hide it from me."

Julia strode to throw the door wide and stood by it, glaring at me as Roy demanded "What are you saying she hid? When could she even have?"

"I've already said, her back. Your shoulders aren't quite what they should be, are they, Bella? Not entirely formed."

"Is that how I am, Roy? What would you say?"

I thought this might be less an appeal than a concealed spell or a means of reviving the effects of one, especially since Roy said "I think you're pretty perfect."

"No need just to think," I said. "You can touch them and find out. Nobody will mind."

Julia made to protest but then aimed just her glare at me as Roy leaned across the stack of books about my aunt to stroke Bella's left shoulder. When he reached further, the stack tottered, slipping awry. He drew his hand across both shoulders before straightening up. His face looked reluctant to admit an expression. "What is that, Bell? It wasn't there last time."

I saw Bella realise as I did that their visits to occult sites had heightened his perceptions. Perhaps she'd been able to block them until now, and her careless invitation had let them in. "I'm sorry if you find me wanting," she said.

"Happy now, Patrick?" Julia said. "Do you think you've gone far enough?"

I feared I might not have, though Bella's protest hadn't been quite immediate enough to hide a hint of discomposure. "I don't care. You're still you," Roy told her, but then the hand he'd reached out gestured as if desperate to grasp the air. "Only how did he know?"

"It was the last time you came to me, wasn't it, Bella?" I saw no point in stopping short now. "Last night in my bedroom," I said.

"Get out, Patrick," Julia said. "Get out this minute."

I watched Roy's hand sink as though its fingers had grown leaden and slump on the topmost book. Bella widened her eyes to display their depths of innocence, but the charm failed to work. The increased sensitivity she'd conferred on Roy was working against her, and I could tell he sensed some of her falseness. "Yes, get out," he said.

"Roy, you said you wouldn't let your father turn you against me."

"He hasn't," Roy said and gave her a feverish stare. "You have."

"Roy, think of all we've done together. Think how close we've grown. Are you really going to believe him when—"

"It's just I don't believe you any more."

"I think you should both leave," Julia said. "I'd appreciate your doing so at once."

To my hysterical astonishment, Bella tried appealing to her, a move I found grotesquely inhuman. "Who do you mean, Julia?"

"Are you seriously asking that? Not Roy. Not my poor son."

For a moment I thought Bella would refuse to leave, lingering until some aspect of her presence overwhelmed everyone in the room. Then she gave a shrug that I imagined flexing the hollows in her shoulders and sauntered past Julia into the hall. I thought it best to keep an eye on her, but I hadn't reached the hall when I heard her open the front door. As I made for it, Julia stayed alongside. "You've excelled yourself, Patrick. I wouldn't have thought even you could be that jealous," she said, and with further loathing "I wonder if you broke the law."

She shut the door as soon as I was out of the house. No doubt she'd seen Bella waiting beyond the gate. I was determined not to be daunted by the sight – by the small face concentrated around those great eyes like emblems of a secret close to revelation, or a threat withholding its words. "Shall I take you back where you live?" I said.

"I've no need of you, Patrick. You'll wish I had." She turned away in the direction of the abandoned hotel, and I made for my car. As it unlocked with a chorus of clicks I heard her voice at my back. "Expect me any time," it said. She sounded close enough to touch, but when I glanced around, the street was as empty as death.

CHAPTER TWENTY-SEVEN
The Constant Visitor

By the time I reached home my hands ached from gripping the wheel, and my neck had grown stiff from twisting my head around whenever a glance in the mirror failed to suffice. I was afraid the absence of any unwelcome reflection needn't mean I was alone in the car. Each time I found myself surrounded by traffic, panic closed in too, a fear that I might be distracted from driving and cause a crash as my father had. When I left the motorway at last I felt just as vulnerable at every junction, fearful I'd be tricked into losing control, crossing the line in front of an oncoming vehicle or lurching past a red light. I hoped the tunnel could offer some respite, but it felt like being buried too far underground for miles. Knowing the river was overhead for much of the length of the tunnel didn't help. Surely even Bella couldn't cause it to be flooded, which simply meant she had some other fate in store for me. I kept telling myself I'd needed to act as I had in order to protect Roy, but until I did I'd failed to grasp how I would be alone with whatever I'd brought on myself.

The whole of my apartment felt as if it housed a threat, even once I'd switched on all the lights. The emptiness of every room needn't mean any of them would remain deserted when I turned my back. Although the bathroom mirror showed nobody behind me, I couldn't help glancing around, for the reflection had started to feel like a trick. I was glad to leave it behind, even if this meant retreating to my bedroom. At least the quilt lay too flat to be concealing an intruder, and I was trying to persuade myself that I should do my best to sleep when I noticed a faint trail glistening on the pillow.

It might have been left by a snail or a slug. Was it meant to tell me nowhere was a refuge? When I seized one corner of the pillow I felt as if I were about to turn over a stone. I jerked the pillow aside, and the object that had left the trail reached to lick my wrist before withdrawing into a mouth. Apart from the wide gleeful eyes, these were the only features the flattened face displayed. With a grin that promised worse to come, it vanished into the mattress as though sinking into a marsh.

I was in the corridor before I had the least idea where I was going. The face had hardly bothered to resemble Bella's – just enough to let me know she could turn up wherever she chose. There was no point in trying to sleep on the couch – she could find me there quite as readily – and so I fell into a chair, which at least had its back to the wall. I tried not to think that the intruder could seep through the bricks or otherwise reappear. The remote control of the television found me a comedy even more monochrome than the night outside the window, but I was distracted from the elegant antics of the wealthy characters, so prosperous in the midst of the depression that they might have been inhabiting a fairy tale, by an incomplete but vigorous figure that kept prancing less than wholly into sight behind them. Was I glimpsing the reflection of a visitor flattened like a cut-out or an insect on the wall beside me? Before long the sideways jerking of my head revived the ache in my neck, and I yielded to closing my eyes. I had a hopeless notion that unawareness couldn't leave me any more at risk than awareness would.

I awoke whenever I nodded, unless slumber sometimes dragged me too deep. Apparently the channel was broadcasting an all-night marathon of comedies, because I kept catching fragments where different performers were enacting similar routines, all of which felt like a joke at my expense. Some of the soundtracks were so worn that whispers seemed to lurk behind the dialogue, and more than once I lurched awake with a sense that somebody had spoken close to me. One thought masqueraded as reassurance: that when day came I should go to my office at the university. It felt like a remote promise of the dawn.

At last the world outside the window grew as grey as the onscreen film, and eventually regained colours – red roofs, blue sea and bluer sky. Switching off the television, I headed for the bathroom, where I stood in the bath and backed away from the shower so as not to be chilled by the initial rush of water. Despite the August day, I felt cold, still more so when a red-hot needle jabbed my shin. It was a splash of scalding water from the shower.

When must I have switched on the immersion heater to make the water so hot? I couldn't recall the last time I had, which might suggest I'd done it in my sleep, unless somebody had meant me to be injured, perhaps disfigured. I leapt out of the bath to crane around the vicious onslaught of water and ease the hot tap nearly shut. Steam rose from the bath, clouding the mirror on the cupboard by the sink. As I cleared the glass with a thoughtless gesture I remembered the moment at my aunt's when I'd revealed a trespasser behind the condensation on a mirror. This time I'd uncovered nothing of the sort, but as my wrist snagged the corner of the mirror the cupboard door swung open, and a grinning face swelled out on a neck like the elongated tube of a balloon.

I staggered backwards and barely saved myself from overbalancing into the bath, where the water that had gathered might have scalded me or worse. Had this been the plan? When I recovered myself I saw the cupboard contained nothing unfamiliar. "Playing games, are we?" I said but felt it best to keep any further challenge to myself.

I let the water out of the bath before stepping in. The mundane action left me feeling trapped between the uncanny and the banal, unable to engage with either. One idea let me believe my behaviour had some purpose: I needed to get ready to go to my office. The bath felt perilously slippery under my bare feet, and I clutched at the handle on the tiled wall once I'd brought the shower up to a timid temperature. If I lost my balance I felt certain I would fall through the glass panel beside the shower – if a face were to thrust itself out of the water into mine. I finished showering as soon as I could, and as I clambered out of the bath a face sprang at me from the cupboard on the wall. My shoulder slammed against the glass panel before I grasped that it was my own blurred face in the mirror.

The realisation didn't stop me feeling spied upon. As I dried myself and dressed I had to restrain a compulsion to challenge the watcher. I was afraid that acknowledging its presence would invite some worse intrusion. Even breakfast felt composed of threats – the water bubbling in the percolator, the red-hot interior of the toaster. How easily could I be tricked into injuring myself with them? I had a growing sense that I would need to be constantly on guard for the rest of my life.

On my way downstairs I took out my car key and then returned it to my pocket. I mustn't risk driving while I could be fatally distracted, and I didn't know if I would ever drive again. I bought a ticket at the station and made for the platform, only to retreat into the booking hall, having seen there was no train. I wasn't about to risk being thrown under the next to arrive. I'd already felt at the mercy of traffic while crossing the road.

A protracted squeal announced a train, and once it crawled to an absolute stop I ventured onto the platform. Just a few passengers left the train, but I had a sense that somebody was using every one of them for cover, dodging behind them all without ever straying into sight. As far as I could see, which no longer meant enough, the carriage I boarded was deserted. When a woman spoke close to me I started as though I'd been wakened from a dream, though it was only the overhead voice of the train. "In the interests of passenger safety…" The advice to stay alert felt like a grim joke at my expense.

I'd still seen nobody in the carriage by the time the train moved off. When it reached the next station someone looked in from the platform, but didn't appear to board. At the following station they loomed outside the window again, and I glimpsed the face that was regaining its features, which were all too familiar. Each time the train halted, the gathering figure grew more recognisable, closer to human. I did my utmost to ignore it, especially once the train sped underground, where the face took to swimming out of the dark between the stations and pressing itself like a perfectly flat mask against the glass. It was only trying to work on my nerves, I told myself, to leave me more susceptible to peril. "Childish," I muttered. "Not even puckish. Not clever at all."

This didn't work. It was no kind of spell. The apparition left me nervous of my next encounter once I was off the train. As I rode up to the station concourse I seemed to glimpse it leaping upwards behind scattered commuters on the downward escalator. I couldn't locate it in the street, where crowds were busy ignoring squatters on the pavement and in doorways. I peered at every seated figure and every supine one to reassure myself their faces weren't familiar, and before long I ran out of change to drop in plastic cups. I had a vague sense of bidding to buy myself grace, but no idea whether that would work.

I was climbing the slope to the university when I found myself straying towards the edge of the pavement. Perhaps this was a symptom of sleeplessness, but it felt as though a companion was leaning against me, so nearly insubstantially that I hadn't noticed they were inching me towards the traffic. I kept having to lurch away from the road as I trudged uphill. When I reached a crossing between sections of the campus I poked the button and gripped the pole until the red light halted the traffic. I'd set foot on the crossing when a van jerked forward to speed through the lights, and I felt the chill wind of the side mirror that had barely missed my head. It left me shaking, and I suspected the driver had been no more to blame for the incident than my father had been responsible for his crash.

A few students were wandering the campus. Since they weren't mine, they must have wondered why I stared at them or more precisely past them in search of a dodging lurker. My card let me through the barrier by the reception desk, and the receptionist said "Dr Semple," surely not alerting anyone to my arrival. I tramped up the bare stairs and unlocked my office, and stared around the room. As I blinked at the shelves of books and the desk occupied by a computer, I felt as if I was very gradually wakening. There was no reason why I should be here today at all.

I remembered imagining I heard a whisper in the night, and now I knew I had. While I was asleep I'd been directed here by a spell that felt close to hypnosis. Perhaps the purpose was to lure me away from my apartment so that some mischief could be perpetrated there – and then, as though I'd wakened fully at last, I knew it was more dangerous. I'd been decoyed into the open, where I would be most at risk.

I locked my room and kept hold of the banister all the way down the stairs, where every step felt like a chance to be tripped from behind. I couldn't begin to anticipate how many opportunities to do away with me the homeward journey might contain. "Dr Semple," the receptionist said as though my departure called for an announcement too. "Leaving us already?"

"That's the idea," I said, feeling as if we'd hastened my demise. I had no time to choose my words, because the traffic lights had halted a taxi outside. Dodging through the barrier, I ran at the automatic doors, only to realise that if they didn't open fast enough I would smash the glass. Perhaps this was to be a variation on the fatal injury I hadn't suffered in the shower, and all the intervening events had been contrived to leave me careless. The doors sidled aside just enough to let me through, and I dashed onto the pavement. "Taxi," I shouted, waving violently as well. "Taxi."

"I hear you, pal."

This was both an acknowledgment and a gruff rebuke. The driver's greying hair trailed over the shoulders of his matching T-shirt, and appeared to have tugged the crown of his squat head bald. With a look that barely rose above morose he watched me clamber into the back. "Can we go to New Brighton?" I said.

"Go anywhere you want long as you've got the price."

I assumed he wasn't prompting me to confirm I had, though his attention lingered in the mirror before he started the meter. The taxi swung away from the kerb rather too close to a car, and I told myself I was safer here than on foot. Whenever the driver glanced in the mirror as we sped towards the tunnel, I hoped he wasn't being distracted in order to put me in danger. The tunnel shut me in with dimness, and I wished I could be sure where he kept looking – at me or the road behind? Surely if he saw I'd acquired a companion from the dark he wouldn't stay as silent as he was. I couldn't see any intruder, even when we emerged into daylight. Once we were past the pay booths I said "Up the ramp and second exit from the roundabout."

We were on the roundabout when the taxi swerved into the adjacent lane, and a lorry roared behind it like a dinosaur. "Make your mind up, pal," the taxi driver said.

I thought he should have directed the reproof at himself. "What did he do?" I asked instead.

"Not him, pal, you. Which way do you want?"

"The way I said. Towards New Brighton."

We veered back into the inner lane and raced around the roundabout while the driver objected "That's the thing you said first."

I stared into his eyes, though willing him to keep his attention on the road. "It's all I said."

"Don't be having a laugh, pal. Nothing wrong with my ears," the driver said and swung the taxi off the roundabout at speed. "Then you told me to go the other way instead."

Although I knew that no response would be any use, I couldn't help retorting "Did it really sound like me?"

He stared at me in the mirror longer than I thought was safe. "You're the only feller in here besides me."

I mustn't add to the distractions that might be brought to bear on him, and I stayed quiet until we approached a junction. "Straight on," I said, and hastily "When the lights are green."

This time his stare was even more prolonged. "Don't need to tell me that, pal."

I managed just to send him onwards at each set of lights, until at last we had to turn right. The road led to the station, and the taxi drew up outside it, not quite what I'd directed. "I'm just across the road," I said.

"Good for you, pal."

He either didn't trust my guidance or had tired of it, and I'd had enough of him. Surely I could cross the street without being run over. I dug in my pocket for notes and handed them through the gap in the glass partition. "Sorry I've no less. Just give me six," I said.

He glared at the handful I'd passed him and screwed his head around on his stubby reddish neck to train all the force of his disfavour on me. "Less of the laughs, pal. That's no joke."

"I'm sorry, what isn't?"

He thrust his hand under the partition, and I saw he was holding torn scraps of paper. I recognised the writing on them – Lumen Scientiae's script – and glimpsed the names Bal and Bel before the driver threw the handful out of his window. "Let's have the cash," he said, "or I'll be calling the law."

I fumbled money out of my pocket, or at least that was what it felt like. Yes, I'd found a scrawny wad of ten-pound notes, two of which the driver accepted with a display of ill grace. He passed me a pound coin and a crumpled grubby fiver, and as I climbed out I saw the fragments of the page under the taxi. I was loitering on the pavement to retrieve them when he moved off, and a trickle of oil from beneath the vehicle blackened every scrap. The sight infuriated me so much that I stalked across the road, and if I'd failed to notice any traffic I might well not have reached the other side. My survival only postponed the next attempt on my life.

Nothing appeared to have changed in the apartment, but this needn't mean nothing was hidden. As soon as I finished searching all the rooms I felt compelled to search again, though what would this achieve? If an intruder was waiting to rear up behind me in the bathroom mirror, unless it revealed its lair behind the shelves of books or produced its flattened face out of the blackness of the television screen, I would know soon enough – when it decided to amuse itself with me again or else exact a worse revenge. Nowhere in the world was safer than my apartment, which was by no means to pretend it was safe.

I sat in front of the computer to persuade myself I had a future I should work for, and succeeded in adding a few sentences but less insight. I heated up a casserole I'd made days ago, and almost dropped it when the oven door sprang open, perhaps because I'd neglected to secure it properly, unless it had been undone from within by the owner of the face I seemed to glimpse shrinking into the dark. Afterwards I sat in my chair against the wall and watched a variety of television broadcasts. The documentaries and newscasts seemed as unreal as the fiction films, every one a brittle shell of narrative that hid a lethal truth. The intrusion could reveal itself anywhere in the room, and the wall at my back felt just as unreliable as protection, but I found the prospect of going to bed more daunting still. I had no idea when I began to nod and flounder awake, nor when I remained asleep.

A change wakened me. There was more light in the room than I remembered having seen. I opened my eyes to find daylight paling the overhead bulb. I had a feeling that it wasn't the only development, but why was I afraid to learn what else had happened? I was alone in the room, and not just in the room. As I made my awareness reach out I sensed no threat of any kind, nor the least hint of a presence.

At first I thought it was a trick, although I didn't see how my sensitivity to the kind of trespassing I'd suffered could be blocked. If

I was really no longer in danger, why did I feel more nervous than ever? Because there was only one reason why Bella would relent, and the possibility dismayed me more than staying endangered myself. I had to know, and I groped for my phone, but the call went unanswered for so long that I'd begun to wonder whose voice any recorded message might use by the time the simulated trill was interrupted. "Yes."

Though the flatness of the word invited no response, I said "May I assume we can talk?"

"You may assume what you like."

"Then I'm assuming I'm to be left alone."

"Quite an assumption after all you've tried to do."

"All the same, it feels as if I am."

"You've opened up your mind a little, have you? Then you should discover for yourself whether you can trust it. It's hardly up to me to provide reassurance."

"If I'm right, I'd just like to know why you've finished with me."

"Patrick, you sound as if you feel jilted." With the same faint amusement Bella said "Because you failed."

As though this weren't enough to confirm my worst fears I heard Roy say "Is that my dad?"

"I'm afraid so," Bella said.

"Let me talk to him." In a moment his voice grew close and harsh. "What do you want now?"

"Just finding out the situation, which I can't pretend I understand."

"That's because you don't understand us. That's why you didn't manage to split us up."

Less like a plea than an expression of dismay I said "So make me understand."

"Bell showed me what she was wearing when you saw her back. She's got it on now."

"I did more than see, Roy, and she let me."

"Why are you keeping up this shit? It won't work on me." A cough delayed more of his protest. "Bell says you never touched her," he said, "and she was never in your room."

In growing desperation I said "Then where did we meet?"

"On the promenade, Bell says."

"And why would we do that?"

"Because she wanted to find out why you're so against us, and she thought it might be easier for you to say if I wasn't there."

I was searching for a way to regain his trust when I had a thought that seemed to offer some hope. "Your mother's been persuaded too, has she?"

Roy's cough let him pause before admitting "She doesn't know."

"Doesn't know you're back together, you mean." Since he let this pass unanswered I said "How do you think she'll react when she does?"

"I expect her situation would be very much like yours, Patrick," Bella said.

I hoped Roy could sense the threat this hardly bothered to conceal, although wouldn't the insight endanger him? Instead he retorted "Tell her if you want. She won't break us up any more than you did."

His voice trailed away into a stutter of dry coughs, and I was sure his energy had been depleted by the spell Bella must be exerting over him. "And where are you now?" I tried asking.

"Where Bell needs to be."

I'd feared so. "How much more of that is there?"

"The last one's tomorrow."

I wanted to believe this would release him, but I was afraid how much it might drain him. Before I could ask their present location he said "Got to go."

It sounded nothing like an invitation to call again, and his companion issued none. "Come and see me, Bella," I said. "There's something we ought to discuss."

Roy had already ended the call, but I knew she would receive my summons, and it was better that he didn't hear. No doubt she would come to me wherever I was, but suppose she assumed I'd found another way to thwart her? Once again I felt safest staying at home. In time shadows crept into the apartment, and then Bella did. Her silhouette appeared against the wall beside the television at least a few moments before she took shape like a cut-out figure swelling plumper. She wore a blouse that exposed her shoulders, or at any rate the apparition of one. "So that's how you fooled him,"

I said in an attempt to contain my shiver. "That's one of the ways you did."

"How concerned you are to reduce everything to your level, Patrick."

"I'm just concerned for my son."

"I presume that's how a parent is expected to behave."

"You're the one whose behaviour is restricted, Bel, or is it Bal? You've admitted that's how you are."

"Not for much longer," Bella said with a smile of careless triumph.

"Tomorrow's the day, is it? What happens then?"

"I shall be free."

"Free to do what?"

"To live as I have every right to do."

"And what will that entail?"

"I shall know that when I'm whole at last."

I found this menacingly ominous, and it mightn't even be the worst development. "What about Roy?"

"What indeed. Another issue to be settled in the future."

I wasn't going to let this lie undefined. "How much more are you going to take out of him?"

"He should live." As my reaction choked off my speech Bella said "And if not he'll have lived more than most of you achieve."

My nails bent as I dug my fingers into the leathery arms of the chair, but I managed to relax a fraction before saying what I'd already vowed to propose. "Use me instead."

"That's quite touching, Patrick. Playing the father up to the hilt."

I didn't know if she was mocking me or simply found my behaviour almost too alien to understand. "You don't need him," I persisted. "You just need someone, and you were after me in the first place."

"I'm afraid you've lost the young mind you once had."

"What does it have to do with minds? All you need is someone's energy to draw on." As a shiver overwhelmed me I said "You're using mine right now to help you be here."

"I find younger is preferable, Patrick. More vital."

Despite feeling appalled by her clinical attitude, I could only do my best to match it. "I promise you I've got enough vitality for your last excursion."

"I wonder. Perhaps you might have." As I dared to hope I'd

persuaded her she said "But I've grown really quite attached to Roy."

"Attached." I had to swallow before I could restrain myself to saying "Not the way I am, or his mother."

"You have no idea of my feelings, Patrick."

Was she feigning pique, or had I reminded her that she wasn't as human as she liked to appear? "Then give me some idea," I said.

"I see no need, and in any case it's too late."

"Not if I take you where you have to go tomorrow. That ought to save some of your energy for where you'll want it most, and you'll be giving me a little of what you say you've given Roy."

Bella widened her eyes as though to make space for my words, and I was afraid my attempts at persuasion had cancelled one another. "Well, I believe Julia is right," she said.

With some reluctance I said "In what way?"

"You're jealous of your son's relationship with me."

"If that's what you need to believe." When this didn't shift her amused look I risked saying "My aunt thought I was worth sharing secrets with. Perhaps you should too."

"You're trying to appeal to nostalgia, are you, Patrick? You want me to indulge you for old times' sake."

"If that's how you see it. However you care to that lets you" – I fumbled for a phrase that might persuade her – "accept my help."

Her amusement was starting to fade. "Perhaps you had an insight after all."

"Which would that be?" I had to ask.

"Being driven by you would conserve some of my energy tomorrow."

"Then you want me to."

I was afraid my eagerness had made her think again until she said "You'd best collect me as early as you can."

I was relieved to think I wouldn't have to spend the night in any sense with her, and she couldn't spend it with Roy while he was at his mother's. "Where from?" I said.

"Where we both know I live. You see, there are insights we share after all." Bella's teeth gleamed, not quite in a smile. "Show me you trust me, Patrick," she said.

I could think of no excuse to avoid asking "How would I do that?"

"Close your eyes while I depart. Don't open them until you feel I have."

This seemed unavoidable as well, to prevent her from changing her mind about tomorrow. I shut my eyes and squeezed them tighter in a bid to fend off a sense of a transformation in the room. I had the impression that my visitor had reared up nearly as high as the ceiling and was determined to make me look, to betray how false my show of trust was. I seemed to sense a face reaching off the head to hover so close to mine that I ought to feel its breath, and hands stretching on their elongated arms to finger the air just inches from my face. My eyes were throbbing with an imitation of light by the time the face and hands withdrew, and at last I sensed how the entire body did, into a distance to which the empty air led. My eyes faltered open, and on seeing I was alone I let out a gasp that left all words behind.

CHAPTER TWENTY-EIGHT

A Final Darkness

"Roy."

My phone spoke his name before I did. I'd just left the motorway and was close to where I had to be, but now I was afraid Bella had delegated him to send me home. I pulled over on a street where most of the parked cars were twice the height of mine, and a hulking dog began to bark through the elegantly twisted bars of a gate. "Yes, Roy," I said.

"She's gone, dad."

His voice was so toneless that I couldn't judge what he meant to convey. Was he accusing me of having separated them or telling me that she was out of both our lives? In the hope of learning more I said "You're talking about Bella."

"Who else am I going to mean?"

Hearing his distress, I felt dismayed to think how much of his life she might represent just now. I couldn't tell him that however devastating separation felt at his age, you soon survived. "How do you know she has?" I said.

"She gave me a bell."

It sounded like a bitter joke, a bid to leave his real emotions behind. "What did she say?"

"She's had enough of me. I mean she thinks she's been using me. That's what you've made her think."

"I can't see how she would," I risked saying, "unless it was the case."

"She says she's used me enough for learning what your aunt did. I tried to tell her that hasn't got to be the end of us, but I couldn't get through to her. She's gone cold on me."

"Perhaps you're seeing the real Bella."

At once I feared I'd said too much, especially when silence responded, but then he said "You didn't know her like I did."

I hoped I was taking enough care by saying "Roy, you have to accept how she's behaved is real."

"Not the way you mean."

"Which way, then?"

"I think she thought wherever she's going today might be too much somehow. She was looking after me, dad."

I heard how much he wanted to persuade me and perhaps needed this himself. I was leaving his belief unchallenged when he said "She isn't answering her phone. If I knew where she was going I'd find her."

I couldn't resist asking "How do you think she knows where to go?"

"Maybe it was in the book we read in the library. I told you she read more than me."

I doubted that Lumen Scientiae had predicted his own place of burial, but I was refraining from making the point when Roy said "Maybe you saw where."

So this was why he'd called. I felt absurdly satisfied to have a chance to tell some truth. "I've no idea where she's planning to go."

"I don't suppose you'll be seeing her again."

I was ashamed to resort to saying "It seems unlikely, doesn't it."

"Only if you should be in touch after all, can you ask her to call me? If she's done what she didn't want to take me to there's no reason we can't get back together."

I could think of several that I didn't voice. Fearing he might ask me to phone Bella on his behalf, I said "Anyway, I should be on the move."

The dog was still barking as though it had sensed an intruder. "Where are you, dad?" Roy said.

"On my way to see someone. Call me whenever you like," I felt obliged to say, hastily adding "Any time at all after today."

Could the prohibition make him suspicious? Might he even guess I was meeting Bella? If he was at his mother's it would take him just a few minutes to walk to the short cut he'd seen Bella use. Surely he had no reason to assume I was going there, but I drove to it as fast as I dared and pulled up opposite the gap in the misshapen wall. At once I saw Bella emerging from the gloom.

As she stepped off the dark path between the trees I had the fancy that she was quitting a canvas of Thelma's, one of those that showed her lurking in a forest. She wore a T-shirt and equally black jeans along with sandals, or at least the appearance of all those, and was carrying her bag. She crossed the road almost too swiftly to watch, and took the seat next to me with a single movement as lithe as water. "I thought I'd see you sooner, Patrick," she said.

"I was talking to my son."

"Ever the concerned father." Presumably she had no reason to keep up her youthful style now that Roy couldn't hear. "Was the conversation private?" she said.

"How could it be when you're around?" Though I wasn't sure she hadn't overheard it somehow, I said "He wanted me to help him get you back."

"I'm the property of no man, and I hope you told him."

"You treated him like yours, didn't you? Dropped him as soon as he wasn't enough use to you."

"He still could be. Shall we collect him on the way? I don't doubt he'd be grateful."

I was already regretting my response. "We agreed he should be left alone."

Bella repelled the notion with the back of a hand, so that I thought she'd changed her mind until she said "Then take some responsibility, Patrick."

Rather than meet this with a retort I said "You need to tell me where we're going."

"Take the highway north."

"The motorway, you mean."

"Whatever speeds us northward."

I was unsettled by a sense that her speech kept reverting to her age. As I turned the car across the road it confronted the gap in the wall, prompting me to ask "Why have you been living here?"

"I was made to live where no man lives, to lie there until summoned. Very soon I shall inhabit your world and more besides."

Her second comment quelled any sympathy I'd begun to feel. "And what will you do then?"

"Make them mine. Bring them together."

While I had no idea what this might entail, it seemed ominous beyond words. I stayed silent as we headed for the motorway, and Bella was as quiet as any of my aunt's paintings, so that I had a notion that for the moment she was no more than a token presence. I could have thought she meant to reinforce it by saying "Shall we travel with some music from my past?"

I wondered if she'd known what was waiting to be heard, because the broadcast that had just started was Purcell – *The Fairy Queen*. "Come, let us leave the town, and in some lonely place..." This sounded uncannily similar to my route, and I had to suppress a fancy that Bella was somehow controlling the radio, unless we were hearing the opera when nobody else could. For a while I listened to the lyrical antics of the fairy folk, which felt dishonestly remote from the behaviour of my companion, but as the characters played their Shakespearian games in the woods I couldn't help wondering "Were you there?"

"In such a forest? Whenever you were, Patrick."

"No," I said, though the possibility I had in mind was just as troubling. "When it was performed."

"I existed then and long before. He who brought me into your world did no more than contain me."

I found I preferred not to enquire further, and regretted learning even so much. By now we were on the northward motorway. "Don't forget you're directing me," I said.

"Set your course for the heights."

I took this to refer to the Lake District, unless it had an occult connotation. In an hour the horizon ahead began to grow mountainous, by which time the sequence of fairyland broadcasts had moved on to Mendelssohn. Fells rose beside the motorway, framing sunlit lakes, but Bella had no word for me. We were approaching the northernmost lakeland town when she said "Now the depths, Patrick."

"I don't know what you mean."

"Leave the highway and I'll guide you further."

Once I took the next exit she directed me northeastwards into a landscape veined with streams and shadowy with forests, rearing its fells high. We'd turned aside from the town without reaching it, and entered a region where the inhabitants were denoted only by the names of unseen villages or sites: Killhope, Heads Nook, How, Long Meg and Her Daughters, Scale Houses, Unthank... I'd met no vehicles for miles of narrow winding road by the time Bella said "Right here."

This sounded ominously immediate until I saw she was indicating the direction at a crossroads, which presumably she'd seen before I did. The pointers of the signpost that protruded from a hedge were so rotten that the words on them hardly resembled language. The lane I turned along was even narrower and more devious than the road I'd left. Spiky hedges shut it in, and the fields beyond them only underlined how constricted a route I was being forced to follow. I'd been constantly twisting the wheel and braking at bends for at least a mile when Bella said "Now left."

Once again she'd anticipated a junction in advance of me. Her voice conveyed less expression than the navigator on my phone would have, but I wondered if she might be hiding some emotion. The pointer at the entrance to the side lane was so weathered and decayed that the illegible word it bore appeared to have been written in an occult script, unless the letters were reverting to ancient symbols. When the lane was made it would have offered just enough space for a car to pass another, but now the neglected hedges left no room. I didn't know whether I was more nervous of encountering another vehicle or of being alone on the secretive road. As my eyes began to ache with the relentless sunlight that the bends in the road kept returning straight into my face, Bella said "Down."

She couldn't have addressed the word more curtly to a dog. I tried to let resentment overcome my nervousness, but her direction sounded threatening as well. The car rounded a sharp bend, and I saw where she meant us to go. To the left an unsignposted lane led downwards between walls composed of jagged stones heaped higher than a man. Beyond the junction the road I was following widened towards a vista of slopes piebald with gorse and heather, and I had to resist an impulse to speed past the side road. "This is it, then," I said.

"As it must be."

Did Bella want to stifle conversation to some purpose? When she used one upturned hand to indicate the route I could have thought she wasn't anxious to be heard. "Let's get it done with," I said.

Hearing no reply, I turned the car down the lane, where the walls closed in at once. Stone fragments splintered beneath the wheels, and I hoped the walls weren't in danger of collapse. Some of the heaped stone looked top-heavy, far too close to overbalancing. The slope grew steeper, and even once I engaged a lower gear I felt compelled to keep tramping on the brake. I'd descended several hundred yards when the lane – little more than a dirt track – began to grow narrower still. "It might be best to walk," I said.

"Driving is swifter. Would you really choose to climb so far?"

I didn't know how far this might be, but I wondered if exertion was really the issue – if Bella simply wanted to be finished and on her way as soon as possible. Even the highest stretch of the lane had been too narrow to turn the car, and I could only hope there would be space further down. The prospect of reversing all the way back to the main road was too daunting to consider, and I eased my foot off the brake.

The right-hand wall came to an end, but the track continued downwards, enclosed on that side by bare black rock. The increasingly haphazard heap of stones crowded closer on the left, where another wall of rock had risen. I'd begun to brake every few seconds for fear of snagging the rickety structure, but it ended abruptly, revealing a valley several yards wide at the edge of the track. The surface underneath the wheels had grown more uneven, and now I was nervous that a wheel might slip over the brink. As black rock towered higher around the car, it seemed to pinch the sunlight off, steeping the route in gloom. When I saw movement on the right-hand wall I thought moisture was streaming down the rock, until I came abreast of it and made out a glistening horde of insects. I shivered as I shut my window, and the sight of the black crawling mass left me anxious to define the situation. "What are we here for?" I said.

"Perhaps you may bring away some memento too, Patrick. I doubt you can remain unchanged."

"No, I'm asking who's down here." When Bella gazed through

the windscreen without speaking I said "I take it Lumen Scientiae is."

"Don't speak the name unless you want to bring him to you."

Her voice had grown so sharp that I wondered why she should be concerned on my behalf – presumably because I might be left incapable of driving. I saw her gaze shift to the mirror, and felt reluctant to look. A generous section of the mass of insects had swarmed off the wall to hover behind the car. It resembled the upper part of a mask or else of a moist blackened face, in which two bulges could have been mistaken for large eyes, unstably hectic and yet imbued with watchful intelligence. The appearance loitered beyond the rear window while I struggled not to speed away from it, and then it swooped back to the wall. The incident made me desperate to speak, and I gestured at the bag resting in Bella's lap. "But you'll be taking some of him away with you."

"That contains him."

Her voice had settled down again, and I was determined to reach past its tonelessness. "You'll be doing what he did to you," I said. "It's your revenge."

"He is a stage of my growth," Bella said with some hauteur. "They all have been."

So was Roy, I thought, and now I was. She seemed to begrudge having spoken, and as the car inched downwards the silence let me hear an echo in my head. It was the name she'd warned me against uttering, though it didn't sound quite like my voice. I set the windscreen wipers working with a shrill scrape of plastic on glass, but switched them off when they didn't shift the darkness. The black walls were amassing it around and inside the car, and I had an impression that the dogged repetitions of the name were helping it accumulate. When I turned on the headlights the beams looked truncated, as if they'd encountered some indefinable barrier. A sudden rush of moisture or a swarm of insects streamed across the section of the track the beams illuminated, and vanished over the edge. "Summon all you will," I heard Bella murmur. "You cannot rise in time."

I wasn't anxious to learn what this meant, not least in case enquiring might help to rouse the subject, though could Bella's observation have done so? Certainly the reiteration of the name in my head was growing more insistent. The headlamp beams fumbled at the track as the car lurched aside from a large hole gouged out of the edge, and the wing mirror scraped the opposite wall. As the beams steadied rather more than my heart did, they found a level stretch at the foot of the slope. I was able to hope that the worst of the journey was over until the car reached the bottom, where the headlights showed a sheer wall at the far end of the track. I drove forwards, searching for somewhere I could turn without ending up in the river, and saw that the gloom or my fears had deceived me. While it resembled a wall, I was faced with a steep upward slope. Surely it wasn't too steep for the car to mount. "Stop now," Bella said, presumably to me.

As I dragged at the handbrake I saw that the river was barely a stream, trickling ahead into the gloom. The summer drought had reduced it so much that its liquid whisper sounded close to parched. Here beside the low point of the track most of the riverbed was exposed, and only the absence of sunlight had saved the mud from drying up. If the site was the resting place of Lumen Scientiae, it might have seemed little better than pathetic, but its lack of vitality felt ominous, the preamble to the revelation of a secret. Eager to be gone as soon as possible, I released my seat belt and was climbing out of the car when Bella said "You may stay at the wheel."

I would have resented this more if I hadn't been glad to retreat, having seen how we appeared to have descended considerably deeper than I'd thought – so deep that the sliver of daylight between the walls far overhead could have been just an illusion, while the blackness that seemed to be seeping out of the walls was the truth. As I regained my seat and fastened my safety belt, I grasped that Bella wanted to leave as soon as she finished her task, and then I realised she hadn't warned me against speaking the name for my own protection. She was concerned if not afraid for herself.

The insistent repetition of the name had started to acquire a depth that made my head feel hollow, and I wondered whether Bella was hearing the voice too. She took an empty screw-topped jar out of her bag, which she left on the seat as she emerged from the car. Her supple movement looked resolute, more consciously performed than her habitual grace. "Leave it, Patrick," she said when I made to shut her door. "And leave the engine on."

I was disconcerted to see her following the headlamp beams to the river. No doubt they illuminated her route, but did she prefer to stay clear of the dark? The ritualistic repetition in my head left very little room for thoughts, and I didn't know how it might be affecting Bella. Her behaviour made the light feel discouragingly vulnerable, a token glow in danger of being crushed by the weight of the dark. I watched her reach the riverbank, where she unscrewed the lid and bent to scoop up mud with the jar. She replaced the lid and screwed it tight before rinsing both her hand and the jar in the river. Straightening up, she gazed about with a triumphant look, and then stooped to drink a handful of water.

I took it for a gesture of defiance until I saw it give her power. As she rose to her full height she appeared to gain stature, growing taller than I'd ever seen her. She wasn't just catching the headlamp beams; she appeared to be absorbing their light, shining as luminous as a denizen of utter darkness. She had her back to me, and I glimpsed movement at her shoulders. Beneath the fabric of her T-shirt, some kind of growth was taking place in the hollows I'd felt there, perhaps a reversion to her true shape. For a moment I expected to see wings unfurl, or the emergence of some appendage still less common. Perhaps realising that the transformation would delay and hinder us, she turned back to the car.

Her eyes were bright as stars, not just with the headlamp beams but with rejoicing. She'd triumphed over everyone she'd used, I thought, and those she'd treated far worse. This filled me with a rage so fierce it was equal to my fears. "He's never seen you look like that before," I said.

Bella sent me a smile I could have taken for conspiratorial, which inflamed my anger. "But I think my parents did," I said.

"Don't spoil the moment, Patrick."

If I'd had any doubts about my course of action, this destroyed them. Though it fell short of quelling my fears, it made me reckless. "And now you don't care if your master does," I said and forced myself to say the name that was nagging at my brain. "Lumen Scientiae."

Bella's smile flickered, only to recover as she strode towards the car. "Patrick, I asked you—"

"No, you ordered me not to call him." I glimpsed activity at the limit of the headlamp beams, a pair of hectic masses surging down the walls to meet in the mud. Partly to protect myself as best I could, I lurched across the seat beside me to slam the passenger door. "Will that be him?" I said, staring along the beams. "Will that be Lumen Scientiae?"

There was movement in the mud, where a shape or at any rate the start of one looked eager to rise up. Bella glanced towards it, and her smile grew fixed. Perhaps this represented an attempt to appeal to me, but it struck me as frightful, the expression of a mask imperfectly concealing fear. "Let me in the car," she said.

"You have to be invited, do you? Not by me any more." I made sure by locking all the doors with a decisive united click. "Stay out there with your master," I said, feeling horribly victorious. "With Lumen Scientiae."

This last utterance of the name silenced the repetition in my head as if its power had been concentrated elsewhere, and at the far edge of the light a figure reared up from the mud. It might have been composed of earth or rotted vegetation or a teeming mass of insects or a combination of them all, but it had some ambition to look human. A version of an arm unstuck itself from a body that swarmed like a mass of hatching eggs, and produced an object reminiscent of a finger to point at Bella. I saw her struggle not to flinch, but I was more disturbed to realise that she wasn't looking in that direction. I glanced in the mirror, and my innards quivered. The same figure had risen behind the car, blocking all escape. It was pointing at Bella, and I could have thought the identical gestures had pinned her where she was, frozen in the headlamp beams. "Let me come in," she said, not quite admitting to a plea. "Roy wouldn't want you to treat me like this."

Was this desperation, or was she so alien that she didn't grasp how it would provoke me? "We'll see how your master does," I said.

The shape behind the car glistened crimson in the glow of the brake lights. As it bent its featureless pullulating lump of a head towards Bella, so did its twin. Though neither figure had produced any kind of mouth, I heard words that seemed to close around the space the figures bounded. They were in no language I recognised, but Bella did. Her aversion to them was so violent that it released her from her paralysis, and she darted towards the car. Her smile was struggling not to collapse while she said "Please, Patrick."

I almost relented. I found myself reaching to unlock the door as I saw the change that was overtaking her. Her wide eyes were growing dull as stagnant water, robbing her smile of all its force. She hadn't reached the car when her eyes sagged inwards, and in another moment they were nothing but blank flesh. She stumbled forwards, and her fingertips thumped the car roof. Her nails scraped the passenger window as she groped in search of the door handle, but the sound was perceptibly dwindling, as if the nails themselves were shrinking into the flesh. She had just begun to fumble blindly at the handle when I heard glass smash – the jar she'd dropped – and she gave a cry of outrage beyond words. As she began thumping on the window I saw the cause of her distress. Her fingers were shrinking into her hands like snails into their shells. In seconds the hands were nothing more than lumpy blobs of flesh.

She continued to dab at the window with increasing feebleness as her arms started to fuse with her torso, and then I watched her concentrate her struggles on her mouth, which had shrivelled to half its width under a pair of noseless nostrils that were visibly labouring to breathe. She chewed at her lips and poked them apart with her tongue to prevent them from wholly closing up. "Please," she said in a withered voice, but I didn't know to whom. Perhaps she was addressing the denizen of the valley, because she floundered away from the car. Although she was naked, having abandoned the illusion of clothes, her gender was uncertain. She staggered towards the figure at the edge of the light but faltered as her legs became a single fleshy pillar. Her attempt to take another pace threw her face down at the edge of the river. I heard a final cry – a plea or a protest – but it fell short of forming a word, and I thought her mouth had gone. In a very few moments her remains lost all their shape, and sank into the mud before the river took them.

I raised my eyes from the dismal spectacle to find that the figure I'd summoned had vanished. The mirror was deserted too, and there was no intrusive voice in my head. I moved the car forward before I'd quite stopped shivering, and drove up the slope. It took altogether too much time for me to feel I was on the way to daylight, and longer still to see it up above. I could have thought that the darkness of the valley was resolved to drag me down, or that my climb was no more than a delusion. At last the louring rock gave way to walls constructed of stacked stones, and sunlight touched the car. I was turning onto a narrow lane between fields when I heard the voice catch up with me. Although it sounded distant despite inhabiting my skull, I couldn't mistake the single word it spoke.

CHAPTER TWENTY-NINE

Safe

"Dr Semple, that was magical."

My student reached out a hand but didn't quite touch my arm. "Well, thank you," I said, only to feel the need to ask "In what way?"

"It made me want to read the book again."

I tried to find neither of his comments ominous. "That's what it should be about," I said. "We'll carry on tomorrow."

Otherwise the afternoon had been less successful. Some of the students had found *The Magus* needlessly obscure, while others had condemned it for a lack of contemporary relevance. Several had questioned the need to discuss magic at all. I'd argued that it addressed moral themes in the book, not to mention how we took reality for granted, but when somebody described the author's previous novel — *The Collector* — another girl protested that the summary should have been preceded by a trigger warning, which provoked a vigorous discussion about how safe a tutorial ought to be. I could only hope tomorrow's session would stay closer to the point, though it wasn't my way to restrict discussion too much. On the whole I was glad to be back at work, especially if it helped me move on from the events of that summer.

As I left the building I shivered. Surely this came just from the chill in the November air, and could revive nothing except memories. I was crossing the car park beneath a thin grey sky when my phone twitched in my pocket and then rang while speaking my son's name. "Roy," I said as well.

"We were just talking about you, dad."

"Nothing too bad, I hope."

"Marie was saying she wishes she was on your course."

I did my best to find this simply welcome, but experienced a twinge of unease as I said "Why's that?"

"Because she likes all the writers you're using."

"I thought she was well read. She's quite a treasure, I'd say."

In case my enthusiasm embarrassed him I tried to quiet it down. I was compensating too much for my behaviour months ago, and was abashed to realise his new girlfriend could hear. "I was hoping I could talk about them with you, Patrick," she said.

"Of course we can. Let's get together again soon." In case this sounded as if I were excluding Roy I said "I'll buy you both dinner."

"We'd like that, wouldn't we, Roy?"

"We can at the weekend. And dad..."

His tentativeness made me uneasy, and the pause did. "Go on, speak up," I said.

"Marie doesn't mind me saying, do you, Marie, but did you ever see Bella again?"

I tried not to recall how she'd atrophied while struggling to remain or become human – that recapitulated lack of shape the river had swept away into the dark. "I haven't," I said as an approximation of the truth.

"If you ever do you can tell her I'm with someone else."

Not unlike a prayer I said "I can't imagine I ever will."

"I'm glad I met her, though. She helped me get over that hang-up I had about your aunt. I don't mean I don't still like her pictures."

Could this really be all he'd retained from his weeks with Bella? I couldn't ask while Marie was listening, and perhaps not even when she wasn't there to hear. "You concentrate on the girl you've got," I said.

"Don't worry, Patrick. He is. He will."

"We'll come to you on Saturday, dad, and now mum wants a word."

"I'll take this in the kitchen while I see to dinner," Julia said.

I deduced this was a ruse to avoid being overheard. The kitchen door shut before she said "So you've made friends with Marie."

"I'd like to think so."

"You won't be taking against her when you've had enough of her."

"I'd like to think I don't know what you mean by that."

"You won't be treating her the way you did her predecessor."

"I'd have no reason that I'm aware of. She isn't the same kind at all."

"You aren't likely to change your mind this time."

"I believe I can pretty well guarantee it. In fact, leave out pretty well."

As I wondered what further undertaking might be required, Julia said "I may as well say I've changed mine."

I would have preferred not to need to say "What's turned you against Marie? I think she's been good for him."

"Not Marie, the other girl. I didn't like the way you nagged her, and I haven't forgiven you for pretending she was in your room." Having given the rebukes time to settle on me, Julia said "But I've come to the conclusion Roy's better off without her."

I felt compelled to learn "What's made you think so?"

"He's been a lot healthier since she left him. I really believe it was as soon as she did."

I was aware that neither of us had referred to Bella by name. Of course it couldn't summon her, and yet the avoidance felt like wariness. In a bid to end the conversation I said "Anyway—"

"Before you ask me, no, we haven't found the book in the archive."

"I wasn't going to. I'm glad at least you know I didn't take it." When Julia let me interpret her silence as I might I said "And I'm glad you've come to agree about Bella."

"I'd rather forget her now there's Marie. Just make sure you can be trusted with her and Roy."

This was one admonition too many. "I'll speak to you again," I said.

"Yes, we'll speak," Julia said, no more than a statement of fact that ended the call.

All the talk of Bella had left her in my mind. As I drove out of the car park I remembered the bag she'd abandoned in the car. On my way home that day I'd looked for somewhere to dispose of it, but couldn't bring myself to do so until I discovered what it contained. At my apartment I'd turned out the contents on my desk. There was my aunt's phone, and a pair of yellowing embroidered gloves as long as half an arm. I found coins several centuries old, and a number of items of jewellery – an oval brooch on which porcelain figures danced in a circle, a necklace dangling gemmed pendants, a ring internally inscribed with symbols that might have related to magic. I'd tried to read a newspaper brown as parchment, where every S rose above the other letters like a weed out of undergrowth, but the pages had crumbled into illegible fragments. I'd consigned their remains to the bin and kept the phone as a reminder of my aunt. The other souvenirs felt like attempts on Bella's part to cling to memories – to pass for human, perhaps to herself. Although I didn't want them anywhere near me, I felt reluctant to destroy them, and so I took them to the oldest museum in Liverpool, where I found an opportunity to leave the bag in the gentlemen's facility while I was unobserved. Days later the local newspaper reported that someone had left several valuable coins and items of antique jewellery in the museum. It was planned to put them on display, but that was the only reference I found.

As I drove home the empty seat beside me felt like a mute rebuke. At least the coins and jewellery were safe, though I'd no idea what had become of the gloves, and I was safe from any lingering influence. I'd thought I would have to return to the derelict hotel and find the jars of haunted earth so as to destroy them – I was afraid that otherwise some trespasser might rouse the presences they invoked – but there had been no need. Before I could nerve myself to venture back, Roy had phoned to tell me the hotel had burned down. I gathered that he felt we were to some extent responsible, given the rumour that people living nearby had started the fire, having concluded that intruders they'd seen in the vicinity were using the place to take drugs or grow them. If the arsonists had failed to realise that cultivation would have required electricity, I was glad of their mistake.

All the keepsakes of my aunt I had were safe. When I reached home her yearly portraits met me in the corridor. The hints of a figure in the background resembled an omen of atrophy now, and I had to fend off memories of Bella's reversion to the earth. Making for the kitchen took me past the portraits in reverse, so that I watched myself grow younger. Perhaps I had the opportunity to recapture some of the wonder I'd experienced in my youth, or even to discover visions I'd never had.

The bitter aroma of coffee lent the air in the kitchen an edge as I filled a mug and took it to my desk. A train intoned its stations before preaching safety while across the bay the windmills scratched the low clouds raw. The sky was only growing red with sunset, and I didn't need any safety advice. My aunt's journal was secure in the drawer of my desk, and I was immune from its influence. I believed I was just as safe with the remains of the other book.

That was the word that had followed me up from the dark valley: book. I'd concluded that the denizen wanted me to return his chronicle to him, but I was never going back. I had no way of restoring it to the library either, but I could at least read it myself; in fact, I felt compelled to do so. One page a day might be enough of a task to decipher, or perhaps I could forge ahead. I retrieved the pages and their binding from the drawer, where they lay on top of Thelma's journal. When I spread the binding wide on the desk, a page slipped out as though eager to be read. *The true mage is conceived by the cosmos, and is its fleshly incarnation...* I thought I felt my mind begin to open like a blossom, and I was already less resolved to destroy the pages once I finished reading them. Perhaps when I came to the end I would know how to proceed.

FLAME TREE PRESS
FICTION WITHOUT FRONTIERS
Award-Winning Authors & Original Voices

Flame Tree Press is the trade fiction imprint of Flame Tree Publishing, focusing on excellent writing in horror and the supernatural, crime and mystery, science fiction and fantasy. Our aim is to explore beyond the boundaries of the everyday, with tales from both award-winning authors and original voices.

•

Other titles available by Ramsey Campbell:
Thirteen Days by Sunset Beach
Think Yourself Lucky
The Hungry Moon
The Influence

Other horror titles available include:
Snowball by Gregory Bastianelli
The Haunting of Henderson Close by Catherine Cavendish
The Garden of Bewitchment by Catherine Cavendish
The House by the Cemetery by John Everson
The Devil's Equinox by John Everson
Hellrider by JG Faherty
The Toy Thief by D.W. Gillespie
One By One by D.W. Gillespie
Black Wings by Megan Hart
The Playing Card Killer by Russell James
The Siren and the Spectre by Jonathan Janz
The Sorrows by Jonathan Janz
Castle of Sorrows by Jonathan Janz
The Dark Game by Jonathan Janz
Will Haunt You by Brian Kirk
We Are Monsters by Brian Kirk
Hearthstone Cottage by Frazer Lee
Those Who Came Before by J.H. Moncrieff
Stoker's Wilde by Steven Hopstaken & Melissa Prusi
Creature by Hunter Shea
Ghost Mine by Hunter Shea
Slash by Hunter Shea
The Mouth of the Dark by Tim Waggoner
They Kill by Tim Waggoner
The Forever House by Tim Waggoner

•

Join our mailing list for free short stories, new release details, news about our authors and special promotions:

flametreepress.com